A Novel

Matt Kuvakos

ADDISON'S MARK
Matt Kuvakos

First Printing, 2014

ISBN: 978-0-9911832-0-3 ebook
ISBN: 978-0-9911832-1-0 paperback

Book Cover Design by Timmy Ham
Book Interior Design: KarrieRoss.com

I'd like to dedicate
this book to my friend,
Brad Harper.

I'll see you soon, man. #2640

I'd also like to acknowledge my close friends and family who believed in me, read this story since the beginning, and supported me throughout this entire process. Thank you dad for the time you dedicated brainstorming with me, and reminding me "writers write." To my mom, thank you for listening to me ramble on and on about my vision for this story. I'd like to thank Megan Hunter, Lisa McMann and Pam Hansen for guiding me through the different stages of this journey as well. Thank you Senator Robert Meza for taking the time out of your busy schedule to read this story. Thank you to my editor, Rose Jackson for taking the time to make sure everything looks as good as it can. Also, thank you Timmy Ham for creating an amazing cover. Most of all, without Jesus Christ in my life I would've given up on this story long ago. Thank you for loving me.

1

My eyes were open, but I saw nothing. I could barely sense daylight through the rough cloth tied around my head, stretched tightly over my eyes. Was the sun shining in a cloudless sky, or was that only my imagination straining to make sense of this terror?

My hands struggled and ached to move, but they were tied to what seemed to be a pole behind me. Leaning against the pole, my legs stretched out in front of me, I wiggled my toes and rocked my legs, feeling that they were still there. Reasoning against confused panic, I forced myself to go through a checklist. How did I get here? Where was here? What did I still have? I managed to stretch out my fingers and bury them in the dirt, searching for anything sharp, since I could feel that the rope was made out of some sort of stringy thread.

"Come on," I heard myself say. Hearing my voice aloud seemed odd, as if I were a ghost hovering over this particular moment or space.

I managed to separate a loose strand from the rope. I grinded and twisted my wrists together, hoping I could free my hands. The rope wasn't going to budge. I gave up trying to break free and listened for some familiar sound to give me some clue where I was. Outside, yes, because I heard high-pitched squeaking and birds chirping in every direction. Warm, humid air clung to my skin; the breeze felt like hot breath. Sweat began to slide down my forehead and neck, soaking my shirt.

"Sam?" I heard my dad's voice in front of me.

"Dad?" Terror and relief crashed into me at once, tumbling like breakers against rocks, creating a larger sense of confusion than before.

"Yeah. Oh, God." His struggled breathing told me he was tied up, too.

"What happened?" I cried in a rough whisper. Before he could answer me, I heard a group of foreign voices creeping closer, shuffling across the dirt somewhere in front of us.

"Stay calm," Dad said through heavy breaths. Was he hurt?

Now the voices were only feet away. One voice separated from the group and a pair of feet walked closer, standing right in front of me. His breathing was calm as he yelled something in Spanish to the group, and they all answered with a laugh. Grabbing my head, he untied the rag, and my eyes blinked against the glare of a flashlight pointed right at me, sending a colorful kaleidoscope into my eyes.

More laughter followed from the splotch of a body in front of me and the voices in the background. The man moved the light off me and, after a few seconds, I could see I was in the jungle, covered by a canopy made of skinny twigs. This must've been a small, camouflaged encampment for this group of men, whoever they were.

The squeaking I'd been hearing came from dozens of monkeys in the trees overlooking the outpost. The tiny, shadow-like animals perched anxiously on the branches overlooking the entire scene.

The man who untied the rag from around my head knelt down near my face, his breath reeking of stale tobacco. His eyes looked like deep craters. He flashed a smile making his teeth glow within the darkness. He was shirtless and covered in mud, as if he was trying to blend in with the night itself. A rifle was strapped to his back, and he pulled out a long knife sheathed by his side. He raised the point of the blade and pushed it against my forehead. I could feel blood slithering down the brim of my nose, coating my lips until it dripped off my chin like a leaky faucet.

Oddly, I realized I wasn't afraid, though. I always thought I would be if my life were threatened. In a way, I felt relieved. Maybe that's what you feel just before you die: relief.

"Hey, hey, hey," My dad called, and got the man to turn his head to look, but he kept the jagged knife pressed on my forehead. Now I could see my dad for the first time. He was still veiled, with his neck tied to a pole behind him so that he could only look upward, his bare neck exposed.

"God is always with us." His voice was strained. I wondered how God could be with us now. The man moved away from me and went over to my dad, swiping the rag away from his eyes. This was not the last image I wanted of my father.

I pictured him as I had when I was a child. A memory surfaced in my mind: dad had randomly decided to do a crossword puzzle as we waited in the doctor's office when I had the flu. He was sitting next to me, pushing back his dark, wavy hair with his palm. His brown eyes searched the puzzle, a small smile forming on his lips. "Don't say anything," he said to me, since he wanted to figure it out on his own. He dropped his head back against the wall as he thought of the answer.

"Don't say anything." That's all I could say now. I kicked my feet in the dirt toward him.

"I love you and God loves…" The man slammed the handle of the knife into my dad's throat, causing him to writhe and cough. I knew why he was saying these things. Dad already knew what was going to happen. I felt the rope cutting into my wrists as I tried to break free.

"I…." my dad rasped, but couldn't get out another word. I noticed the man with the knife nod his head once toward the other men, as if he was showing off to them.

"No." I lunged forward as hard as I could, bending the pole behind me with a strained creak that echoed my unspoken cry, but I went nowhere.

"Vete a tu casa, pastor." The man knelt down next to my dad and held the knife up to his neck.

"Dad!" The way I said it sounded like "Stop."

My dad gasped for a breath and tried to say something. Before he could, I slammed my eyes shut and wished I could slam my ears shut as well. The only way was to scream.

2

"Are you OK? Sir?" My head leaned against a window and someone next to me was shaking my arm. The smell of exhaust and the whining blare from a passing car's horn opened my eyes. I remembered I was not in the jungle, but on the bus. Tears ran down my cheeks as I straightened in my seat. This was the seventh day in a row I'd had to relive that night as I slept.

"Yeah, yeah. I'm sorry." I wiped my eyes. "Bad dream."

"Looked like something worse." The person holding my arm was an older lady with a kind face. The bus started to slow down. I was lucky I woke up when I did or I would've missed my stop.

"I'm OK. Thank you." I nodded toward the aisle. She let go of my arm cautiously and stood up so I could get by. I could feel her concerned eyes following me as I stepped off the bus. She probably thought I was going to admit myself to be evaluated, since this was the stop for the institute.

"I'm visiting my mom, lady." I said, pretending she heard me, and secured the beanie on my head as it started to rain.

My footsteps echoed hollowly down the hall and I shut my eyes before I walked into mom's room, not to sleep but to think of how my life should've been. I wanted to be an artist whose work would be acclaimed and written up in all the papers. I would go on tours promoting my work to the finest galleries and find a beautiful girl to marry, a woman with dreams of her own that I would support. On weekends we'd travel to my parents' cabin in the woods and have barbeques, where I would watch my mom paint and listen to my dad as he talked about God, like he always did, but I would listen the way a birdwatcher listens for the distant chirp of the next big find. Then I would grab my girlfriend's soft hands and kiss her lips before returning to filling my notebook with sketches of my own. The funny thing is, I truly believed that would happen. For being only twenty, I guess that dream wasn't too far-fetched. Reality hurts even more when it's shredded by denial.

My eyes opened and locked on my frail mom lying on the faded white bed she'd trapped herself in by convincing her mind that she couldn't walk. Her once thick and shiny blonde hair now hung like thin strings of yarn over her bony shoulders. I knocked on the door to get her attention. Her green eyes lit up as she turned her head and saw me standing in the doorway.

"Hey, Mom." I sat in the chair next to the bed and rested my hand on hers.

"Sammy." Her voice was tired, but she smiled as she flipped her hand over and squeezed mine.

The wires and tubes connected her thin body to glowing and blinking monitors as if she was part of some sort of diabolical experiment. The constant beeping and ticking of the machines drove me crazy. I hated that these modern institutes smelled and looked way too clean for what they really were: a place to rot. It pissed me off that this was where my mom was living. She didn't deserve this. No one did.

I stood up and sidestepped past the bed to the only window in her small cubicle of a room. "Let's get some light in here," I said, masking my anger with cheerfulness as I pulled the string beside the window and the blinds folded upward, allowing some gray light in to join us. Drops of rain speckled the window and clung to the glass. I took off my beanie and looked back to my mom as if she had said my name. "The nurse told me you're barely eating." I walked back to the chair and put my hand in hers again. "You need to eat."

"I'm just not hungry anymore," she replied, shrugging her left shoulder. "Don't worry about me."

How could I not worry about her? I knew if I told her that, the conversation would end. Even in her current state, she wanted me to believe that she could still take care of me.

"Have you done any drawing today?" Mom asked. I reached for the red sketchbook both of us - mostly I - would draw in every time I visited her.

She nodded her head as I flipped through the pages. I held the corner of the last page between my fingers and rubbed them together where she had drawn the ankh symbol: a cross with a loop on the top. She'd shaded in the loop red, and in the body of the cross were other symbols I had never seen before, drawn in great detail.

I had forgotten just how good an artist she was. I lifted my eyes back to her. "I like it, but why'd you draw it?"

"I keep seeing that in my dreams," she said. "I don't even know what it is." She turned away suddenly and stared up at the ceiling.

"It's the ankh, an Egyptian hieroglyphic," I explained, though I didn't know what the symbol meant. I just remembered seeing it a lot in the one art history class I took before I dropped out of school when mom got sick after my dad's death. I shut the sketchbook and put it back on the nightstand.

"I've been dreaming a lot again," she said, her eyes searching the ceiling like a security camera combing over a vacant lot. I wanted to say "Me, too," but I didn't.

She rolled her head to the side and lifted her stare above me. I watched her smile and her eyes widen. She pointed to something behind me. "Sammy, they're back. Those angels are back."

I watched her face twitch with excitement. "Look, please look." She tightened her lips together, glanced at me and then behind me, like a child wanting a toy.

I turned around in the chair and saw a nurse pass by the door in a hurry, but nothing out of the ordinary.

"Do you see them?" My mom's voice became strong. "Do you? They're looking right at you."

I turned back and faced her. "I see them," I lied, bringing her hand, which had been raised pointing at nothing, back down on the bed.

"They're still following you and only you." She shook her head in disbelief. "Do you ever ask them why?"

"No, I haven't," I said. "Why don't you?" I had learned to just play along with her, even though the doctors advised me not to. This was why she was admitted in the first place. After my dad's death, Mom started to see these beings, or "angels," floating above me, following me. She didn't just see these angels, but also a few times she saw "demons" following me, too. I used to believe in that stuff, but now I realized it meant nothing. My mom still believed, though.

I was "lucky" to be spared. I was a "miracle." That's what everyone told me. My dad's dead body was eventually shipped back to us like a misplaced, forgotten package. The funeral was closed casket.

I still dreamt about that night all the time even when I got some help. No help can erase the memory of death, though. What bugged me the most was why the terrorists just let *me* go and not my dad, too?

"Vete a tu casa." I could hear that man's voice in my mind like he was right next to me. I still couldn't remember how exactly I did "go home." That's how the whole miracle talk began in the first place. I wasn't going to tell my mom I was dreaming again, because I knew that would light a fire in her mind that I'd never be able to extinguish.

I used to try to fight off her outbursts - I knew if there was a God, he wouldn't want any of this - but it didn't do any good, so I stopped. I just wanted her to be as happy as possible. If that meant for me to pretend I was being followed by imaginary creatures, then that's what I would do. I must admit that a tiny part of me wanted to believe her. Maybe it's because I just didn't want to believe that my mom's beautiful mind was now distorted, or maybe I just didn't want her to end up like my dad. She was all I had left. Yet, in a way, she didn't even exist anymore. Was this what God wanted, too?

She took a deep breath and said, "OK, I'll ask them." She was nodding her head, breathing deeply, preparing her question for these beings that were not even there. I gently patted her hand. I hated seeing her like this, so fragile.

She licked her pale lips and slowly opened her mouth, thinking of the right words to say. "What do you want with Sam?" She blinked her eyes multiple times and held her breath, waiting, even I listened for any sort of answer, but all I heard was the Velcro wrap crinkling around her arm to take her blood pressure.

"He's staring at me," she gulped. "His eyes are so beautiful, so green like yours, but bright like they are on fire. He looks like a gladiator, a giant gladiator, or like Goliath. Can't you see him?" She dropped her eyes to stare at me for a split second, and then returned her eyes to the space behind me. "He's covered in… what are those, markings?"

I looked to the beeping heart monitor that was now flashing red.

"What do you want with Sam?" She raised her voice, wiping sweat from her forehead.

"Mom, take deep breaths," I urged her softly. The beeping machine was now buzzing behind her.

"He's right here. Look at him." She sat up in the bed with her arms straight out, then collapsed onto her back as if she was shoved down.

I shot up out of the chair, sending it crashing to the ground, "Nurse!" I held my mom's face, now drenched in sweat. The whites of her eyes filled with red from broken vessels.

"Look at his hand," she whispered, her arms and legs stiffened by her sides. "He's fighting," her teeth clenched, "over you." Her eyes shook as they rolled back of her head. I slammed the emergency button on the wall. Every machine squealed down at my mom as she started to convulse.

I ran and tripped into the hallway, desperately calling, "Nurse!" There wasn't a damn nurse in sight. I started to sprint down the hall to look for one until I heard my mom scream, "Saaaaam."

I scrambled back, but the door was shut. I pulled on the handle, but it didn't open. Grabbing my head, I backed away, "You idiot, why did I shut the door?"

I lunged toward the door to try to open it one more time, squeezed through and ran back to Mom as the door barely pushed open. She was gasping for air but starting to calm down. Her breath became normal and her eyes were no longer shaking. She reached for my arm and held it, looking right at me. Her face and body relaxed, but the machines were still shrieking as if every car alarm in the parking lot was going off.

As she brought her hand up to my face I noticed the color of her hair and skin seemed to be shining; amazingly, she looked healthy. I looked into her eyes, the same eyes I have, and for the first time since she'd been sick, I saw life.

"You'll be all right," She said as her hand dropped from my face and her eyes closed like she was only going to sleep.

A mob of doctors and nurses pushed me out of the way and hovered over her, like lions around a dead gazelle. Stepping back to the wall, I slid down to the ground. I could still feel her hand on my face as all of the monitors chorused one single, high-pitched note.

The doctors pounded my mom's chest and screamed orders at each other for a few panicked moments until they were out of breath, leaving that one long beep, the only sound I heard. I looked up at the ceiling as if I was looking at God and shut my eyes again, knowing that He wasn't there. I tried remembering my parents' imaginary cabin. Instead, I only saw blackness. I pressed my eyes closed, refusing to reopen them to the insane reality that my family was gone.

3

A bead of sweat trickled down my neck as I stared vacantly out the wall of windows in front of the grocery store where I worked. I watched the lines of heat squirm above the parking lot surface as if they, too, were looking for relief. Phoenix in the summer made Mars seem like a better place to live.

I watched my manager, Tammy, set up another giant fan, hoping to fend off the heat from penetrating deeper into the store. She was always red-faced, but today was an extreme case. We were the only two people working, since our store was small, and the fact was that we were probably going to be out of business soon anyway. Not a lot of people had money to shop regularly, and not a lot of producers were selling their product to anybody else. That's just how it was.

I leaned my hands forward on the counter in front of me. My sleeve lifted on my left arm, partially revealing my tattoo. This was the only thing I liked about myself. It was one of the last designs my mom had drawn. I couldn't believe six months had passed since losing her. I traced the intricate designs on my lower arm with my finger down to my wrist, where my parents' initials were: J.A. for Jack Addison and C.A. for Catherine Addison. I raised my hand to my cheek, the last place my mom's hand ever touched. I couldn't really grasp the idea that I didn't have a family anymore. I felt like I'd been thrown overboard in the middle of the ocean and told to swim back a thousand miles to shore. I could only tread water for so long before I started to drown. I pulled down my shirtsleeve, hoping that would cause those thoughts to leave.

A quiet female voice did that instead. "Excuse me?"

I looked up, and BAM! I felt like I had been punched in the gut. Her blue eyes were all I noticed. They were the kind of eyes that needed to be framed in a showcase for people to see, not just glanced at to acknowledge their beauty, but to observe them, as if her eyes were handcrafted diamonds. "Uh, sorry, I didn't see you come in," I stammered, unable to take my eyes off her. She was thin and petite, with long dark hair that hung down her shoulders.

"Oh, it's fine," she smiled as a few items started to come towards me on the conveyor belt. "I have this pack of water on the bottom of the cart. Do you need me to get that, too?"

My mind went blank as I watched her unload her items. I felt like I knew her already. I wanted to jump across the counter and kiss her like I was picking her up from the airport after a long trip. For this one moment, I forgot about everything.

"No, no, you can leave it there. I have a code for it." My voice seemed too loud. I waited until her cart was empty to start scanning the products.

"Wow."

I kept my head down. She probably noticed me gawking at her like a fool. I slowly looked back up at her.

"You have incredible eyes," she said, smiling. She had a small, thin, freckled nose with soft pink lips. I was shocked she had noticed something about *me.*

"Thank you...you have...even more incredible eyes," My tongue forced that sentence out of my mouth like I was speaking English for the first time. A behemoth of a man dressed in an all-black suit walked up behind her.

"Thanks." She smirked and looked down at her feet briefly. She put her purse on the counter in front of me and then turned to talk to the man in the suit.

I bagged her items and put them in her cart, trying not to look at the two talking. The giant seemed to shadow her every movement.

"I'll be outside in the car." He walked out of the store, looking at me while he exited.

"How much do I owe you?" she asked, digging in her purse for her wallet.

"Huh, oh." I wouldn't care if I had watched her steal the entire store. "It's going to be $32.52."

She swiped her card in the machine in front of me and as she waited to see if the card worked, she puckered her lips and moved them from side to side. "Hmm... ." She swiped her card faster the second time and raised both of her eyebrows as she watched the screen. "It's not really working." She glanced up at me and then to the machine again.

She was so cute. "Let me give it a try." I said. "Sometimes it doesn't want to work." I walked around to the other side of the counter beside her. She reached to hand me her card, but dropped it on the ground. We both bent down to pick it up at the same time, both realized this, and stopped for the other one to go. We both stood there waiting for a few seconds to see who was going to be the brave one and try for it again.

"I got it." I smirked and picked the card up. I peered down and saw her name, Ashlin R. Ammon.

I had heard that last name all over the radio for the past few months. I tilted her card back and forth like I was trying to get the perfect angle for a picture. Marcus Ammon, Senator Marcus Ammon? That was the name being repeated on the radio every day. He was supposedly the "answer" to all of our problems. I had never followed politics or world news, but I knew that name. I had to stare at his face on magazines lined up like clones on the shelf in front of me some days. Plus, his face was unforgettable. He, like Ashlin, had piercing eyes, but his were light brown, a shade darker than his permanently tanned skin that made him look like an avid hiker or explorer who was always in the sun. He was well groomed with strong, structured features. His dark hair was neatly styled but not like most politicians when they look like plastic. There was just something about him that made him look honest.

As I remembered the senator's face plastered on magazines and posters everywhere, I wondered if this was his daughter. Why the hell would she be out here in the city and in this store? I guess that would explain the giant guy in the suit, though.

"You OK?" She asked, grinning.

"Yeah, yeah, I'm fine. I like your name; it's pretty." Was I flirting now?

"Oh. Well, thanks. Let's have a proper introduction. I'm Ashlin." She reached out her hand.

"I'm Sam." I met her hand with mine and felt my heart do a somersault inside my chest.

"So, are you going to try and get my card to work or…. " She glanced at the card, then to both of our hands that were still in each other's.

"Yeah, I'm sorry for how long this is taking." We let go of each other's hands, and I turned toward the credit machine.

"No worries, take your time. I'm in no rush."

I was in no hurry to get this fixed either. I didn't want her to leave. All I needed to do was press the reset button and it would be fixed, but I couldn't bring myself to do that. No one really talked to me, and I had no one to talk to. For some unfathomable reason, though, she was.

As I played mechanic, I felt her staring, like she was examining me. I liked it. I smacked the side of the machine, hoping I looked like I knew what I was doing. I wondered if she really was related to Senator Ammon. I didn't want to seem like an idiot asking about that and being wrong, though.

"It's too hot out there." She leaned on the counter next to me.

"You took a page out of the cashier's handbook with that statement," I smirked, making sure I didn't look at her.

"What do you mean?"

What *did* I mean? I pressed the reset button on the machine and faced her. "Rule number one for a cashier." I raised my index finger. "State the obvious when you don't know what to talk about with a customer."

"I never knew cashiers had a 'handbook.'" She made the universal sign for a quotation with her fingers and laughed. When she laughed, she squinted her eyes and brushed a strand of her hair out of her face. It had been a long time since I heard a girl laugh. Actually, since I heard anyone laugh. Maybe I hadn't been paying attention, or maybe there was just nothing really to laugh about around me.

"Well, now you do. In fact, I'll give you a copy if you want."

I swiped her card on the newly reset machine and felt a smile form on my face. Another first for me in a while: a *real* smile. Whenever I did smile before, it never came with a warm, bubbling feeling flowing through my body.

"Thanks, I'd really appreciate that," she teased. "I want to learn about the dark underground ways of a cashier."

I gave the card back to her. "You'd be surprised how dark those ways are. Cashiers are dangerous people, ya know?" I didn't know where I was coming up with this stuff.

"Whoa, I better watch out then," she stepped back, accidentally bumping into a shelf holding the magazines and candy bars, almost knocking the entire thing over. She held the rocking shelf steady.

"Like I said, very dangerous." I walked back around to my side of the counter.

Her cheeks were ruby when she turned back to me. She brought her hand up to her forehead, embarrassed. "I'm sorry." She shook her head slightly. "Anyway, did it work?"

"Don't be sorry. Did what work?" We were both new at whatever this game was we were playing.

"The machine," she nodded, raising her chin toward the little box.

"Oh, yeah, yeah. Just enter your pin."

"Cool." She pushed in her pin number and then stuffed her card into her purse before swinging the designer bag around her shoulder.

"Well, Ashlin. I really enjoyed our little talk." I held out her receipt toward her. I didn't want her to leave.

"Me too, Sam." She slid the receipt out of my hand and then tore a tiny piece off the bottom. "Do you have a pen?"

My hands had a mind of their own now and like a two sniffing dogs, they searched until they found a pen in one of the drawers.

"I hope you call me." She looked up at me with her big blue eyes. BAM! There was the slug to my stomach once more.

"I… I definitely will." I was still holding her eyes with mine. As she pushed her cart outside I reached for the paper she had written and saw her phone number scribbled across it. I watched her get into a fancy, black SUV. That weird warm feeling flowed through my body again. I folded the shred of paper and stuck it in my pocket, checking every few minutes that it was still there.

4

Once my shift was over, I walked to the bus stop in front of the store, passing a few homeless begging for money I didn't have, and sat down on the metal bench next to an old man with a beard that looked like a piece of stretched out cotton. His skin was leathery from the sun, and he had on a pair of aviator sunglasses resting crookedly on his nose. He was always there the same time every day, waiting for the bus with me. I nodded my head, acknowledging him, and he did the same.

I had decided that I was going to stop by the cemetery, only the second time I could bring myself to go there since my mom had died. The first time I went, I just got too depressed seeing both of my parents' graves. I hated thinking of them buried in dirt. Sometimes I pretended that they never died and that they just went on a long vacation. But my memories usually destroyed that within seconds.

"Why you always look so sad?" A haggard voice asked and out of the corner of my eye, I saw the old man staring at me. I turned my head toward him and saw my reflection in the dark lenses of his glasses. My brown hair was disheveled, but I didn't think I looked that sad. Maybe I pout a lot?

"I look sad to you?" I asked, relaxing into the back of the bench while keeping eye contact. This was the first time he had ever talked to me. He covered his mouth as he coughed and moved his sunglasses to the tip of his nose, revealing gray eyes. As I looked in his eyes, I wondered what he had seen in his lifetime. I wanted to know if he had a family. I had never wanted to know anything about him before, but there was just something about how he was looking at me, like he cared.

"You sure do. Every day I see you, you look sad. Why?"

"Well, I don't try to look sad. I think everyone is sad though. We are all just sad people roaming around this place in search of things that make us less sad."

"What are you looking for then?" His eyes followed mine carefully.

"I'm not sure. I think I gave up my search before most people, I guess."

He leaned forward and moved his glasses back to covering his eyes. "So, you're done looking to be happy?"

"I just think it's a waste of time to search for happiness. I forgot what being happy even felt like, until today." I reached into my pocket and felt for the crinkled piece of paper with Ashlin's number, just to bring another smile to my face. "If happiness wants to find me, then that's great. If it doesn't, then I guess I'll be considered a 'sad' person." I did enjoy the way I felt the few moments I was with Ashlin, so maybe that *was* happiness finding me. I didn't know why I was even having this conversation with this guy in the first place.

"Oh," he turned and faced the street, stroking his scraggly beard in thought. "I'll see you around, kid." He got up off the bench and started to walk down the sidewalk. I could've sworn I heard him laughing as he walked away. What a weird conversation. Actually, what a weird day. Most days I resembled a gnat living on stagnant water, just existing, hoping for something to come by and stir up that water. Today was definitely throwing some ripples in my little pond.

I sat up straight and stretched my arms along the back of the bench. Surges of heat blew in my face from each speeding car that passed by. I unbuttoned my shirt and leaned forward to see if I could spot the bus coming down the road.

The sky started to blister with red as the sun set. I pulled out my phone from my pocket to make sure I still had time to make it to the cemetery. "I should have an hour," I thought aloud, leaning back against the bench again. I started to think about when I should call Ashlin. I didn't know what to do next. I had never really had a girlfriend, let alone have a girl show some real interest in me. I mean, I never really had much time to pay attention to girls. My boss, Tammy, would always tell me I didn't have a girlfriend because I came off "intimidating," whatever that was supposed to mean.

I turned back and glanced at our small store, with the "H" in the sign for Hunt's flickering on and off. Tammy was a lifesaver for hiring me during a time when finding a job was like trying to find the lost city of Atlantis. I just didn't know how much longer our store would remain open because all of the other Hunt's stores had shut down already.

I nodded my head toward the other bus stop "regular" I saw most days. He sat down next to me and lit a cigarette perched on his lips. He was a short, stubby, balding guy who worked at the bank next to my store. He still had his nametag hanging loosely on his shirt pocket. His name was Dale. I knew the bus would have to be coming soon now.

"You hear the news yet?" Dale took a drag of his cigarette, not looking at me.

I wasn't sure if he was talking to me, to himself, or someone on the phone. I answered him anyway. "No, I haven't."

"Senator Ammon decided to run for president, man." He turned to me with his stubby legs bobbing up and down all excited. "Do you know what good news that is?"

Ashlin's eyes came into my mind. "No, I really don't. I don't follow politics."

"Well you should, man. This guy is going to save our country. He'll even save the entire damn world." He chuckled and sucked on his cigarette. "I'm serious."

He kept on talking about how great Marcus Ammon was, but I still didn't care. When I heard that name, Ashlin was the only thought I had. "Does he have a daughter?" I interrupted Dale's lecture.

"Who, Ammon?" He looked at me puzzled and flicked the cigarette into the road.

"Yeah." I leaned my elbows on my knees, staring at the smoking butt rolling along the street with the cars, and then looked at him.

"Um, I don't think so. He's not even married. He *was* but his wife died, so I doubt it. Anyway…" He was about to start ranting on how perfect Ammon was when the bus screeched to a stop in front of us. I made sure to let Dale get on first so I knew where *not* to sit. But I thought I had gotten my answer. Ashlin couldn't have been Ammon's daughter. The huge guy that was with her was not just a friend. Plus, what was with the fancy, black SUV she had gotten into? I needed to know more.

I sat in the first seat available near the front of the bus. I hated getting on the bus and seeing the emotionless faces staring back at me, all of them hoping I wouldn't sit next to them as if it were middle school all over again. That's the thing – people may get old and look old, but really, everyone still has the same heart they had when they were ten. In a way, the world is one big schoolyard filled with kids. I leaned my head against the window, thinking of these things, and watched all the small restaurants and businesses blurred within the dusty haze that constantly covered the city in the summer.

The cemetery was only three stops away. With each bump in the road, my heart inched forward in my throat. Two stops away, I watched a few more miserable-looking people come into the bus, with my head still against the window. I felt someone sit down next to me as the bus started to move and I smelled the spicy cologne my dad always wore. I assumed it was coming from the person sitting next to me, since the fragrance was so strong. I didn't mind though.

The smell triggered a memory of watching my dad get ready for work when I was probably only five years old. That morning, I climbed into my parent's bed. Their bed always seemed more comfortable than mine. I watched as he stood in front of the mirror by his wide dresser combing his dark hair back, making him look like a businessman. He straightened the red tie around his neck and grabbed the bottle of cologne, with gold liquid swishing around inside, and sprayed it multiple times, filling the entire room with the aroma, stinging my nose, almost making me sneeze. He looked at me in the bed and whispered, so he wouldn't wake up my mom, "See you after work, bud." That was before he became a pastor.

I moved my head off the window and held it in my hands, with my elbows resting on my knees. Now the smell was starting to piss me off. I looked next to me to see who the culprit was, but the seat was empty. I turned behind me and no one was there; no one was across the aisle, either. The closest person to me was a few rows behind me -no way he was the cause. I turned my eyes back to the seat next to me and the smell became even stronger. I could've sworn I felt someone sitting there.

Maybe it's the driver? No, the driver was a girl. The bus was now at the stop before the cemetery. I stuck my hand out over the seat, allowing another rush of the cologne to flood into my nose. What the hell? Was my dad sitting next to me? I squinted my eyes, focusing on the empty space like I was trying to spot a sign far away, and I imagined him looking right back at me from some other dimension. "It's just your mind." I turned away as the bus rolled to a stop; this was where I needed to get off. I stood up and stepped right through the smell. Nothing stopped me because nothing was there.

I looked up at the entrance of the cemetery as if I was looking up at a judge about to sentence me to life in prison. I didn't go in, but decided to just walk the two blocks to my apartment, with my hand in my pocket clutching onto Ashlin's number the entire time. I needed to call her.

5

I don't know why, but imagining myself calling Ashlin turned my stomach into a Tilt-A-Whirl. I was sitting on my apartment balcony, reclining in a cheap lawn chair, with my feet propped up on the railing, my phone in one hand and Ashlin's number in the other. I didn't have a clue what I would say to her, but I just wanted to talk to her again.

I'd never felt like this about a girl. I only ever had one girlfriend, and that was when I was a freshman in high school. Her name was Erie. I couldn't ever remember her last name, even when we were so-called "dating." I wasn't even sure what dating was - still don't even know. All I remember is holding hands with her walking down the crowded halls of school feeling nervous. But it was a good kind of nervous, like how I felt meeting Ashlin. I think when a girl makes a guy feel a little nervous, that's the first and most important spark in a relationship. The only time my mom ever talked to me about girls was when I was telling her about Erie. She told me, "The spark is everything." At the time, I had no idea what she meant, but I definitely understood now.

I scanned the night sky with my eyes, using them like spotlights, as if I was trying to find the courage to make the call somewhere within the blackness. The dark outline of a plane glided across my view, with its red strobe blinking down at me. Ever since the collapse of the economy before my dad died, planes were rare. I wondered where it was taking the lucky people that were in it. Maybe some place cold and rainy? I kept my eye on the flickering light and thought that, in just a few hours, that same light will be winking in some other person's sky, hundreds of miles away, and they would watch it like I was, wondering about where it was going. The plane slowly blended within the night. I wanted to be on that plane with Ashlin. I knew I had just met her, but thinking about going someplace new with her, and being close to her, just seemed right.

I started to dial her number, grinding my teeth with each ring. What if she didn't answer? Should I leave a message? What if she answered? What the hell should I say? It rang and rang some more. "How many times does it have to.... "

"Hello?" BAM! There was the slam to the stomach again. Apparently, I got beat up even if she wasn't in front of me. My eyes slammed shut, thinking that would make this easier.

"Uh, hey Ashlin, it's Sam."

"Sam?"

"Yeah, Sam from Hunt's." I sounded terrified. Did she not remember me?

She laughed. "I know, I remember. What's up? I'm glad you called."

Instant relief, then the nerves came sprinting back. "Oh, nothing. Just hanging out. But, really, you're glad?"

"Um, yeah, of course I am. I didn't give you my number to *not* call me."

"Well good. I'm glad that you're glad that I called. I'm glad too," I said, wondering if I could've said glad another time. Idiot.

She laughed her cute laugh, and I imagined her blue eyes squinting like they had in the store. "So, what's the reason for your call?"

What *was* the reason? I felt my face turning red. What the hell was wrong with me? "Um, I wanted to ask, to see, if you wanted to get coffee or something?"

"Awesome, yeah, I would love to. Does tomorrow afternoon work for you, or do you have plans?"

Me? Have plans? I was off work, and that's pretty much all I do. "Tomorrow is perfect, like two o'clock, at Jason's Coffee by my store?"

"Sounds good to me. I'm looking forward to hearing more about the dark ways of a cashier."

"Only if you're ready to hear them."

"I'll be ready. See you then, Sam." I could tell she was smiling by the sound of her voice.

"OK, bye." I hung up and realized I was pacing back and forth. But it was over. This was all a first for me. Maybe things were finally starting to change for the better. I wanted it to be tomorrow so I could see her.

Lying in bed that night, I couldn't sleep, so I started to think of what had happened on the bus earlier. Was it my dad? I concentrated on a water spot above me on the ceiling and tried not to think about my parents as much as possible, since it always ended the same way, them still being gone. But lately they seemed to be on my mind a lot. I rolled over onto my side and shut my eyes. As soon as I did, I heard my dad's voice say my name. He sounded like he was in a spacious tunnel. My eyes burst open, and my heart pounded against my chest like an angry prisoner wanting freedom.

The sun shot an arrow of light through my window, directly onto my face. No way was it morning already. I sat up in my bed, trying to calm my heart from this odd wake-up call. The aroma of bacon and coffee hovered like fog in my small apartment. Sliding the covers off, I heard the clanking of dishes. I peeked around the edge of my door to look down the hallway to my kitchen. I saw nothing but the front door and the pale light creeping in from the blinds of the balcony window. As I inched out of my room, I heard a baby whimper.

"Who's there?" I called and forced myself to keep moving forward. I listened for anything, my heart pounded in my ears like a war drum. Then I heard my dad's voice singing, "The eensy weensy spider climbed up the water spout…"

"Dad?" My voice broke as I cautiously walked into the front room, turned toward the kitchen, and saw my dad sitting on the tile with his legs spread out next to the stove, holding a small, wiggling baby in his arms. "Dad?" He didn't respond.

My dad's eyes stared lovingly at this mystery child squirming around, giggling, and unleashing Dad's boisterous laugh. They were both in bliss. Without looking, he acknowledged me. "Hey, Sam." When I took a step toward them, my dad faded, becoming transparent, but not the baby. I stepped closer again and Dad faded even more, as if a thin sheet dropped in front of him.

The closer I got, the more he disappeared. I sat down only a few feet from him and the baby. He looked something like a hologram, but Dad's face was filled with life. I missed him more in this moment than I ever had since his death. He moved his eyes off of the baby and onto me for the first time.

"Dad," I breathed, "am I really seeing you?" I ached to hug him. I couldn't believe he was sitting in front of me.

He held out the baby toward me. "Take him."

I looked from the baby bundled in a blue blanket back to my dad, "Who is he?"

He then started to flicker like a flame in the wind. "Take him before it's too late." He was holding the baby out in front of him, with a serious look on his thin, drawn-out face, as if my life depended on me taking this mystery baby. Then my dad vanished. I sank to my knees as the baby's tiny body floated in nothingness and suddenly started to drop before my dad reappeared, catching him.

Crawling closer without moving my eyes off of my dad's, I positioned my hands underneath the baby. When I looked back up, Dad was gone, like he was never there. I held this baby I had never seen before gingerly as if I was holding a bundle of sharp, rusted knives. The baby stirred in my arms and mumbled, opening his tiny green eyes.

"What's this?" I said out loud as I noticed a white smudge covering his wrist. I brought the baby to my chest and, with my index finger and thumb, turned his hand over. "Is that a scar?" I leaned in closer and saw that the marking was in the shape of the number seven. My eyes pulled away from his wrist into his intense green eyes, opened wide, unblinking. I knew I was holding a baby, but it felt as if I was holding something dangerous, like a grenade or something. He was small and looked innocent, but something was happening. I couldn't look away.

The baby's pupils became smaller and smaller, eaten

by the green pools of his irises surrounding them, until both of his eyes were submerged. Both of his eyes began to glow, dimly at first, but then brighter, causing me to turn away, the intense glow seeming to burn a hole through me as if I was only inches from the sun. I snarled in pain, but no sound escaped my mouth. Then, like someone had thrown a bucket of ice water over me, I felt complete relief. I tried to reopen my eyes, but they wouldn't budge, as if they were welded shut from the agonizing burn. I couldn't feel the baby in my arms anymore. I collapsed onto the ground, wherever I was.

"SAM," a strong voice I had never heard before boomed inside my head. "Come home," the voice commanded.

My eyes opened and I was in my kitchen, sitting next to the stove, right where I had seen my dad. I didn't know if I was dreaming or if that had actually just happened. Intense fatigue clamped onto every part of my body, as if all of my limbs were tied together with metal chains. Falling sideways onto the kitchen floor, my face slammed against the tile. My eyes were open slits, hardly perceiving the pale light coming in from the balcony door and back window. Then a silhouette of a man walked into my view and stood by the window, looking down at me.

"You're going to make an impact on this world, Sam. I feel it." My dad's voice was coming from the shadow. I tried to speak, but my eyes closed, and I fell asleep.

6

The morning's odd events were still pricking at my brain, diverting my attention from thinking about anything else as I sat in the back row of the city bus, staring blankly at a wad of gum smashed to the seat in front of me. I felt just like that wad of gum, chewed up and abandoned, clueless to what was going on. I pressed my hand below my right eye and winced from the soreness of the purple bruise rapidly bulging from my face-first fall in the kitchen.

I dreaded the inevitable - Ashlin asking how it had happened. I knew I'd have to lie to her so I wouldn't sound like a maniac. As I looked out the window at the few colored tops of cars passing the bus, I imagined myself telling her what really happened.

We would be sitting at a table in the coffee shop. She would be looking at me with her pretty blue eyes and ask me, "How'd you get that bruise?"

Then, I'd start to tell her the truth. "Oh, this bruise on my face? I got it this morning when I saw my dad, who's dead by the way, holding a baby I never saw before, with eyes that blasted out a scorching light."

She would probably ask, "Was it a dream?"

"Dream? Nope. I thought it was, but I saw my dad and heard him again, even when I knew I was awake. So, yeah, I might be losing my mind, just like my mom, who died only six months ago, seeing angels and demons hovering over me. Anyway, the most beautiful girl I have ever seen, what do you like to do?" I'd smile and give her a thumbs-up. By then, she would have a terrified look on her face and walk away for good.

"Why am I even doing this?" I hadn't really had time to think about the date with Ashlin because of whatever-the-hell had happened earlier, but now that I had just opened the floodgates, all the pent-up thoughts came rushing out of my brain. I cocked my head back against the rearmost wall of the bus. I probably looked like an opened Pez dispenser, with my mouth gaping as I continued to battle with myself, like I always did.

"She's not going to like you," I told myself, sat up straight and wiped my sweaty hands against my jeans. The nerves buzzed through my heart like bees swarming around a hive someone had thrown a rock at, sending hundreds of bees scattering in every direction. Every nerve in my body flew in frenzy, looking for a safe place to land with none in sight. I never let anyone get to know me too well, but I knew Ashlin was going to be asking questions to try. That scared me, not because she'd want to know, but because I wouldn't have any answers for her.

Before I could think of something to say, the bus pulled over and stopped. I stepped off and into the searing heat, smoothed my black t-shirt and made sure there were no noticeable wrinkles, then headed toward the coffee shop, trying to keep my mind as clear as possible. "No more thinking about this morning," I said to myself as I pulled open the door. A sign had been taped across the front, saying: "CLOSING NEXT WEEK." This was a normal sight throughout the city.

I walked in, and the potent smell of coffee and cinnamon intertwined in the air like two skaters performing an ice dance routine.

"Can I help you, sir?" A skinny blonde guy wearing an apron stood behind the counter, which held an assortment of pastries and chocolates displayed in the front. He looked at me as if I had just lectured him about how grass grows.

"Not yet, thanks." I searched the small seating area, with tables to the left of the front counter and to the right in the lounge area, where a few other people were sitting on a beige leather couch sipping drinks and talking. No Ashlin yet, so I stuffed my hands in my jeans pockets and sat at an open table in the corner, looking over the entire place. I tapped my fingers on the table to the drumbeat in the song that was playing. I didn't want to look as nervous as I felt. This was when it would've been nice to talk to my dad or mom for some tips. I never really thought about some of the experiences they would miss and I would miss, now that they were gone.

The silhouette from this morning crept back into my thoughts, along with the last words from my mom, "You'll be all right." I hadn't thought about my mom's final words until now. I wondered what she had really seen in that last moment for her to speak those words to me. Even if she was hallucinating, I liked to think that those words still held some sort of meaning within them, like an old photo that didn't seem important when it was taken, but took on a richer value when rediscovered years later.

I shook my head as if there was a bug in my hair. I wasn't doing a very good job of not looking nervous, but I was probably doing a great job of looking nuts. As I continued to wait, I noticed a middle-aged man wearing a white polo, eating a slice of cake by himself at the table next to me. He cut into the cake with a fork and shoveled it into his mouth as if each bite was the last. I don't know why, but I felt sad as I watched him eat. I wasn't as sad thinking about my parents as I was watching this normal-looking guy eat cake. Why? It wasn't because he was alone either. There was just something so innocent and childlike about the scene. I pictured this man as a little kid happily eating cake that his mom had made him, but now he ate it to bring his mind back to those better times as a child. Maybe I wasn't the only one stuck remembering what used to be. At least, that's what I thought. He probably just liked to eat cake.

"Hey, Sam," that sweet, bright voice said, breaking into my thoughts.

I jerked my head up, surprised, and saw Ashlin flashing her perfect smile down at me. I had forgotten how beautiful she was. She was wearing a purple tank top and white shorts. Her sunglasses were perched on top of her dark hair, which highlighted her blue eyes even more than I remembered.

"Ashlin, hey." I stood up, causing the chair to squeak against the floor.

"I hope you weren't waiting long." She stepped closer and wrapped her arms around me.

"Oh... ." I tried to remember how hugging went again. She fit perfectly into my chest. The scent of vanilla rushed into my nose from her hair. "Not long at all."

"Did you order anything yet?" She stepped back, still smiling.

"Not yet." I peeled my eyes off hers and moved them to the scrawny guy at the front counter. "After you," I motioned my hand like a waiter would at a fancy restaurant. She laughed and we both headed toward the counter. I had no idea what to get, so I got what Ashlin ordered.

"I think he's in love with you," I joked as the guy at the counter almost drooled over Ashlin as he made our drinks.

"Do I sense some jealousy?" she played back.

"Maybe a little?" I pinched my thumb and index finger together. We both held each other's stare. I didn't want to look away.

"Two iced coffees," the guy yelled out. I grabbed our drinks and brought them back to the table, with Ashlin following. When we sat down, I noticed the little, faint freckles on her nose as she took a sip from her drink. I wasn't the biggest fan of coffee, but the iced version was surprisingly refreshing.

"I'm glad you asked me out. This is nice." She slid her sunglasses off the top of her head and put them on the table.

"I was just happy you said yes, to be honest."

"Why wouldn't I say yes?" she asked, one corner of her mouth turning up slightly.

A little celebration erupted inside of me. "I don't know. I guess I'm not used to this." I lowered my eyes to the table and took a drink of coffee.

"Used to what?"

I was still looking at the table and fidgeting with the plastic cup in my hand. "I don't know what I'm saying."

"Well, most people never know what they're saying anyway," Ashlin said. "So, what're you not used to?"

I raised my eyes to her and saw her smirking. "I'm not used to...good things."

"No one's called me a 'good thing' before."

I took a big gulp of coffee, hoping to calm the nerves that I still felt fizzing inside of me like a freshly poured soda in a glass.

Her eyes lowered to my arm. "I love your tattoo. Why'd you get it?"

"I, umm." I didn't want to get into my dreary life already. "I got it for my parents."

She looked at me, puzzled. "Is there a special meaning?"

Here we go. "Yeah, it was one of the last designs my mom drew before she passed away." I turned my arm over and showed her their initials on my wrist. "They both...passed."

Her face dropped. "Sam, I am so sorry, I didn't mean..."

"It's fine; don't worry. It's probably good I'm saying this now," I smiled to reassure her. "What about your family?" I hoped to change the subject to a lighter one.

Her eyes were still looking down at my arm. "I actually never met my real parents. I was told they died when I turned seven. I was adopted as a baby." She glanced up at me, then back to my arm. "You might have actually heard of my dad."

I already knew the name she was about to say. I had thrown out the idea of it being true.

"He's a senator, Marcus Ammon. Maybe President Ammon soon. God, that's weird to think about." She widened her eyes briefly, before taking another sip from her drink.

"This is crazy. I never knew he even had a daughter." I played dumb. She didn't need to know I had been trying to figure out if she was related to him.

"I bet you knew of his dead wife, though."

I cleared my throat, hoping that would count as my answer. "I do."

"The tragic American love story," Ashlin continued. "Never gets old." She plucked out the straw from her cup and put it in her mouth like a cigarette, pretending to blow out smoke. "I never met her and he never talks about her." She shrugged and slid the straw back into the cup. "But the reason you didn't know about *me* is because that's how he wanted it. He wanted to keep me out of all the popularity madness. I'm thankful for that, in a way." She brushed a few strands of her hair that dangled in front of her face aside. "And I'm not at the same time."

"Do you mind me asking why?"

"Well, I'm thankful because I see him get attacked by reporters every day. Doesn't seem too fun, ya know? But then, he pretty much sheltered me my entire life, 'protecting' me. I can't go anywhere without the suits following me." Ashlin nodded her head toward the front window where I saw a giant dressed in black, much like the person with her on the day we met, trying to blend in. It wasn't working. "I hope this doesn't change what happens with… . " Her eyes mirrored mine.

"No, no, not at all," I said, wanting to know everything about her. But it was pretty cool to finally know that she was indeed *the* Marcus Ammon's daughter. I almost felt like I was breaking a law. Everyone wanted to know about the great Marcus Ammon, and his story. Yet, here I was, talking to his daughter.

"I was nervous I'd scare you away telling you that." She said.

"Remember, I'm a cashier. We have no fear."

"Sounds like a lame slogan to me." She laughed her cute laugh, with her eyes squinting.

That warm feeling rushed through my veins when she did. The nerves started to diminish inside of me. "I like it. It's catchy."

"Sure it is," Ashlin smiled, shaking her cup and rattling the ice against the sides like some sort of percussion instrument. "What do you want to do, though?"

"For a job?" I asked.

"Yeah, like what do you want to be?"

I saw myself drawing in the middle of the woods, surrounded by enormous trees and the smell of a fire drifting in the air from my imaginary cabin's chimney.

"I wanted to be an artist… a painter like my mom. I loved taking an image I saw in my mind and bringing it to life."

"Why are you saying 'wanted' and 'loved?' Don't you still want to paint and love to paint?"

"I do, but I mean I have no time outside of work. Plus, I haven't painted anything in a long time. I don't even know if I'm that good anyway." The last time I drew was when my mom was in the hospital. After she died, my only audience was gone. I thought about her last drawing, the looped cross. I never did find out what that meant.

"Well, I think you should start again. I love art." Ashlin arched her eyebrows. "So I expect to see your work soon."

"We'll see. What about you?"

"I want to be a writer, an author. I love creating stories and, especially, reading them." She nodded her head, agreeing with herself.

"Who's your favorite writer or writers?" I didn't know a lot about books, but it was refreshing to see someone with a passion like Ashlin's. She seemed to be pulling me out of a murky hole I had put myself in.

"Hmm." She raised her eyes to the ceiling in thought. "Books were a huge part of my childhood, since I was sheltered; remember?" She raised her hands just above her head and ducked, like she was protecting herself from falling objects. "So, this is a tough one, but I'd have to say C. S. Lewis is my favorite. I found one of his books, The Great Divorce, tucked away in one of my dad's boxes in his office."

I pictured the Oval Office, even though he wasn't president yet. "I never told him I took it, but he never even noticed. My favorite line is, 'Those that hate goodness are sometimes nearer than those that know nothing at all about it and think they have it.' I've read that book a thousand times."

My dad always talked about C.S. Lewis. I wondered just how close I was to goodness. "I like that. I haven't read anything from him, though."

"Well, you... ." She stopped mid-sentence when one of the "suits" towered over us.

"Miss Ashlin, we need to go. I'll be outside in the car." He wiped the beading sweat off of his bald head with a white handkerchief and eyed both of us, basically saying "hurry up" with his stare.

She let out a frustrated breath. "I'm sorry," and tightened her lips together. "That was the man my dad put in charge of me today. I have to cut this short. Want to walk me out?"

"Yeah, sure. I hope everything is fine."

"Everything is always OK," she said flatly.

We exited the shop and stood in front. The "suit" was already pulling the SUV around.

"I really want to see you again. I like hanging with you," Ashlin slid the sunglasses off the top of her head to cover her eyes.

"You'll see me again."

She leaned into my chest, and I felt her arms around my back. I wrapped mine around her and felt my heart doing double time. We both held onto each other like we had met a thousand times before. I realized that I was comfortable.

"I should get going," Ashlin sighed, "since he seems to be in a rush." She leaned back and glanced behind to the approaching SUV. "Call me." She walked backwards while still looking at me. I think every guy wants to hear those two words said by a beautiful girl. It was confirmation that she enjoyed her time with me. I liked that.

"I will." Watching her go further away was like watching that plane in the night sky. I wanted to be wherever she was going. All of that worrying I had done before she even came was useless. I touched my bruised cheek and wondered why she didn't ask about it. I could already tell that Ashlin was going to make me wonder about a lot of things.

7

That night I went to bed with a new feeling growing in the pit of my stomach. I pictured the feeling as a white flower with blue specks on its pedals. Ashlin had planted that feeling in me the day I first met her, and now it was sprouting. It was hope. I was feeling hope.

But when I shut my eyes to try to sleep, a thick presence hovering around me in my room plucked and squashed that feeling. I opened my eyes and noticed the smell of mold, as if I were in a damp basement. I couldn't see my hand in front of my own face, though usually the streetlight outside would provide some sort of lighting. The darkness that consumed my room was the kind that lives in hidden caves deep in some massive mountain.

My mattress compressed as if someone had just sat down. I listened for a breath or any kind of movement, but there was nothing but the sunken place by my feet. Even though I couldn't see anything, I felt a pair of eyes searching me, wanting me to see. Then, as if I had been drugged, I fell asleep.

When I woke the next day, I told myself it was only a dream, that I was sleeping the entire time. I didn't convince myself, but I couldn't convince myself of anything these days. I was starting to dread sleep, since it brought me no rest, only confusion. That feeling of hope from last night was already rotting in my gut like a piece of trash baking in the sun. I walked into my store for work feeling completely defeated.

I stood at my register in a daze helping the few people who came in. My thoughts bounced around my head like a pinball: from seeing my dad, to that baby, to my mom, to last night's event-until finally settling on Ashlin, repeating like that for hours.

"Long day, huh?" Tammy asked as she came up to the counter and dropped her head. I hadn't seen her all day, unless I just didn't notice her.

"Isn't every day?" I said.

I couldn't tell if the sound she made was a laugh or a cry. "It finally happened, Sam." She had her hands on the counter, with her head buried between them, hunched over.

"What happened?"

She slowly lifted her head out of her hands and rubbed her eyes like she was just waking up. "They're shutting us down. We're done."

My stomach shriveled inside of me, as if it were a raisin. "When?"

"End of the week. And then," she moved her finger across her throat. "we're screwed."

This was the last thing I needed to end the day. I only worked one more time before the end of the week. In this economy, I would be homeless sooner than later. I just stared at her blankly. I didn't know what to say.

"Go on home. I'll close up." She massaged her forehead and closed her eyes. "I'll let you know when I get your last check."

"Thanks" I said, trying not to sound bitter as I untucked my shirt and headed for the door. I knew this day would eventually come, but, in a way, I guess I didn't want to believe it. Tammy followed me out without saying a word and lit a cigarette.

"See you later," she said.

Without turning around, I just waved. I walked with my head down through the parking lot, watching my feet. "What the hell am I going to do?" I wondered.

"Sam." I heard Ashlin's voice behind me, stopping me mid-step. I spun around and saw her getting out of the driver's seat of a black SUV.

"Ashlin?" A smile stretched across my face. She was carrying a paper bag as she hurried over to me, leaving the driver's side door open.

"I don't want you to think I'm a creep, because I know I didn't even give you time to call me. But I wanted to finish our date." She held up the paper bag. "I brought cookies."

I wanted to kiss her right then and there. "You just made my day so much better. Cookies sound great right now."

"Rough day?" she asked with concern in her eyes.

"Something like that, yeah."

We both sat in the luxurious SUV, which smelled like leather, and ate chocolate chip cookies while watching the sun melt away in the sky. "Where are the suits?"

"Back at my house, probably looking for their car," she laughed while taking a bite of cookie. "I told them I'd be right back. They'll get over it."

"What about your dad? Will he?"

"He's much more understanding than you think. He's too busy to think about anything else anyway."

"Even you?" I reached into the bag for my second cookie, keeping my eyes on her.

She dropped her head slightly and moved a strand of hair behind her ear. "Even me."

The urge to kiss her came again and seemed to grab my mind and take control. I leaned in closer to her with my hand still in the cookie bag as she turned and faced me. Without hesitation, our lips touched. My thoughts of loss and despair, all of my worries about the weird things that were happening, plus my job, were gone. Her lips brushed them away like the gentle stroke from a paintbrush. We both pulled apart gradually, as if our lips were made of fragile pieces of glass.

"That was a *good* thing," she whispered, with her lips still lingering on mine.

"Yes, yes it was." I whispered back.

"You know, your hand has been in the cookie bag for like an hour?" she chuckled as I pulled my hand out of the crinkled bag, and we both laughed.

"Can I ask you something?"

"Sure. I love questions." She twisted her entire body to face me, tucked in one of her feet under her leg, and rested her head against the seat. She moved her eyes from the windshield back to me, waiting.

"How come you haven't asked how I got this bruise on my cheek?" I pointed to the small splotch of purple underneath my eye.

"Well, I don't think anyone should ask how another person got bruised. We're all bruised enough as it is, only we can't see the ones that really matter." She tore off a shred of the paper cookie bag and rolled it between her fingers. "Unless you want me to ask."

"No, it's OK. You're right, I was just curious." She was right. I had plenty of invisible bruises that made the one on my cheek look childish. I could tell Ashlin did too.

"So," she threw the paper wad at me, hitting my shoulder. "I will ask why your day was so rough."

I wasn't sure if I wanted to tell her that I was now a jobless fool. Well, technically I wasn't yet. "Just a long day."

"It's never *just* a long day. There had to be something that happened."

"It's always a long day as a cashier."

"Is that in the cashier handbook, too?"

"Of course." We talked as if this handbook was a real thing. I watched the parking lot lights flicker on and off like a lightning bug dancing in a summer night sky. "Where're we going?"

Ashlin turned on the SUV and shrugged as she shifted into drive. "Does it matter?"

"No, I guess not."

"Good. Because when there's no set destination, you'll always end up where you needed to be." She squeezed the steering wheel with both hands and turned hard onto the main road.

"What if that destination isn't what you wanted?" I reached for the handle above the window to steady myself.

"But what if it is?" She pushed down the gas pedal even more as we flew through a yellow light. I watched her cheeks rise as she smiled. She glanced up at the rearview mirror and back to the road. Her smile was quickly replaced with an earnest look.

"We could play the 'what if' game forever." I gripped the handle tighter as she turned right into a neighborhood and accelerated even faster. Was she trying to kill us?

"Well, let's play." Her eyes continued to shift between the rearview mirror and the road.

I cleared my throat. "OK, what if we die because you're driving like a maniac?" Houses were flying past us on both sides.

"Then we'd both be having a family reunion very soon." She slammed on the brakes, causing the wheels to screech and throw up smoke and rubber. She turned left and onto the main road again, barely missing a concrete island in the middle.

"I guess we would," I said. I felt like I was on a roller coaster. She was driving as if this was only a game, as if life was just a game. Maybe it was, because this was the first time I felt like each breath I took mattered and counted for something other than simply using up air. We were both laughing as we swerved in and out of tiny spaces between other cars, as if the SUV was a thread sewing the lanes together. Ashlin jerked the steering wheel all the way to the right, and we screeched into a parking lot like a stunt car in a chase scene. She pulled around a building and shut off the lights and engine, out of breath.

"What just happened?" My knuckles were white and seemed to be cemented to the handle.

"Was this where you needed to be?" Ashlin asked. Directly in front of us was a dimly lit, cracked sign with the three bold words I had heard my parents tell me my entire life: "**God Loves You.**"

"Nope." A church parking lot was not where I needed to be, and those three words hadn't proved anything to me yet, so why should I believe them now?

Ashlin started the car again. "What if it was?"

8

It was July, a few weeks after the little joyride Ashlin and I had taken. My eyes examined a canvas set up in the middle of my apartment. I had to dig it out of my storage closet on the balcony. I felt the need to paint an image that Ashlin had described the evening after the joyride. She had picked me up from work not knowing it was my last day.

Before I even got to the SUV I could hear music blaring. When I opened the door, she motioned for me to come in. With the music still turned up she turned to me and started to say something. I wasn't sure if she was singing along with the echoing voice in the song, or if she was talking to me.

"What!" I tried to out-yell the singer.

With a serious look on her face, she held her hand up to her ear and shrugged.

I started to think the volume control was broken. I tried yelling again and as soon as I did, she muted the volume from the steering wheel right just as I screamed, "WHAT ARE YOU SAY.... "

She tried to hold in a laugh but couldn't. "No need to yell, geez." She had this goofy grin on her face.

"Good one."

"Where to today, Sir Yellington?" She poorly imitated an English accent.

"Does it matter?"

"You're right, it doesn't." She put the SUV in drive and turned onto the road, not as crazy as the joyride, though. "We have company today." She pointed over her shoulder to another SUV following us. "They think that we won't notice." She exhaled and shook her head slightly.

"Let's take the 'suits' to South Mountain," I suggested.

"Let's. They need some beauty in their lives. And I've never been."

"Now's the time, then," I said. We turned around and drove toward the mountain.

"I can just keep driving?" Ashlin leaned forward on the steering wheel. We had just passed the gate to the base of the mountain.

"Yup," I replied. "Follow the signs all the way to the top."

"This is crazy," she laughed nervously as we started to drive upward on a thin dirt road that zigzagged along the edge of the slope to an outlook at the top of the mountain. As we got higher, the city became smaller until it wasn't even relevant to look at anymore. The neighboring mountains and the massive red and orange dessert took the city's place. Ashlin couldn't stop looking as we drove, so we decided to just pull over at the first outlook and not drive all the way to the top. This forced the suits to continue to drive past us since there was no room for them to pull over. Ashlin waved to them as they went by.

"I can't believe I've never been up here." She moved to where a massive red boulder lay overlooking the view below.

I walked up next to her. The wind hummed across the jagged mountain, whistling its way to us. For a few moments, we didn't need to speak. The view filled the silence.

"See that dead tree down there?" Ashlin pointed to her right. I followed her finger and saw the tree she was talking about. It hung off the side of the mountain with each of its crooked limbs reaching over the edge as if it wanted to jump.

"Yeah, why?"

"I used to have this dream all the time when I was little." She leaned against the boulder still looking at the dead tree. "I would be standing on this path with my dad. He would be on my left side and grab my hand. We would then start to walk toward this massive tree in front of us." She held out her hands in front of her, moving them over her head while she stood on her tiptoes. "The tree was the biggest tree in the world. I know it doesn't exist, but still…. " She relaxed her arms by her side. "The crazy thing is, this tree has one side that is alive and colorful, with leaves that look like they are covered in snow on a sunny day. But the other half of the tree is rotting and dead, with drooping branches and dark purple leaves." She nodded, remembering correctly. "I've always wanted to know why that one side of the tree was dead, though." She moved her hand onto the boulder, brushing something off of it. "Even in my dream, I turn to my dad and ask. 'Why is that side of the tree dead?' He looks at me and says 'Ask him.' Right before I wake up, I feel someone on my right take my other hand."

Then she took her hand off the boulder and moved it into mine. "That was a big detour for what I wanted to ask you." She faced me and clasped her other hand around both of ours while resting her chin on my arm.

"What did you want to ask me?" I looked at her out of the corner of my eye.

"Do you know why that tree is dead?"

"Because it's too hot?" We both laughed until Ashlin moved her chin off my arm and looked up at me.

"No. Because it was meant to be." We both stopped talking after that and went back to just looking at the view in front of us.

I wanted to paint that tree Ashlin dreamed of for her. I sat on my couch with a slender paintbrush between my fingers trying to decide how to start my first painting in a year. I felt like I was seeing a long lost friend, trying to remember what they liked and realizing just how much they had changed.

I tightened my grasp around the paintbrush and pictured the image in my mind on the canvas, as if I could copy and paste it from my brain onto the blank sheet in front of me. I saw the massive tree Ashlin described. It looked like one of those thousand-year-old redwoods, but bigger, with bark as strong as steel and so thick, no machine could destroy it. One side of the tree had white and gold leaves that emitted bright colors like they were pieces of glass reflecting the sun. The other half was dark and rotting, with drooping vines with purple and black leaves reaching for the ground. The background that I saw in my mind was a splotched sky with tints of red and orange, as if the sun was setting behind the massive tree. There's just something about the sunset that would make any painting or picture better; it's the final image of the day. If the sun could speak, the swirl of red and orange throughout the sky would be its last words.

"You'll be all right." I thought of my mom's last words, again. Then I thought of my dad, standing in my apartment like he never left.

I shook my head slightly, erasing the previous thoughts like an Etch-A-Sketch. I concentrated on the canvas again and imagined the enormous tree, seeing each stroke in great detail. I could almost feel the tree in front of me. I needed to get this image out of me as if I was about to be sick. My heart quickened, and the brush dropped from my hand, a sudden stinging pain stabbed into my brain like a nail through a piece of plywood.

I shut my eyes and held my breath, my head in my hands. My body was shaking uncontrollably, causing me to collapse onto the floor. I didn't know what was going on. I felt overwhelmed with this image, like I was in the middle of a crowd all going in different directions, pushing and shoving, trying to get out of each other's way. I tried to calm my heart and ease the pain by taking deep, controlled breaths, but nothing helped. I felt the urge to just run, run away from this tree and whatever this pain was.

I launched myself off of the couch and opened my eyes as if I had been in a coma for years. What I saw stunned me. The blank canvas and my small apartment were somehow gone. I was standing underneath the colossal tree.

"How.... " I dropped to my knees in awe of this gigantic tree. I noticed that one of my knees was in soft green grass with vines covered in colorful flowers sprouting up by the second, all the way to the base of the tree's trunk, and my other knee was in charred ground, with long barren vines twisting up toward the other side of the tree's trunk. I was right in the middle of the dividing line. I looked to my left with the fresh grass and felt a crisp breeze caress my face with the smell of the ocean. I turned to my right and my face was wrapped in a warm breath of air and the smell of smoke.

"This isn't happening," I mumbled, pushing myself off the two distinct surfaces. I stood about a hundred feet away from the tree, looking straight up at this incredible sight. I could hear the rustle of the white and gold leaves rubbing against the thick branches from the breeze and saw that each leaf was throwing off rays of colorful light like the reflection of a rainbow in mist, just the way I'd seen it in my head. A streak of lightning darted across the red sky behind the dark half of the tree, but the lightning didn't cross over to the colorful side; it stopped right at the dividing line, as though halted by some sort of invisible barrier. For some reason I couldn't walk to either side; I was stuck directly in the middle.

I saw two figures standing still up ahead of me by the base of the tree. The closer I got to them, the taller they both became. I felt something like a rope around my chest attached to something ahead pull me forward. Was it some force from the two figures, whoever they were? I tried to take another step toward them and the tree, but I was stuck in place only twenty feet from them now. I still couldn't tell who they were because they were both concealed in the shadow of the tree.

"Come home," I heard the two voices speak within a gust of wind from both sides of the scene. I recognized one of the voices as a voice I heard when I saw that baby with the scar. It was strong, like a soldier's voice should sound, but the other one was a smooth, poetic voice.

I tried to speak, but some force seized and held the words in my throat. Then, as if a camera was inches from my face, a blinding light flashed in my eyes. All I saw were blue and green spots. I rubbed my eyes vigorously to wipe away the spots and see what had just happened. When my vision cleared, I was back in my apartment, sitting on my couch, with my head in my hands. The random stinging pain was gone.

"You're losing it." I laughed nervously as I leaned back on my couch, still rubbing my eyes just to make sure I was actually there. The blank canvas was right where it was before, staring at me. "Come home," this time I heard the voice of my dad's killer echoing in my head.

Three taps at my door stopped the echo. I knew it was Ashlin. I got up, took the canvas off of the easel, and called out "Door's open," as I walked to lay it on my bed. Ashlin came through the door, holding her laptop by her side and balancing two drinks in the other, her purse around her neck. She was wearing a sexy gray shirt with black jean shorts. I was glad to see her, but at the same time, scared. I *knew* she was real and in front of me, but that tree felt the same way. I rushed over to her and helped her with the drinks.

"Hi." She threw her purse on the ground and put the computer and her sunglasses on the kitchen counter before turning to me with the two drinks. "You like tea?" She took one out of my hand and took a few gulps.

"Yeah, I do." I sipped the drink and put it on the counter next to her computer and glasses.

"You OK?" Ashlin asked. She put her drink down, too, and came close, wrapping her arms around me. She looked up at me with her chin against my chest.

"Yeah, I am. Why?" I was doing a horrible job of trying to hide the fact that I was losing my mind. I could still hear the leaves and those voices. Who were they? Whatever happened seemed so real, as real to me as holding Ashlin now. I needed to shake off that vision or brain attack, whatever it was. I couldn't let it affect me. Nothing happened, anyway, I told myself. I could've even fallen asleep.

"You're staring at me like I have three eyeballs," Ashlin broke in.

"You do have three eyeballs. You didn't know that?" I said, touching the spot between her eyebrows with my finger.

"You're not that funny," she pretended to scowl. I could tell she was holding back a smile.

"I was just trying to paint for the first time in a long time, and I couldn't," I explained. "No inspiration, I guess," I shrugged, with my arms wrapped around her waist.

"Well, that's normal. True inspiration is like an illusion: you think you have it, but you don't. When you get it, though, you *really* know." She squeezed me close to her before letting go and grabbing her drink. "When I get inspired to write, nothing else matters until it's out and on the page." She stood in front of the couch and plopped back like a tipped-over domino. "So, I apologize in advance if you're around when that happens." She sipped from her drink while looking at me.

"No need to apologize. I know how that is."

"Don't be discouraged though, Sammy. What you did today was a big step back into your art." She waved for me to come and sit next to her.

I had definitely taken a step into my art, all the way in. I smoothed back my hair, which must've looked like I just woke up, and sat next to Ashlin.

"You're right." I forced a smile. I was a professional at doing that. "Yesterday you mentioned that you had something to ask me, but you never did." I changed the subject while I had the chance. She cuddled up close next to me with her drink in her lap.

"I do have something to ask you." Ashlin turned and sat cross-legged, facing me on the couch. She seemed nervous as she looked down at the drink in her lap.

"Did you have plans for the Fourth of July?"

I would've had to work I'm sure, but now I had nothing but time. I wasn't sure how to tell her that either. "No, why?"

"Well, would you want to go to this park dedication to meet my dad? He's going to be speaking, but there will be fireworks too." She closed her eyes as if she was anticipating a scary scene in a movie.

"Of course I would. What's wrong?"

"I don't know. I was afraid you wouldn't want to meet him. I'm happy you want to, though. He wants to meet you."

I was finally going to meet Marcus Ammon. It was still hard for me to grasp that he was her father. Ashlin had told me before that he had his campaign tour planned and would be leaving next month. That was another thing I tried not to think about, since that would mean she would probably be leaving as well.

"Sounds cool to me," I said.

Her face brightened. "I'm excited for you to meet him. No need to be nervous either." She smirked and cuddled close to me again. I rested my head on hers, which was still on my shoulder.

"I think you're more nervous than I am," I said.

"Well, It's just weird, you know? I've never introduced a boyfriend of mine to him before." She intertwined her hand around my arm.

My heart turned into an acrobat in my chest. "I'm your boyfriend?"

She took her head off of my shoulder and her cheeks filled with crimson. "If you want to be."

"Of course I do." We brought our lips together, like that was the seal on the deal. The whole weird event earlier seemed like it never had happened.

"I have an idea." She scratched below her chin like an old philosopher with a beard, and pushed herself up from the couch, then disappeared into the hallway. I just sat on the couch with a smile on my face that no eraser could've rubbed away.

"What's your idea?" I looked down the hall from the edge of the couch and saw nothing.

"Sam?" Her voice came from my room. She almost sounded frightened.

"Yeah?" I headed into my room, where I saw her holding the canvas. She spun around to face me.

"Why did you say you couldn't paint?" She arched one of her eyebrows.

"Um, because I couldn't. What's wrong?"

She looked like she was about to cry. "Sam." She turned the canvas around in her hands and showed me. "This is stunning." I felt like a tidal wave was about to come crashing down on top of me. She was holding the exact image I saw in my head, the colossal tree I had heard and stood underneath. The tree was painted as if DaVinci himself was the artist. It was perfection.

"Thanks." I couldn't speak, so I whispered. I wanted to say it was hers. But, I didn't paint this. This wasn't right.

"How long did this take you?" Ashlin seemed to be in shock too.

"Not long." My voice was still hushed. I took the painting from her and looked closer. I saw the two tall figures standing underneath the tree, waiting.

"This... this could be in a gallery. This is just like my dream. This nee...." Ashlin kept talking, but her voice was overrun by the two figures' voices calling to me inside my head. I definitely *felt* missing, that's for sure.

"I'm serious." Ashlin took the painting out of my hand and placed it on the bed, staring at it like it had the value of a bar of gold. "You have to show this to my dad." She glanced back at me in the doorway before gawking over the painting again.

"Sure." I turned away, just to try to escape the voices repeating, "*Come home, come home.*"

9

I lay in my bed that night, anxious, with my eyes patrolling the ceiling back and forth like some spotlight advertising a grand opening. I started to wonder if I was experiencing the same things my mom had. Did I need to admit myself to the institute?

"I'm not going crazy," I told myself, but not with any confidence. "Come home?" I covered my eyes with my hands and wiped my face up and down. "Where is home?" I grabbed a handful of my hair. If I wasn't crazy yet, I was surely going to drive myself there thinking about the painting and the two figures with their statement that made no sense. All that had happened seemed real, and in some supernatural contradiction, the painting now was. I knew I couldn't have done that. I was too busy hallucinating that I was *in* the painting. I laughed at myself. Why was I even hallucinating?

I shut my eyes and gave up, but that only lasted a split second when I heard what sounded like a mouse scratching in the ceiling. I tried to ignore the pestering sound, but it grew louder. Instead of a mouse, maybe a raccoon was somehow trapped up there. I folded my hands behind my head and stared up at the ceiling, trying to pinpoint the exact location of the scratching. The water spot that had always been there began to darken. I focused harder on the splotch, which was definitely getting darker and even growing across the ceiling like a virus. Something syrupy oozed from the middle of the stain and poured down onto my bed, forming a puddle by my feet. I tried to get up and move out of the way, but my body felt strapped to the bed. I struggled to get free of whatever was clasping me down, but I still couldn't move an inch. The puddle grew by my legs as the pour of the liquid became quicker, the stain now stretching across the entire ceiling. Flakes of plaster drifted onto the bed like dandelion seeds caught in the wind. The thick, brown gel engulfed my legs. With one loud crack, the entire ceiling gave way and collapsed. I slammed my eyes shut and braced myself against the falling debris as the liquid submerged my entire body. I coughed and choked for air, still held captive by some pressure keeping me down. Suddenly the thick gel slid off my face and body; I could see and breathe again. All of the pieces of the ceiling hovered suspended above me, weightless, and blinding golden light exploded through the void in the ceiling with a swirl of wind, splattering the gel in every direction. Like the eye in a hurricane, as if a switch had been flipped, everything stopped. I was finally released from the mystery hold and rolled off my bed onto the floor.

I stood, gel dripping off every inch of my body, staring into the green eyes of a small boy. He wasn't covered in the sludge. He had dark, wavy hair and was wearing a bright white garment. His skin illuminated the room like the moon in the night sky, his face cold and expressionless, frozen. Only his eyes moved, mirroring mine wherever I looked. Then his stare caught fire, burning green, and the child started to walk towards me. With each step, parts of the ceiling debris crashed behind him, as if he controlled what fell and what didn't.

"What do you want?" I shouted, wiping the thick gel off my face, my eyes glued to his. He raised his hand toward me, and I saw a scar in the shape of the number seven on his wrist, the same as that baby my dad was holding. I realized this boy *was* that baby. "Who are you?" I demanded, holding my ground. He stopped right in front of me, grabbed my wrist and shut his eyes, extinguishing the burning glow. He tugged my arm down, over and over, each tug stronger than the last.

"What, what?" I winced and knelt down to hopefully stop the tugging, but he continued with his eyes still closed. I turned away for a second to look at my demolished apartment, and when I looked back toward him, his eyes were open and blazing once more, blinding me. He pulled my arm down again, but this time it felt like my hand was attached to an anchor sinking deep into the ocean. I fell face-first onto the ground with this sinister child trying to tear my arm off of my body. A burning sensation wrapped around my wrist where the boy was holding me, smoldering along my entire arm. I tried to pull back, but his grip tightened. My flesh could be nothing but ashes by now.

"Please." I snarled like a trapped animal and wrestled to free my arm from what felt like an iron press. Why and how was this happening? I had to be asleep, having a nightmare. This wasn't real. "Wake up, wake up." I heard myself screaming, as if the louder I screamed, the faster the pain would go away. Finally, the child slowly released his hold around my wrist.

"Thank you, thank you." I was trying to catch my breath. I was afraid to look and see my entire arm ravaged raw. I buried my face in the carpet, absorbing the cool relief. I rolled over onto my back, exhausted, and opened my eyes to see the ceiling intact, as if nothing had happened. The gel-like liquid was nowhere to be seen. Along with the boy, it had vanished. I sat up, still breathing heavily. I knew I was in my room, but I felt like I was in a stranger's place. The room only contained a tattered-looking bed and wooden desk, but they seemed misplaced. My whole life seemed misplaced. I just sat in the middle of my room in a trance, watching the blinds on my window sway side to side from the air-conditioning vent humming above the door.

I glared down to my throbbing wrist resting on my leg, sending a sharp pain through my entire arm. I knew I needed to see the source of the pain. I expected to see skin dangling off my arm. My hand started to shake uncontrollably as I slowly twisted it around so I could see.

What did he do to me? A scar, neatly shaped like the number seven, exactly like the boy's, was embedded in my skin. It was faint, but it was there, about the size of a bottle cap and smooth, like it had been there for years. "What did he do to me?" I asked the empty air, my voice rising as I rubbed the skin around the marking, trying to erase it, like it was only ink from a pen.

"How?" I stood up to my feet in a panic and dug my nails into the scar, trying to scratch it off. This couldn't be *really* happening. Once I realized scratching didn't do anything, I went into the kitchen and opened up a drawer, throwing utensils out of the way until I found a small knife to cut this mark out of my body. I washed the blade in the sink and laid a towel on the counter, placing my hand on top of it like I was preparing a fresh slab of steak, resting the tip of the blade right below the seven on my wrist.

"What're you doing?" I came to my senses, stepped back and threw the knife into the sink. Whether I liked it or not, this *was* happening. Fishing for sanity, I rationalized this was just a birthmark resurfacing; I'm sure that's happened before. I quickly remembered a teenager I worked with at Hunt's who showed up one day with one eyebrow bright white, like he had bleached it. But, he hadn't; he woke up with it like that.

I shuffled back toward my room, calming myself down, thinking of that lanky teenager with the white eyebrow.

"Weird stuff happens all the time." I walked into my room, and the first thing I saw was the painting of the tree, propped up on my desk where Ashlin had left it. I approached my desk, as if I'd been called to the front of the class against my will, put both of my hands on the sides of the painting and stood over it.

My eyes switched from the tree to my wrist, with the fresh scar staring back, mocking me.

10

"**J**oin us for the grand opening of Liberty Park, dedicated by Senator Marcus Ammon." I read one of the thousand posters I had seen all day as I walked downtown trying to find a job, with no luck. I still hadn't told Ashlin I was jobless, and I wasn't going to tell her tomorrow, the day I was going to be meeting her dad. I couldn't picture myself meeting him.

Slouching down on a bench at the downtown bus stop, I moved my eyes away from the poster and looked up at the buildings surrounding me. They were quiet and still, like the mountains that surrounded them. The streetlights flickered on, buzzing above me. Before the country's economic collapse, this city was booming and always working, like a human beehive. Now the city seemed deserted, except for a group of homeless people sprawled out on the pavement against a building across the street. One of them was the old man with the aviator sunglasses and scraggly beard. I hadn't seen him since the day we'd had that random conversation. He was resting on his side, bracing himself up on his elbow, and moving his head left to right, scanning the area for something. They were all silent, all defeated and hungry. They passed a bottle around and took swigs from it. I needed to find a job or else I would be the newest member of that group. I pictured myself sitting with them, I already felt like them, in a way. Sometimes all I wanted to do was just sit against a building and watch. I wondered just how much people missed when they weren't looking.

I didn't realize I was massaging the scar on my wrist until it started to sting. This was my first full day with the newest addition to my body. I had convinced myself somewhat that it was only a birthmark and all that I had seen was just a dream, and when thoughts that there was something more to this crept into my mind, I distracted myself with thoughts of Ashlin. Nothing in particular about her, but I would just picture her in my mind until those other thoughts subsided. I missed her.

I thought about a night from a few weeks ago and remembered one of the stories Ashlin had told me about her dad. We had been bored and decided to just go for a walk around my run-down apartment complex.

"Do you think we'll get mugged?" She smirked like she always did as we walked down the stairs from my apartment.

"Everyone is too poor to be mugged, unless we have food in our hands. I think we'll be OK, though." It was the truth. The entire city and country were plagued by poverty. "What were you even doing over here when we met? I'm sure you don't live nearby."

"You're right. I don't," she said. "I live in the middle of nowhere, it seems." She kicked a rock that was in the street. "I just like to *go* sometimes. I don't like being motionless. Just like the cliché says, we'll have plenty

of time to stay still when we're dead, you know? Plus…"
She kicked the same rock again when we walked up to it.
"I've always felt out of place. With the lavish life my dad
brings with him, it gets on my nerves if I'm around that
too much." She slowly turned around on her heels and
walked backwards, facing me. "He plans on making all of
this better, making the entire *world* better." She crossed
her eyes and made her voice sound like a radio news-
caster advertising something absurd. We both laughed.

"You don't think he can?"

She stopped walking backwards and walked beside
me again. "Well, I think he'll try, and I'll support him,
along with every other person in this country. But one
mind cannot change how the world spins, and the way
this world spins is in a self-destructive way. That's how it
got to this point in the first place. Even if by some miracle his plans work out and change everything we know,
it'll just change again over time. The world will end up
just how the world wants to end up. God's the writer
of this story, no one else. My dad doesn't think like
I do, though."

"No one thinks like anyone else." I hated thinking my
life was controlled by some other force. If that were true,
then God must really hate me. I didn't want to offend
Ashlin saying that. "Maybe *you* should run for president."

"I'd win that election." She nudged me lightly with
her shoulder.

"You'd have my vote." I wrapped my arm around her.

"Thanks, I appreciate the support." She clenched her
fist with her thumb on top and motioned her arm up and
down like she was using a hammer.

"What the hell are you doing?" I laughed at her as she
continued to do it.

"You don't know about the political thumb?"

"No, I can't say that I do."

"It's every politician's go-to move when they want to get something across when they're speaking. A sentence isn't powerful unless the political thumb is used." She did the "political thumb" after the last three words she had said.

"Does your dad do that?"

"I told him I'd punch him if he ever did. He hasn't used it once." She leaned her head closer into me. "I do hope he does some great things if he's elected, though."

"I know he will." I hugged her tighter as we both walked in silence. Those few moments of walking quietly with Ashlin made me realize even more just how much I liked being near her. Just the sounds of our shoes tapping against the pavement and the drone of cars in the distance were peaceful, as if we were walking down the beach alongside the ocean. I was OK with life as long as I was walking with her.

"I remember, I had to have been only four or five years old," Ashlin shifted away from me and slid her hand into mine while talking, "when I asked my dad, 'What's a mommy?' It was after my first day in preschool: this was before he was in politics and the madness that came with that. Anyway, I asked him that, because my teacher, Ms. Dober, was explaining to us at the end of the day to tell our mommies everything that we did. I was all excited to tell my dad. I remember wondering if she meant 'mummy.' I knew what that was and thought that everyone had a mummy and I didn't. So when my dad picked me up, I put all of my hair in front of my face; that's what I did whenever I was sad. I know I'm weird." She twirled her index finger in a tiny circle by her temple. "He knew that and asked what was wrong. I was silent the entire car ride, just sitting there with my hair covering my face like a curtain." She chuckled and ran her hand through her hair, scratching the top of her head, smiling as she remembered the rest.

"I even walked into our house like that, bumping into things, until I finally asked him why we didn't have a mummy like everyone else, so I could tell it about my day. He laughed like crazy. He is half Egyptian to begin with, so he got a kick out of that question. I just got mad that he was laughing and not answering me. I thought I asked the wrong thing." Her smile disappeared off her face. "I realized that Ms. Dober had said 'mommy.' So, that's when I asked him, how come we didn't have a mommy." We had stopped walking and were standing below my building.

"He instantly stopped laughing, dropped down to his knees, and looked right into my eyes. He started to cry, not sob or anything, but he cried. That was the first and last time I have ever seen him do that. He hugged me and held me for a while, never answering my question. I didn't ask it again either." Ashlin sat down on the curb.

"But do you know what my dad did after?" A smile stretched across her face once more. "He wrapped himself up in paper towels so he looked like a mummy. I laughed until my stomach hurt. That's the first memory I can remember." She glanced up to me, then down to her feet. "Of course I eventually found out I was adopted and that when I had turned seven, my real mom had died. I knew I'd never have one." She paused. "I miss a mom I never even met. It doesn't make sense to me." She scrunched her lips together and made a popping noise. "I guess if everything made sense, though, there would be no point in living life. Since that *is* the point, right?" She shook her head slightly. "Trying to make a little sense out of what seems like nothing sometimes." She pulled her legs close to her chest and looked up at me. "I don't know why I just told you all of that."

I sat down next to her on the curb, my feet straight out in front of me. "I'm glad you told me. Your dad sounds like a good man. I... ." I wasn't too sure what to say to her. I wasn't good at opening myself up, but she did, so I was going to try. "I remember my mom would take me on these bike rides with her. She had this enormous rusted green bike with a small plastic seat attached behind her where I would sit. She would strap this floppy red helmet on me that always slid down onto my eyes after every bump." I felt Ashlin rest her head against my shoulder, listening.

"We would ride for hours. I used to hold my arms out and pretend they were wings. I loved feeling the air slide through my fingers. When we would turn, I would tilt my arms that way and attempt to make the best plane propeller noise with my lips." I looked up to the cloudy night sky. "I never told her how much I loved those bike rides. That's the first memory I can remember." Still looking at the sky, I laid my head on Ashlin's, which was still on my shoulder. "My mom would've loved you. Both my parents would've."

She moved her head up to face me and kissed my cheek. "It's the freeing moments in life that stick with us the most. Those moments are what keep people from giving up during the ugly times. We all want to feel freed again, no matter if it makes us sad or happy. When we are freed, we know we are alive."

We sat there on the curb outside of my apartment, completely fine with not saying another word. I had forgotten what it felt like to feel free. I had forgotten about those moments. I had let the ugly times consume me until I had been drowning in them.

Another sharp pain raced through my arm from my wrist, snapping me out of the memory. Lately it seemed like the harder I tried to free myself, the tighter the hold around me became. I wrapped my hand around my wrist and squeezed to try to numb the pain. I felt someone staring at me and noticed the skinny old man with the aviators looking in my direction. He nodded his head and smirked, almost like he knew what I was thinking. I waved to him, but the bus pulled up in front of me before I could see him wave back. Once I was on the bus, I saw him walking away from the group. I wondered again where he was going.

I rested my head against the bus's window, with my wrist still in my hand, trying not to think about meeting *the* Marcus Ammon the next day.

11

must've walked around my apartment a thousand times, waiting for Ashlin's knock at the door like I was waiting for an important package. I wasn't sure if Mr. Ammon would be with her or if he was already at the park. I hoped he wasn't with her so he wouldn't see the absolute dump I lived in. I had been thinking all day about what I would even say to Marcus when I met him. I mean, I doubted that anything I'd say would interest the front-runner for the presidency, anyway. I'm sure in his mind I was just his daughter's stupid boyfriend, and he had probably forgotten that he was even meeting me. I was pacing up and down the hallway like a caged animal when I heard Ashlin knock.

"Hi. Happy Fourth of July." Ashlin was already smiling when I opened the door. She was wearing a light blue sundress, with her hair resting in front of her left shoulder. I probably looked like the guy in the coffee shop, gawking over her.

"Hey." I awkwardly leaned in and kissed her, causing her to laugh.

"How nervous are you?" She lifted her sunglasses to the top of her head. BAM! The slam to my gut returned when I saw her eyes. I was never going to get used to that. I looked out the square opening in the apartment building, where down below was the street, and I imagined the senator was right down there, waiting.

"He's not here. He's already at the park." She read my mind. Her voice was soft and comforting. "You ready to go?"

"Yeah," I shut the door behind me and struggled to lock it, since the door wouldn't shut all the way. As we walked down the stairs, at every tier I saw the black SUV by the curb. Ashlin folded her hand into mine as we walked up to the vehicle. I made sure my scarred wrist was hidden in my pocket. I opened the back door, and the lush smell of leather greeted us. Ashlin climbed in first, and I followed. Two giants were in the front and neither of them acknowledged us. We drove off, and Ashlin slid her hand into mine again. I watched out the window as the sun welcomed the night, turning the mountains into distant shadows.

"When is your dad speaking?" I asked.

"Right before the fireworks begin," she explained, "so probably right when we get there." She bent forward. "How far are we?" The suit in the passenger seat turned around.

"Not far, Miss Ashlin."

The closer we got, I noticed more and more people walking down the street, flocking toward the park. Some were carrying signs with "Ammon" written on them. All of the faces that we passed were smiling. Seeing so many people smiling and cheering was weird to me. Just the day before, this city had been empty; now it reminded me of when this city was filled with life. I started to smile myself, observing all of the people and realizing just how much they loved Ammon. The car stopped, and I looked through the windshield to see the street overflowing with people and cops directing any traffic that came.

"Is this how it always is?" I turned and faced Ashlin next to me. She squeezed my hand tighter and nodded her head slightly. She was obviously used to this.

"You're going to have to go around the back way to get there," the passenger suit pointed to his left, and the driver followed his direction, turning away from the mass of people. I could see multiple lights through a cluster of thick trees, which bordered the entire park, as we drove past. I just wanted to get out of the SUV and walk around with all of the people. I felt like when I was little again, waiting to get my birthday presents. I could see all of them wrapped neatly, but I would have to wait until after the cake to open them. I could see the park right next to us, but I would have to wait until we stopped to go in. I noticed we were driving further away for some reason.

"Where're we going?" I asked. The park was now behind us.

"Where my dad told him to go." Ashlin nodded toward the driver. "We aren't going to be inside the park." Her thumb gently stroked my hand. I wanted to ask why not. I wanted to be a part of that crowd. I knew Ashlin did too. But the way she was looking at me told me to just be quiet for now. The SUV swung into a restaurant parking lot a few blocks away from the park. Ashlin leaned forward again.

"Is this where we're stopping?"

The driver nodded. "Don't go far."

Ashlin reached across me and opened the door. I was a little confused as to what was going on. We both got out of the SUV.

"This is my dad's favorite restaurant." She shut the door and turned toward the small, dirt-stained, stucco building behind us, which was positioned in between two alleyways and looked like it had been deserted years ago. The name of the restaurant, Forester's Steakhouse, was written in green paint across the side and looked as if the owner himself had climbed a wobbly ladder and written it freehand.

"What's going on?" I asked, still hearing the murmur of the crowd at the park two blocks away.

"Come on." She took my hand, and we walked away from the restaurant. "I knew as soon as I saw how big the crowd was that there was no way he was letting me in there." Her voice was hushed as she glanced back at the SUV, like they were listening to us. "He told them to wait here until he was done and could meet us." She let go of my hand and wandered across the street, waving to me to follow her. "I told you he was super protective of me."

She was standing in the middle of the street, facing the towering, gleaming lights of the park. "I don't know why I thought this was going to be different – maybe because you were with me. I don't know." I stood right next to her, with my hands in my pockets, imagining the massive crowd in the park spilling out into the streets like a tipped-over jar filled with marbles. I was also getting more nervous about meeting Ammon. It hadn't hit me just how protective he was of Ashlin. That, to me, meant he was automatically going to hate me.

"Doesn't he know that if he's elected, people are going to know who you are?" I asked.

"I think so. It's not so much people knowing me. He just doesn't want me involved, yet." She shrugged. "So I involve myself in other ways, like stealing the SUV." She put her arm in between mine. "We'll be able to hear him from where we're at though. My dad told me they're shooting the fireworks out of the old baseball stadium. It should be a good show."

I was more interested in hearing what Ammon had to say than the fireworks.

"AMMON, AMMON, AMMON!" The crowd started to chant. It sounded like an army before a battle.

I looked at Ashlin, just to check to see that she was hearing this. I thought the chanting impressed her, like it did me.

"Welcome to my life." Her face was emotionless as she stared toward the park, as if some boring teacher was in front of us, lecturing. She really didn't seem to like all of this. She was only there for her dad. It still didn't make sense to me why he was so protective of her. I mean, I understood to a point, but eventually he'd have to let Ashlin in the spotlight, especially if he was going to win the presidency. The chanting grew louder, bouncing off the walls of the restaurant and the surrounding buildings. I thought I could feel the ground shaking from the voices.

"The entire city must be there," I said.

"One, two, three," Ashlin motioned her hand like she was throwing a Frisbee toward the park, and a giant roar from the crowd answered. He must've walked out onto the stage or whatever was set up for him. After the cheers, the chanting resumed, but not as methodically. I pictured Ammon trying to calm the crowd with his hand raised in the air. Ashlin held onto my arm tighter. Then I heard Marcus' voice come through the speakers for the first time.

"Thank you, thank you." He was trying to speak over the cheers. "Please." Chants of "Ammon" began once more. I pictured the enormous crowd like the ocean in a middle of a storm.

"Welcome to the new and beautiful Liberty Park. This is another step in making our city great again." Another roar from the crowd, but Marcus cut it off before it had time to build.

"I am honored to dedicate this park to our wonderful city and declare it officially open. Most of all, I am honored to be here with you tonight." I heard enthusiastic clapping.

"I know it feels like we have no freedom anymore. I know times are rough and seem hopeless. I know you are sick and tired of hearing the same promises from Washington, only to be forgotten as soon as the words leave their mouths. Forget about them, friends. I am asking you to not give up on *yourselves* yet." His voice was powerful and confident.

"Let's declare war on what our country has become, and together we can change our country and our world to make it what it was meant to be." A cheer erupted throughout the crowd. I found myself wanting to clap with them. I turned to Ashlin, who looked at me out of the corner of her eyes. Marcus waited for the crowd to quiet.

"I cannot do it alone. *You* are what matters to this nation. *You* are what matters to me. I am nothing without you. We can only get stronger, and we will, but strength is nothing without hope, friends. If a small park opening can cause all of you to come out together, then that is proof that our country is not dead. Not yet. Our world needs us."

A few short cheers rang out but quieted quickly. "Many years ago we fought to get away from what is happening in our nation today. I am here to take back what was supposed to never be taken away. Our freedom, friends, our freedom has been stolen from us. This doesn't need to be how we live anymore. This collapse has lasted far too long. It's time to shed our dark, destructive past and start the new era of America. This new era is what our forefathers truly envisioned when they bled into the soil Washington has abandoned." Silence.

"Do not call me Senator. I am just a man who wants to see the country he loves rise to where it belongs. I ask that you join me in this vision and together we will make sure it becomes real. Thank you and enjoy the show." All of the lights turned off and the park seemed to disappear. More wild cheers along with our national anthem roared across the starless night sky.

"Short and sweet; I'm inspired." I leaned over to Ashlin.

"He's good. I know. Now, you'll get to meet him."

Before I could say anything, a burst of red and blue exploded above us. The fireworks show had started. Ashlin squeaked next to me out of excitement. With each firework, I felt it rumble within my chest. I thought about Ammon on his way over to us. I watched the bright colors shimmer across the sky like glitter, and I could only think of my scar for some reason. After each BOOM, I felt my scar throb on my wrist, shooting pain up my arm.

"I love fireworks," Ashlin leaned her head on my shoulder and wrapped her arm around my waist.

A pair of headlights turned down the street we were standing in the middle of, and I knew that it was time. I was about to meet Marcus Ammon.

12

wo black SUV's drove past Ashlin and me in the middle of the street and turned into the restaurant's parking lot. The smell of sulfur from the fireworks show carried over from the breeze. Ashlin still hadn't even moved; she was watching the show intently as I was halfway turned around, watching the SUVs park. The reflections of the fireworks burst in the sky off the windows of the restaurant and vehicles. I started to wonder why we were even there.

"The finale," Ashlin gasped, as multiple explosions and crackling sounds filled the sky. I turned back around and watched the final seconds of the show with her. The bombing stopped, and I could feel her dad watching us from the parking lot. Another loud cheer from the crowd echoed from the park. Once it was over, Ashlin slid her hand off of my waist.

"Ready?" Ashlin took my hand, and we walked toward a group of murmuring shadows standing by the SUVs.

"Hey, Dad," she called.

One tall shadow raised his hand and waved as he continued to talk. Right before we got to the group, Ashlin squeezed my hand.

"My beautiful daughter, how'd you like the show?" The tall shadow stepped away from the group and moved closer to us. I couldn't really get a good look at him, since we were standing in an unlit parking lot. But, from his outline, he looked just like he did in the magazines.

"Surprisingly good," She let go of my sweaty hand. "Dad, this is my boyfriend, Sam. Sam, this is my dad, Marcus." She moved her hand back and forth between us.

"This is *the* Sam? I've heard a lot about you. It's nice to put a face to a name. Once I can see it." Marcus laughed and extended his hand to me, and I met his with mine. When our hands touched, a sharp pain wrapped around my arm, like he had crushed every bone in it. I realized I was using my scarred hand. I hid my discomfort. I was glad it was dark out there.

"It's an honor to meet you, sir." The sharp pain made me short of breath, so I tried to hide it as well as I could.

"I hope both of you are hungry." He gestured toward the restaurant. "This is my little secret. I bet you didn't know this place existed, Sam."

I didn't think this place was even open for business, by the looks of it. I wasn't that hungry, but I wasn't going to say that to Marcus. It's not every day you get invited to eat with a man like him.

"I think you're the *only* person who keeps this place open, Dad." Ashlin held onto my hand again.

"Let's go, then. I'm starved. I let Dean know we would be coming to eat tonight." We all walked toward the entrance. When Marcus tried to open the red wooden door, it was locked. He knocked firmly three times.

"Where's the inner circle?" Ashlin asked.

"The inner circle?" I saw Marcus' shoulders bob up and down as he chuckled. "They're busy making the final plans for the campaign. Erica says hi, by the way."

"Aw, well tell her hi when you see her," Ashlin said, leaning in close to me. "Erica is the brains behind the campaign."

"It's true. No more talk of my campaign tonight." The door swung open and sounded like a dying bird. A short, pudgy, white-haired man unleashed a huge smile, causing his face to ripple with wrinkles. He stood with his arms open, as if he were waiting for a hug.

"Mr. President," the old man wheezed from laughing. His already huge smile grew even bigger.

"Let me get voted in first before you call me that." Marcus hugged Dean like he was his father. "Thanks for letting us come, Mr. Dean."

"Jiminy Cricket! You've known me for two decades, and you still call me 'Mr.'" Dean patted Marcus on the back. "Come in, come in." He waved with both of his hands, as if he were directing traffic.

"You remember my daughter, Ashlin." Marcus shut the screeching door.

"Do I remember your daughter?" Dean repeated Marcus, as if he had just asked the most obvious question. "Of course I do. It's been awhile." Dean wrapped Ashlin's hand in both of his like he was holding a baby bird.

"This is her boyfriend, Sam." Marcus gestured to me.

"You're a lucky man, Stan."

"Sam, sir," I corrected.

"Huh? Oh, I'm sorry, Sam." He placed his hand over his heart and smiled again. "It's nice having you all here. Come sit." He walked us all in past the front counter and into the dining area, which smelled like new carpet. The place looked like an old western bar. The walls were wood paneled, with classic photos of cowboys everywhere I looked. "We were closed today, but when Marcus called and told me he wanted to eat here tonight, I came rushing over."

We all sat down at a table, but Dean remained standing.

"We appreciate you doing this for us," Marcus said.

Dean scrunched his face and swatted the air. "Anytime for the next president of this damned country."

"Well said." Marcus laughed his crisp laugh and brought his arm up to Dean's thin shoulder. "We'll eat whatever you make us."

"Good thing. I just killed some rats back there, so I'll whip those up." Dean wheezed again and patted the air as he walked toward the kitchen. "I'm kidding, I'm kidding."

This was the first time I had a good look at Marcus in person. He was sitting across from me with his elbows on the table, hunched forward. He was looking around the restaurant as if each direction he looked held an old story. Marcus seemed youthful, though, in the way he moved. What I noticed the most was that I knew that I was sitting with a powerful man, but I didn't feel like I was. Marcus just emitted comfort from him, as if there was this protective bubble that would absorb anyone around him. I was nervous all day, but now those nerves were gone. Yet, after hearing his brief speech, I knew that power was there, and here I was sitting across from the man this country seemed to adore.

"Twenty years I've been coming here, and it looks exactly the same. This place almost feels like home to me." His eyes drifted in thought. "Anyway, now I'm glad

I can put a face to a name." His eyes turned to me and stayed this time. "So Sam, what do you do?"

"I'm… a cashier at Hunt's." I certainly wasn't going to break the news that I was jobless now.

"I can already tell that you hate it. What is it that you *want* to do?

"Um…."

"He's an amazing artist," Ashlin interjected as she unwrapped her napkin and silverware came clinking out onto the table.

"Really, like a painter?" Marcus leaned back in his chair keeping his hands on the table.

"Yeah, I love to paint." I nodded, not knowing what else to say or do.

"Here, look what he made." Ashlin took out her phone and showed it to Marcus. "I thought about bringing it but I took a picture of it instead." She turned to me and smirked her usual Ashlin smirk. The image of the tree forced itself into my mind again. I hadn't looked at the painting since the night I got my scar. I hated thinking of it. I rested my scarred wrist on my lap, trying to force the image away like a pestering fly.

"How fascinating," his eyes moved to me, then back to the phone screen. "This could be sold in a gallery."

"That's what I said." Ashlin put her phone back in her purse on the floor. "Sam doesn't think it's that good. I don't get it."

"True artists *know* they can be better; the false artists *think* they're the best, and every artist *hopes* their work speaks to many." Marcus pushed his chair away from the table and stood up. He didn't seem that tall, now that I met him, but when he was standing, he seemed to soar over everyone else. "You guys want something to drink?"

"Water is fine, thanks." I probably looked at him like I was looking up at a statue.

"Me, too," said Ashlin.

Marcus nodded. "You need to start paying me, Dean." He yelled toward the kitchen as he walked through the swinging door to get the drinks. The image I had of Marcus before this was of a man waited on every second of the day like he was an emperor or something. But he seemed just like a normal guy to me.

"I like him." I turned to Ashlin, who was folding the napkin into a triangle on her lap.

"I can already tell he likes you, too." She looked up at me briefly and placed the napkin on top of the table. She looked distant to me. She was right next to me, but the look on her face made her seem far away.

"Are you OK?" I touched her hand with mine and held it. She dropped her eyes back to her lap then up to me, like she was debating to herself where to look, until she settled on looking at our hands in front of her.

"I just think way too much, and... ." I watched her eyes focus harder and she moved her hand out from underneath mine and flipped my wrist over. "What's that?"

You freaking idiot, I thought when I realized my scar was showing. If the scar wasn't causing me pain, I forgot about it. I tried to keep my face calm. I kept my eyes on her as she examined my wrist like she had never seen one before.

"It's a birthmark. I've always had it," I lied.

"I never noticed it before. It looks just like the number seven. Pretty cool." She flipped my hand back over. Relief quickly followed. I slid my hand off of the table. I was glad I didn't have to hide it anymore, though.

"Yeah, I just think way too much," she said.

"What're you thinking about now?" I asked as I heard Dean wheezing and Marcus laughing in the kitchen.

"What if we were fireworks?" Ashlin leaned forward slightly and rested her chin in her hand.

"What do you mean?"

"Like, instead of being humans, we were fireworks." She shrugged, like it was an everyday question she was asking me.

"I never thought of that. I guess I'd be afraid."

"Why?"

"Because you'd never know when you were going to blow up."

"That makes sense, but isn't that how most people feel every day? People are afraid of life because they don't know when they're going to die. If you were a firework, as soon as you were launched, you would know you were going to die, but what a last few seconds you'd have, flying through the air, then bursting into colors and leaving your mark on the world to see." She sat up straight when the kitchen door swung open, and out came Dean and Marcus with the food and drinks. I didn't have time to really respond to her, and I felt like she didn't want me to with Marcus around. I wanted to ask why she was thinking about that. Maybe, she just wanted to get out of there?

"Dean makes an incredible steak." Marcus laid the plates of food in front of Ashlin and me while Dean poured the water into the glasses. Who would've thought Marcus Ammon would be serving *me*? I noticed Ashlin start to stir in her seat like she was trying to get comfortable. She got up right when her food was placed in front of her.

"I'll be right back." She was looking at me when she said it. Marcus just nodded as he cut into his steak. I watched her walk toward the front door and heard it squeal open. I knew I was right: she needed to get out of there. I started to get up to follow her, but Marcus' voice sat me back down as if I was bungeed to the back of the seat.

"Enjoy your food. She'll be back." He was slicing his steak into tiny slivers of meat. I picked up my fork and knife. This was apparently a normal occasion for Ashlin to just get up and go.

"Did she not like the food?" Dean was pouring the last bit of water into a glass for himself.

"The food is delicious. She gets anxious sometimes, that's all." Marcus hadn't looked up from his food once yet. I wasn't really that hungry at all anymore. But I could feel Dean eyeing me for my approval, so I took a bite and smiled, allowing him to walk off back into the kitchen. Marcus looked up from his plate, and his eyes were thin. I was nervous for the first time since meeting him. I felt like I was sitting in an interrogation room after being caught stealing money or something.

"I can tell you really like Ashlin. I can tell that you'd take care of her, too." He glanced back to his food and then to me again.

"I do like her, sir. She's wonderful and… ."

"I don't know what exactly it is yet, but there is just something about you that seems so familiar. Have we met before this?"

"I don't think so, sir. I would've remembered meeting you."

"Please, please. Don't call me sir. It makes me feel old." He took a swig from his water and kept it in his hand as he sat back in his chair. "I haven't seen Ashlin a lot lately, but when I do, you're all I hear about. Maybe that's why I feel like I already know you."

"Hopefully, you've heard good things?" I slowly cut the steak just so I had something to do.

"Good things, but also tragic things. I'm sorry for the loss of your family." He put the water down softly. "Like you," he raised one finger toward me, "my parents died when I was young. I raised myself after the age of seventeen. I lived with lowlife aunts and uncles for a year, but I was by myself most of the time. I realized there had to be more to life. I told myself I wasn't going to stop looking until I found whatever *that* was."

"When did you find 'that'?" The nerves subsided.

"Ironically enough, as soon as I stopped looking. The 'that' was never missing. It was me." He pointed to himself with his thumb. "I needed to find me, and once I did, things started to make a lot more sense." He laughed and moved his mouth to the side, trying to get a piece of food out from between his teeth.

"Come on." He stood up and walked to the front. I followed. "I can tell you're worried about her." I *was* worried. She could've walked off anywhere. He opened the squeaking door. "She's right there. She's always right there."

Ashlin was sitting across the street where we had stood watching the fireworks. Two suits were already eyeing her. I wanted to go over to her and sit with her. We didn't need to talk if she didn't want to, but I didn't like seeing her alone. I didn't count the suits as company either; they might as well have been concrete pillars.

"She'll come back in, trust me. She's OK." Marcus walked back to the table.

I didn't understand what was happening between the both of them, but I couldn't get over how normal Marcus felt about his daughter having to get up and leave.

I let the door shut behind me as I walked over and sat with Ashlin. We didn't speak, but she smirked her usual smirk. After a few minutes, she said, "I'm sorry, I just needed to go."

"If you need to go, then I need to go too."

"Thanks." She placed her hand beneath my chin and turned my head toward her to kiss me. I hoped her dad wasn't watching. As we kissed, I pictured my heart bursting silver like a firework, but in my mind, this one would never be extinguished. I understood a little bit more what Ashlin meant about being a firework.

We need to live each moment like it's the last moment before we explode. So when we do burst, we burst into the most extravagant color anyone has ever seen, making our mark on the world.

Ashlin slowly pulled away from my lips. "I wonder where we can get a free steak around here?" She tried to hold in a laugh through her nose, but couldn't.

"Let's go eat, weirdo." I pulled her up to her feet and we walked back in the restaurant. We finished our dinner with Marcus as if nothing had happened. Definitely not a normal night, but I couldn't say anything that had happened to me recently was normal, so this was just another night for me.

13

The day after the dinner with Marcus, knocking on my door awakened me. I wasn't expecting to see a suit standing there sweating with a stern look on his face.

"Follow me, please." He wiped his bald head with a handkerchief and started to walk down the stairs. I rubbed the sleep out of my eyes, grabbed the first shirt I saw, and stumbled down the stairs. I saw one of the black SUVs waiting for me as soon as I got to the bottom. I knew it wasn't Ashlin, since she would've just walked in. The back door swung open right before I reached it. I climbed in, and Marcus was sitting in the back.

"Sorry to wake you so early. This is the only part of the day I have some time." He reached out his hand and shook mine.

"How're you, Mr. Ammon?"

"Please, call me Marcus, and I'm doing great. I hope you don't mind me showing up unannounced." The SUV pulled away from my complex and turned down the street. Now I started to wonder what was going on.

"No, it's completely fine." I rubbed my hands against my shorts just because I was nervous. I started to wonder if Ashlin was OK.

"Good. The reason why I'm doing this is because I have an offer for you."

"An offer?" What could he possibly offer me?

He smiled and turned to look out the window. He put his finger against the glass, and as a tree blurred by, he swiped his finger across like he was using a touch screen computer.

"You know what my least favorite thing is about living in Phoenix? There is no real change of seasons. Every month seems to be the same. After a while, it gets boring. Life should never be boring. If it ever is, that's your cue to shake things up." He turned to me briefly before looking back out the window. "Yesterday, at our dinner, I saw that you were bored."

"I wasn't... ."

He lifted both of his hands barely, stopping me. "I know you weren't bored at the dinner, but with your life. I saw what I used to look like in you." He chuckled to himself. "Even though we just met, I see a lot of myself in you. This is your cue. Accept the change that is about to come your way. You deserve it." Marcus patted my shoulder as he faced me once more.

I wasn't sure what change was about to come my way. I was a little confused.

"I know you work at Hunt's, but would you be interested in a new job?"

"Yes, yes I would. What's the job?" I probably sounded like he had just offered me a million dollars.

"After I saw your painting, I knew you had talent."

The image of the tree screamed back into my mind.

"And after I saw how you went out to sit with Ashlin, I knew you cared about her for herself, and you're not with her because of me." He reached in front of him in the back seat's back pocket and pulled out a piece of paper.

"I talked to Erica already. You haven't met her, but you will soon." He handed me the piece of paper. It was a contract of some sort.

"I asked her what she thought about bringing on an intern once we were on the road." He pulled a pen out of his shirt pocket and started to click it.

"She said she was already thinking about that and had a few candidates in mind." He handed me the pen. I was skimming the contract, but mainly listening to him.

"I told her early this morning that I found who I wanted to join us and help out." He nodded toward me and pointed at the contract. "I can never pass up on talent when I see it. All you need to do is sign on the dotted line, Sam. This is a career opportunity. Plus, I knew Ashlin couldn't go three months without seeing you." He clapped his hands and rubbed them together like he was trying to keep warm. "It's a win-win. Only if you want to, of course. Feel free to ask me any questions you may have."

I just sat there, holding the pen in one hand and the contract in the other, which was flapping like a banner from the air-conditioning.

"This is too good to be true." I looked up and met his stare. "You just met me. I don't get it, to be honest."

"I understand, but do you really *know* anyone at first? No. In order to change, you need to take a chance. Like I said before, I see potential in you, and I think this could be a fresh start." He looked behind me. I followed his stare and saw that we were back at my run-down apartment complex. "Everyone needs one fresh start. It's normal to get caught up in the... the. . . " He looked like he smelled something rotten, "gunk of the world, especially now. There is not a lot to be happy about, but you're going to have to want to shed off all that you're used to and welcome an entirely new feeling. Trust me, it's worth it."

He was right. Marcus would know more about the "gunk" of the world than me. I had a hunch he was thinking about his wife while saying that. I thought of the night I saw my dad sitting in my kitchen with that child. I thought of my dad's silhouette I had seen looking out of my window and what he had said: "You're going to make an impact on this world, Sam." Even if that really didn't happen, I still heard his voice. I pictured my mom in my mind nodding her head in approval like she always did when she listened to someone she agreed with.

I wanted to make an impact and I wanted to make my mark on the world; maybe this was my chance. I didn't know what was happening to me lately. Nothing seemed real, but this, this meeting with Marcus, felt very real. He honestly believed in me already. I didn't know what he saw in me that I couldn't.

"I'm in," I smiled. "I accept." I flattened the paper out on my leg and signed at the bottom. I was ready for a change and felt that Marcus wouldn't lead me wrong. I handed him back the contract and the pen.

"Welcome to the team. We leave in a week. Make the arrangements you need to make." He clicked the end of the pen. "I'll let you tell Ashlin the good news. I'm sure you'll be seeing her before I do, anyway." The suit that awakened me got out of the car and opened my door for me. I guessed the meeting was over.

"Thank you. You don't know how much this means to me, really." I held out my hand to him.

"I'm looking forward to working with you," Marcus said. "Have a good day, Sam." He met my hand with his and shook it once firmly. I got out of the SUV, and called Ashlin, and told her to come over later for some good news.

14

As soon as Marcus had dropped me off, I caught the bus and went to the store to use up most of the money I had left to buy pasta and make dinner for Ashlin. On the way there, the bus passed where Hunt's used to be. The sign was still hanging where it always was, but this time each letter was unlit.

I had just got back to my apartment and put the two plastic bags of groceries on the stove for later. I walked to the balcony door and turned back to face the kitchen, remembering the image of my dad standing right where I was. I looked out the glass and saw the skyline filling with a brown haze. I slid open the door and stepped outside, right into a gust of warm wind. I leaned on the railing, holding on to it, smelling dirt mixing with rain in the air. The horizon darkened by the second with a towering wall of dust rapidly bearing down on the city. I could already feel tiny particles of sand grinding against my teeth.

I sat down on the flimsy lawn chair and propped my feet up on the railing, watching the brown cloud inch closer and closer. I kept thinking about my new job and I wondered what was waiting for me. I didn't consider myself a man of many skills or anything, so I was already nervous. I couldn't wait to tell Ashlin, though. From where I was sitting, I could see her SUV turn into the complex. I got up just as the dust storm was about to engulf everything in sight, hurried to my front door and opened it, waiting for Ashlin to come running in. It felt like my hallway had turned into one of those wind tunnels.

"Come on, come on," I said, with Ashlin laughing and sort of screeching as she made her way up the stairs. Instead of running right inside, she ran into me and wrapped her arms around my waist. She had a plastic bag dangling from her wrist that bumped against my leg. Our lips found each other's as her hair whirled around our faces as we kissed. I then felt the dust storm impact as it violently threw specks of debris around us.

"Let's get inside," I said as I pulled her into my apartment and shoved the door shut from the whining wind.

"You saved me, Mr. Addison." Ashlin threw her head back in a pretended faint and fanned herself with her hand, giggling the entire time, of course.

"You're weird." I took the bag off from around her wrist and kissed her again.

"Yeah, well I'm OK with being weird. If you're *not* weird, then you are *really* weird," Ashlin teased.

"What's in the bag?" I held it up.

"Why are you asking me? You have it in your hand." She smirked and leaned forward, letting her hair fall down, and shook off any bits of dust that were trapped. "My dad told me to give it to you. Well, actually a note *from* my dad told me to give it to you."

"Cool, cool." I didn't open it yet, but brought it into my room and put it next to the painting of the tree, which still hadn't been touched since the day it appeared on the canvas. I wished Ashlin would take it but she didn't want to remove it from its "birthing place." I stopped and looked at it as if hypnotized. I don't know if it was my eyes playing tricks on me or what, but the two shadows seemed to be closer in the picture than before.

"What's for dinner?" I heard Ashlin searching the bags in the kitchen, along with the wind slamming against the window in my room.

I ran my hand down the painting, feeling the roughness of the canvas against my fingertips, and stopped right on the two shadow figures.

"I'm starving. Let's cook." Ashlin tapped lightly on my door with her nails.

I nodded and forced a smile as I turned away from the painting, which felt like it wanted to pull me inside it, and forced my hand off the picture and into my pocket. I followed Ashlin into the kitchen and felt better the farther I got from that damned tree.

"I'm making my specialty dish, you know." I turned on the sink and filled the only pot I owned with water. Ashlin propped up her elbows on the kitchen counter, like she was sitting at a diner waiting for her food. I could feel her watching me.

"You OK?" She sounded like she knew I wasn't but wanted to hear it from me.

"Yeah, why?" I asked, turning the knob on the stove, which caused some clicking noises, until I felt a burst of heat coming from the burner.

"Just checking, that's all."

I put the pot of water on the stove and turned to face
Ashlin, who had walked around the counter and stepped
closer to me.

"So," she brought her arms up onto my shoulders and
loosely wrapped her hands around the back of my neck,
"what's this good news you wanted to tell me?"

I slid my hand around her waist and onto the small of
her back. "You sure you want to hear it now, or do you
want to wait until after dinner?"

"Now, please." She batted her eyes at me over-dram-
atically on purpose.

"First, you know how you're leaving in a week for
your dad's campaign?"

She sort of flinched and grimaced. "I don't want to
talk about that."

"I know, but you are, right?"

"Yeah," She was looking at me like I had told her she
was dying in a week.

"I hope you won't mind if I come along."

Her already big eyes grew even more as she smiled.
"What? How?"

"You're dad offered me a job."

Her smile shrunk, but it was still there. "A job?"

"Yeah, I'm not quite sure of the position, but still.
That means I get to be with you now." I pulled her closer.

She didn't say anything else, but just kissed me.
"You sure you want to do this?" She leaned back with her
arms still around my neck.

"I'm positive." I was more than positive, actually.
I needed to take this job.

She smirked and nodded her head. "OK." She
massaged the back of my head and tilted her head to see
behind me. "Water is ready."

I went over, and poured the box of pasta into the water and stirred. When I turned back, I saw that same distant look on Ashlin's face I had seen the night at the restaurant with Marcus. I walked over to her and stroked her cheek with my thumb.

"If you feel like you need to go, the weather might be an issue." I smiled and nodded toward the back window, which was smothered in dust. She held my hand against her face.

"Just be careful." She squeezed my hand.

"Careful with what?"

"Just say you will be."

I felt my mouth open slightly. I wanted to ask why, but I didn't. Asking why never seems to give me a clear answer, so I just bent down and pressed my lips on her forehead.

"I'll be careful."

15

he weeklong wait was about over. Tomorrow morning would be the start of my new life. I was only bringing one suitcase onto the bus with me, which was stuffed with anything I wanted to keep - mainly just clothes and the sketchbook my mom and I drew in. I made a deal with my landlord, since I couldn't pay rent, that I would leave all the furniture and anything else of value in the apartment after I moved out. He agreed. He was an old, white-haired Italian who rarely spoke.

With a cigarette bouncing in his mouth, he said, "You're the only one who paid rent on time anyway." He took a long drag, and before shutting his door, he told me, "Good luck." I had never understood why people told each other good luck. Almost always, if someone told me that, it was never sincere, and I could tell the old man wasn't sincere either because of the faded smile drawn on his face. Good luck is the nice way of saying, "Don't die too quickly," or, "Just quit already." I didn't understand. Maybe I wasn't supposed to, though.

I sat at my desk and put the painting of the tree facedown so I didn't have to look at it. Ashlin was planning on leaving it at her house while we were gone. If I had it my way, I'd leave it for the next poor guy who was going to live in this rat's nest.

I was observing the little box Marcus had told Ashlin to give to me. When I eventually opened the bag, there was a tiny shred of paper with a note that said, "Don't open this until the night before we leave - Marcus"

So I waited. I don't know why I did. It wasn't like he would've known I opened it beforehand or not, but I waited nonetheless. I took out the tiny, white, cardboard box and lifted the lid.

Inside the box was a lapel pin: the ankh cross, the last drawing my mom had ever produced. I held the black-and-gold pin between my fingers. Written boldly on the inside of the box was "**Do Not Lose This**." I held it in my palm and kept thinking it was going to crawl away. I'd never found out what the symbol meant. Since I didn't have access to a computer I was planning on asking Marcus as soon as I saw him. This was obviously an important symbol for him, and it seemed to be following me. I placed the pin back in the box and opened the front compartment of my luggage and set it on top.

I sat down on the floor next to the suitcase and used it as a pillow for my head. I stretched my arms and legs out. I had never lain on the floor the entire time I had lived in the apartment, but now, for some reason, it seemed appropriate. I held my wrist up and stared at my scar, hoping the longer I stared at it, it would eventually disappear. I wished that I could somehow replace all of the bad memories I had with any thought I wanted to. Whenever I thought of my mom, my brain made the same trail to how she died. I couldn't think of my parents without remembering that they were not here anymore. Tomorrow would be the first time I had ever left Arizona. I was also leaving my parents for the first time, in a way. I was ready to leave some of my life behind in the apartment.

Turning my head toward my bedroom door, I thought I saw something standing in the doorway out of the corner of my eye. All the lights were off in the apartment, except a single desk lamp that barely lit my room. I kept my stare on the doorway, where I could feel that something was there, like the way a fish leaves a ripple in the water even though it has already left. I sat up, still looking at the doorway, and started to feel sick. I clutched my stomach and started to gag. I hurried into the bathroom, which was just outside of my room in the hallway, and heaved into the toilet. I hugged the side of the toilet and saw my scar glowing on my wrist, throbbing to the beat of my heart and glowing brightly. I puked one more time and felt my scar burning against my flesh. I lifted my head away from the toilet and felt like I had been upside down. I saw splotches of purple and flashing sparks until my vision went black. I felt my body collapse onto the bathroom floor. Then silence.

My heartbeat broke through the thick silence, sounding far way, but I heard it. I could feel the scar still throbbing on my wrist. My heartbeat grew louder. I felt like I was swimming underwater and coming closer to the surface, hearing the muffled noises getting louder above the water. My eyes shot open, and I saw my arms and legs flailing in every direction. The sensation of falling squeezed my gut for a second, and then the feeling was gone. I knew I was no longer in my bathroom because

I saw a shining light standing in front of me. I blinked my eyes rapidly to try to wake myself up and see if I was dreaming.

Nothing happened. I stared at this light, shaped like the flame from a candle, as it slowly started to flash like a strobe. It threw off cold gusts of wind from it every time it pulsated and began to move around me, radiating gold and a sparkling green. The light resembled a twister, destroying the darkness that surrounded it. After writhing around, the light came to a complete standstill, though it continued to burn brightly. Wherever I was, I felt as if I was standing on top of mountain peak. The light's force seemed to pull me closer toward it. I noticed even the blackness surrounding me bend and blur toward the light. A burst of heat flared out from it, causing the light to collapse inward, sucking the air like some sort of black hole in space. I was lifted into the air and reached for anything to hold onto as I was dragged toward this blob of light.

Then everything became still. I dropped to the ground, then slowly stood back on my feet and saw a single tall shadow shaped like a man standing in front of me. The mystery light was still there, but it was much smaller and duller behind the tall figure.

"Who are you?" I tried to sound like I was asking a regular, every day person in front of me this question. Instead of an answer, a piercing, whistling sound, like the feedback from a speaker, was all I heard, but the noise was coming from the inside of my head. I gripped my forehead with my hands, wincing in pain, hoping for the noise to subside.

"You've seen me before," the shadow spoke from within the high-pitched noise, drowning it out. I had heard this forceful male's voice before. The painting of the tree popped into my mind as if this shadow had placed it there. I instantly knew he was one of the figures standing underneath that colossal tree.

"What do you... ." Before I could finish what I wanted to ask, I saw the shadow walking closer to me. I heard a loud clanking with every step he took, like he was dragging chains behind him. I couldn't see what he looked like, but I saw he had tiny, shining markings covering his entire body, none of which I had ever seen before. They all began to flash brighter.

"Your wrist," the shadow indicated, stopping only feet from me, raising my arm without touching it. I saw my scar flash rapidly on my skin. I looked back to him and noticed that he had raised his massive arm and saw, where his wrist would be, the same flashing symbol, just like mine. My arm dropped back to my side.

"What are you? What's happening to me?" I shot, needing answers now. I was tired of confusion. Something was happening, and I needed to know what.

"I am here for you." The light behind the shadow burst into a giant, golden flame once again, blinding me.

When my vision returned, I was on the floor of my bathroom, soaked with sweat. I pushed myself up and sat against the wall, the toilet between my feet.

I was convinced I was losing my mind this time. I just sat there listening for the shadows voice. "I'm going crazy," I told myself again. I flipped over my wrist and saw the scar puffed out. I laughed in shock until my stomach burned. I definitely looked insane now. Once I stopped laughing, I took a deep breath and shook my head slightly, still looking at my wrist.

"You're not crazy," I mumbled, as I stood up on my feet. I wasn't going to let myself go crazy. Not now. I flipped on the shower to see if I could at least wash off everything I had just seen. I leaned my head back against the back wall and watched the steam drift upward, searching for an escape.

16

took one final look at my apartment and then shut the door for the last time.

"Are you gonna miss this place, Sammy?" Ashlin slid her hand into mine. She had driven to my apartment with a suit in one of the SUVs. This was where Marcus' tour bus was going to be picking us up with an entire army of suits and members of the campaign team following. I had no idea what to expect, but I never really did, especially lately. I thought of the massive shadow being. I wanted to know what he was, even if he wasn't real.

"Sam?" Ashlin moved her finger against my palm, getting my attention.

"Huh?"

"Are you gonna miss this place, you think?" We both stood outside the closed door. I grabbed my luggage and turned to walk down the stairs.

"No, I'm not. I'll never forget it though, that's for sure." I peered down to my wrist. "It's time for a fresh start."

Ashlin nodded in agreement. We walked down to the entrance of my apartment complex, where two SUVs were already parked.

There were no clouds in the sky, just a sheet of blue. The sun was our only audience. I was reminded of when I was little, when my bed had blue sheets with clouds all over them. I would pretend that I was free-falling out of the sky every time I jumped on the bed face-first. One day I would be Superman, the next I would be an eagle. It didn't matter as long as I was flying in my mind. That's what I wanted most as a child: to fly. I think kids want to fly in order to escape bullying at school or getting punished by their parents, any situation at all. If the sky was available, I think every kid would be flying around. An image of a bunch of kids racing each other through clouds and flipping around in the sky made me smile. I wished to fly with Ashlin. I pictured us having lunch on top of skyscrapers and reaching for the moon on mountain peaks, away from everything and everyone. We would have the best views every single day. She wouldn't feel that need to leave anymore either.

Back in reality, we both sat down on a curb underneath a few trees to wait for Marcus' bus to arrive. We watched some of the suits smoke and laugh about nothing. This was the first time I wondered who they actually were. I mean, all these men did was follow either Marcus or Ashlin wherever they went. That was their lives. I wondered what they liked to do for fun or if they had a families of their own to protect.

"How's your wrist?" Ashlin asked as she held onto my hand in her lap, tracing the scar with her finger.

"It's OK. Why?"

"I notice you keep looking at it like you're expecting it to explode any second." She shrugged, pushing her sunglasses down from the top of her head to cover her eyes. I think she knew that I didn't always have the scar, but I also knew she wouldn't say anything unless I did.

"It's fine. It just gets sore, sometimes."

She brought my hand up to her lips and kissed the scar. "And you call me weird?" She stuck her tongue out at me when I looked and leaned her head against my shoulder. "I'm glad you're coming with me. I would've died not seeing you for months."

I turned and pressed my lips on the top of her head, burying my face in her hair and the smell of vanilla. "I'm glad too. It would've been hell without you here."

She moved her head off my shoulder and lifted her eyes up at me. "Can I ask you something?"

"Of course, anything."

"Do you believe in heaven and hell?" She plucked a weed that was growing out of a crack on the curb between us.

"I don't. That's all made up." I leaned back and propped myself up with my hands.

"Why do you think that? I'm just wondering. We never really talked about it, so… . " She ripped the weed into tiny pieces and tossed them aside like she was throwing candy during a parade.

"I think we've been through enough hell already. What would be the point of its existence if I already know what it feels like? And is there a heaven?" I clenched my jaw. "If there is, God isn't there."

"So you don't believe in God at all?" She leaned back just like how I was.

"If there is a God, he isn't anywhere near me." I looked up and saw the sun through the drooping branches on the tree above us.

"You're just like my dad." She looked at me and then sat up straight again and tapped her feet against the pavement. "I think there *has* to be something else out there, guiding us through life." She stopped tapping her foot and tilted her head upward, absorbing the sun's warmth. "I don't think we could survive without some sort of help, whether that help is physical, like someone pulling you out of the street when a car is coming, or emotional help, having someone there to talk about whatever you want, anytime you want. Even during crappy times, like now, I think there is something pulling us along. I feel it."

"I don't feel it. That's why I said that if there is a God, he's nowhere near me." I cleared my throat, even though I didn't need to.

"You might be closer to God than you think. It's like whenever you get used to something always being there, you take it for granted. I'm not saying you take God for granted, but maybe you're just used to the fact that He's there and you don't want Him to be." She shrugged. I knew she was just thinking out loud, like she always did.

"I don't think so, Ash. For me to do that, I would first have to know that he is actually there. I still haven't been shown anything to prove that he actually exists. All I ever got was my parents and whatever they told me." I pushed myself up and sat straight, letting my arms hang over my knees. "I hate to say it, but my mom *was* insane, and my dad… the point is, how could I trust anything they would tell me about God?" I shut my eyes and saw my parents' faces. They looked different to me. They started to look like strangers. Was my dad's hair graying? Did my mom have a tiny mole above her lips? I quickly opened my eyes again.

"You can't." she said.

"I can't what?"

"You can't trust anything they said about God. But you can't trust anything, *anyone* says. I guess it's just faith."

"I guess you're right," I said. "Can we talk about something else?" What was faith anyway? To me, faith was just an imaginary promise to an imaginary force.

"Sure, I was just curious." She kissed my cheek and rested her head on my shoulder again. We didn't talk for a minute or so; the birds and the suits were the only ones speaking.

"Have you seen the bus yet?" I rested my chin on the top of her head.

"No, I haven't, but I think we're both about to." she stood up.

I followed her gaze and saw, turning into the complex, a mammoth vehicle, its engine roared as if it were a beast making its presence known. It rumbled to a complete stop in front of us.

"I think this is bigger than a house." My mouth sagged open as I looked. "Marcus Ammon For President." I read the bold printing on the side of the bus. The bus itself was red, white, and blue, with flashy stars spotted across the sides.

"We'll have no problem getting attention in this." Ashlin laughed. The engine's deep growl was silenced and out stepped Marcus, smiling his bright smile.

"Whadaya think?" He turned and faced the huge bus proudly.

"Fits you perfectly, Dad," Ashlin grinned as Marcus hugged her. She seemed to be swallowed by the bus when she climbed in.

"So, Sam, you ready?" Marcus extended his hand to shake mine.

My arm was halfway extended toward his when I noticed his eyes lock onto my wrist where my scar was. I stopped my hand as if it were a bird shot down in midair. I flipped my wrist over and forced out a smile. Did he notice my scar? Why didn't I where long sleeves?

His stare bounced between my wrist and my eyes one last time before shaking my hand. "Follow me. I have some people for you to meet." His voice became stern.

I really needed to be more careful flaunting this scar around like it was normal. I was still clueless to what this marking even was. I didn't need anyone else asking questions. Thankfully, it wasn't glowing like it had been last night. That's all I needed to happen, to be the insane guy with the glowing wrist.

I followed Marcus and entered the bus. Once on top of the stairs, I saw how incredible this thing really was. On the entire right side of the aisle were big luxurious chairs, but the left side resembled an office. The bus was extremely wide and spacious. I wasn't sure how it would fit in the lane on the road, although not as many people owned cars anymore, so there wouldn't be traffic.

Two desks were bolted into the floor along with the chairs. On the left, at one of the desks, a blonde woman typed away on her laptop.

"Sam, this is Erica's main assistant, Kelly." Kelly looked to be in her thirties. She had a pretty, thin face with sad-looking brown eyes. Her hair was curly, but neat.

Marcus swiveled around in the aisle and had his hand on her shoulder. "Kelly, this is, Sam. He will be helping me out a bit. But his main priorities will be with Gabe and... . " Marcus' forehead scrunched in thought. "What's his name?" He snapped his fingers on his other hand as if that would help him remember.

"Oh, the designer?"

"Yes, the moody one. Odd name," Marcus let out a quick laugh.

"Kale," Kelly pointed at Marcus and nodded her head.

"Yes, Kale." He looked back to me. "They'll both be meeting us in Iowa."

I was glad to finally hear some clarity of what my job would be during this time.

"Welcome to the team." Kelly smiled and continued typing away.

"This'll be your desk. We'll meet in my office most of the time, though. But you can put your things here." He pointed underneath the desk where there was a floor compartment and waved for me to follow again. I shoved my luggage underneath the desk and caught up to Marcus down the aisle. I couldn't believe how massive the bus was. It was like a traveling building. I heard Ashlin laughing along with other voices talking all at once.

"Here's the main office. It may sound cliché, but I call it the war zone." Marcus turned to face me quickly, before walking in. The office was carpeted throughout, with a dark mahogany desk in the middle. A leather couch lined the back wall with an older man and a redheaded lady about Marcus' age sitting on it. Ashlin was sitting cross-legged behind the desk in a brown leather chair. If it weren't for the engine starting up again, I would've forgotten I was on a bus.

"I'd like to introduce Sam Addison to you all." Marcus wrapped his arm around my shoulder. "Sam, this is my good friend and running mate, Dante Wess." He opened his other hand toward the older-looking man, who was neatly dressed, like a college professor. He was partially bald, but the hair that he had was brown. His dark eyes were thin slits, like he was trying to stay awake. Narrow glasses rested on the tip of his nose. His mousey face was covered in perfectly trimmed facial hair. When he stood up I was a little surprised he was going to be Marcus' running mate.

"Nice to meet you," His voice was sharp and calm.

"Nice to meet you, too." I was expecting to shake his hand, but he just sat back down on the couch.

"Dante is hitching a ride with us to Iowa to link up with the other half of our team, where he will then fly around the country with them and spread our movement," Marcus looked at him proudly.

"And this," Marcus then motioned toward the lady next to Dante, "is Erica Andrews." Her reddish hair was pulled up in a tight ponytail. She stood with perfect posture in her black skirt and white, buttoned shirt, which was unbuttoned at the top.

"This is *the* Sam?" she asked with a slight southern twang. Her light eyes shifted to Ashlin as she smiled.

"Erica is pretty much my brain during this tour. Actually, she has been my brain for my entire political career." Marcus rubbed underneath his chin and nodded slightly. "Anyway, this is my team. There will be a lot of faces you'll meet during this thing and then never see again. I appreciate the work they all do, but not how I appreciate these two."

"Nice to meet you both, I'm excited to have this opportunity." Erica and I shook hands. She had a strong, firm grip.

"We're glad you decided to join in on the fun. Welcome to Team Ammon. Now, I need to talk with Dante and Marcus." Her eyes drifted to the door, basically telling Ashlin and me to leave.

"She's all business." Marcus walked around to his desk, kissed the top of Ashlin's head, and picked up a coffee mug. Both Ashlin and I turned to walk out.

"Sam?"

I looked back at Marcus, who was holding his mug up in the air. "Coffee, please." I hurried over back to him. He started to laugh.

"I'm kidding. I'm not going to treat you the way Erica treats her assistant, or should I say, slave?" He reclined in his chair, still chuckling, while looking at Erica, who held her hands behind her back and smirked. "I can't speak for Gabe but I have a feeling he won't either. I'll need to talk to you in a few though, once we're done in here. Bring that pin I gave you too."

"I'll come get you." Erica folded her hands in front of her.

I simply nodded and shut the door on my way out. I felt a little out of place being in the same room as all of them. But I also felt important. I felt needed for the first time in a long time. I liked that.

Ashlin was in one of the luxurious chairs, on her knees facing me, holding the back of the chair. Before going over to her, I went to my desk and pulled out my bag. I unzipped it and took out the little white box with the ankh pin.

"What's that?" Ashlin's feet slid into my view as I zipped up the bag.

"Some sort of pin your dad gave me." I shrugged and put the bag back in the floor compartment.

"Humph, lets pick out our seat-slash-bed for the next three months." I watched her walk down the aisle and pat the top of each chair. I glanced down at the white box and saw my scar begin to glow. Why now?

I stuffed my hand and the box in my pocket and followed Ashlin down the aisle. Erica came out of the office with her eyes locked on mine.

"Marcus and Dante are ready for you." Was *I* ready for them?

Ashlin stepped aside to let me through to the office, where Erica was holding the door open for me. "I'll save you a seat."

17

ante stood by the door and cleaned his glasses with a fancy-looking rag before shutting the door on his way out. The bus was now on the road, so anytime it turned or stopped, the desk would creak and strain against the bolts holding it down on the floor. I sat down on the couch beside Marcus' desk. Marcus was on the phone with someone as he opened the blinds of the back window and watched the road, nodding and trying to get a word in.

I checked my wrist, hoping the scar wasn't still glowing like I was some sort of alien. Thankfully, it wasn't. I opened the little white box and lifted the ankh-cross pin out, interested in knowing what this little thing was all about. I rubbed the pin and started to think of my mom's last drawing of the same thing. I remembered when I was little and how I would always watch her draw or paint. If she were painting, it would be in the garage. After my dad died, the garage turned into a full-time studio. The floor was splattered with colors. Even with a sheet down, it didn't do any good.

"You cannot create something beautiful without getting messy first," she would say, while looking over the multicolored mess with approval.

A bump on the road startled me back to reality and the fact that I was sitting in Marcus Ammon's office, waiting to speak to him. He hung up his phone, stuffing it in his pocket. He untucked his shirt and sat down in the chair, almost like he'd fallen in it.

"This is going to be interesting." He reclined back and ran his hand through his hair, rubbing the back of his neck with one hand. "I see you have your pin," he commented as he pointed his finger lazily to the white box in my lap.

"Yeah, right here." I raised the pin up for him to see. "If you don't mind me asking, what's it for?"

"I'm not sure if you know this already, but that symbol is the ankh. The ankh means a lot to my heritage. I'd like it to be the symbol of my campaign." He smiled and leaned forward in his seat. "I'm sure you don't remember since you were probably just a child, but years ago I'd have been chastised in this country for embracing this symbol." He pointed his finger up to the ceiling as if he just remembered a lost thought. "While suffering from the collapse, our country began to re-shape itself without even knowing." He picked up a pen and twirled it between his fingers slowly. "As you know now, no one cares about what you believe, as long as you can provide some answers." He pointed the pen at himself. "Now is the perfect time to unite." He clenched his fingers around the pen as if he was trying to crush it.

"What does the symbol itself mean though? Why would you have been chastised?" I leaned forward awaiting the answers.

"At that time, our nation fell into a dangerous trap of looking for anyone or something to blame but ourselves. The ankh is somewhat linked to the Islamic culture, that is 'something' our country blamed for its issues." Marcus tapped the tip of the pen against the desk. "But the symbol itself could mean a lot of things. No one really has a legitimate meaning. They call it 'the key of life.' But, to me, the ankh is a reminder of what I want to become when I start to forget." He leaned to the right in his chair, and barely tapped the pen against the bottom of his chin, lost in a thought.

I vaguely remembered what life was like before the collapse. All I knew is if the economy hadn't collapsed, my parents would still be alive. My dad wouldn't have ever tried to start a church in Honduras and I would never have gone with him, causing my mom to lose her mind. I felt myself getting angry. "What is it that you want to become, besides president?" That sounded stupid. I just wanted my thoughts to go in another direction. I still didn't know exactly what the ankh mean, so now I guess I wanted to know what Marcus was all about.

"Good question. Let me answer that later though, if you don't mind." He placed the pen down and stood up. He straightened out the bottom of his shirt, which was crinkled. "For now, I just wanted to talk to you about your job."

"Sounds good to me," I replied, wondering if I should stand up as well.

"You are my extra pair of hands and feet, like how Erica is my extra brain. What exactly that entails, I don't know yet. You'll find that out during the campaign. It's hard to keep organized." He chuckled as he turned to look out the window. "Also, as we discussed earlier, you'll be working with our advertisement designer, Gabe and maybe Kale, if he comes around." He turned to me and half-shrugged. "You obviously have talent with painting. So, I believe Gabe and you will create some stunning signs, especially with the ankh." Marcus nodded slightly. "Most importantly, you'll need to keep me sane." It was going to be hard enough to keep myself sane, since I already felt like I was just about to board the train to Insanityville already.

"I'll try, Marcus." I laid my arm across the top cushion of the couch. "Thank you, again, for this opportunity."

"That right there is the last time you'll thank me." He sat on the edge of his desk and held on to the corner as the bus slowed down then sped up again. "Keep that pin close to you. We'll be in Des Moines tomorrow."

"Iowa, right?"

Marcus nodded. There was a knock at the door before it opened, and Dante came in. Marcus didn't say anything, but looked at him, waiting to see what he wanted.

"I need to speak with Marcus, if you don't mind, uh… . " He was trying to remember my name.

"Sam." Marcus completed Dante's sentence for him.

"Yes, Sam." Dante was holding the door open. "I do hope you understand that this is not a vacation. You're here for Marcus." His thin eyes seemed to get even thinner as he looked at me. I stood up from the couch and nodded at Dante.

"He understands," Marcus patted Dante's shoulder. "I'll get you if I need you, Sam. Thanks." Marcus smiled as I walked past both him and Dante. I heard the door shut as I left and balanced my way to the seats Ashlin had picked for us and sat down next to her. She was listening to music and writing in a notebook. She pulled out one earphone when she saw me and put the notebook in the seat's pocket in front of her. I could hear the buzz of her music, since it was so loud, until she turned it off entirely.

"How'd it go in there?" She wrapped the white cord of the headphones around the device.

"Not too bad, but that Dante is kinda weird, huh?"

"Oh, yeah, I know. He's always been close to my dad. They went to law school together. Dante was the one to convince my dad to go into politics." She fixed her hair into a ponytail. "I don't know how he was able to convince him, since he barely talks when anyone else is around." She moved her lips from side to side, like she was trying to scratch her nose. "He's just creepy. He'll be leaving us soon though."

"That's what I've heard." I rested my head back. "At least these chairs are comfortable." They really were too. They seemed to mold to my body.

"You better get used to this." She twisted her body to face me in her seat. I leaned across, pressed my lips against hers, and then kissed her forehead.

"What was that for?" She smiled and ran her hands along the back of my head, pulling me close to her again. She had her hand on my cheek, stroking my face with her thumb. She smirked the usual Ashlin smirk.

"Trust me, I'll have no problem getting used to this. It's already been better than the last few years of my life."

"You say that now, but in two weeks you'll be scratching to get out of here, trust me," she said.

"You're probably right. But if you can do it, I'll manage." I took her hand off of my face and kissed it.

"We can be miserable together." She made a goofy face.

"Sounds fun."

"Oh," Her eyes lit up. "I'm sure you've heard, but I was listening to Erica on the phone and we are headed to Des Moines first." She made her face look bored. "Exciting, I know. Erica was also saying-"

"Eavesdropper," I joked.

Ashlin smiled and continued. "She was also saying that my dad has risen in the early polls, even with the controversy of him running as an independent. So it begins." She did the political thumb and made her voice deep.

"Yes, it does." I tilted my head back against the seat and took a deep breath.

"Now, you need to listen to this song." Before I could even respond, Ashlin had put an earphone in my ear and the other in hers. There was no singing; it was an electronic instrumental band. I hadn't realized just how long it had been since I had listened to music. I used to all the time while I painted, but not even music could've lifted me out of the dark hole my life had become. I turned my head slightly and looked at Ashlin, her eyes closed as she listened. I shut my eyes too and let my mind wander with the melody of the music.

Then I felt a gentle tingling around my scar, like tiny bubbles were popping over it. The slow bouncing of the bus made me feel like I was floating, and my head dropped to my chest. There was nothing but blackness and the sound of the music gradually fading away turning into an echo, until silence was all that remained. I felt blood rush through my veins, using them like a racetrack, causing my muscles to twitch and stiffen.

"Addison." A fierce, low voice spoke into my ear. When I opened my eyes, I was standing in the middle of a desert.

"Walk." The voice spoke again.

I listened, and started to trudge forward, fighting the deep sand with each step. The sun's rays whipped my bare neck, and I could feel its heat reflecting off the sand that blew into my eyes with every dry gust of wind. I approached a small mound and heard faint voices coming from the other side. I peeked over and saw two figures facing each other. Dropping to my stomach, getting a mouthful of sand in the process, I couldn't really tell what either of them looked like, but they wereboth enormous.

I inched a little closer on my stomach to get a better look. This reminded me of the only time I had gone hunting with my dad a few days before we had left for the Honduras jungle. Instead of lying in sand, we had been lying in snow in northern Arizona.

"You got this one, Sammy." I remember my dad's voice was hushed, but intense. About twenty yards away was an elk resembling a small brown minivan. I couldn't believe I was as close to the creature as I was. I could see the elk's back muscles twitching as it bent forward to sniff the frozen ground. I couldn't grasp that this thing was actually alive, and that in my hand I had the weapon to end that life.

"Trust your sight." My dad rested his hand on my back.

I took aim and tried to steady my shaking arm. I held my breath.

"Hold on." My dad nudged me. Another monstrous elk moved into view, its head down, heading right toward my target. I lowered my gun and looked at my dad. I'll never forget the look on his face. His eyes were wide, as if he was making sure to take all of what he was seeing in. His lips formed that familiar half smile. He lowered my gun with his hand. "Look at this."

The two elk stared each other down, puffing their chests out at one another, making them seem even bigger, even more fake. I remembered not believing that an animal like that existed. That's how I felt as I looked upon the two massive beings in front of me in the desert.

An awful, high-pitched scream erupted above me, erasing the hunting memory. I looked up into the sky and saw another being floating in midair. I heard an explosion, like two cars colliding, from the place the two figures on the ground stood. I saw them both crash into each other and dart around one another far quicker than any human could. The third figure floating in midair blurred past me and seemed to fall right on top of the other two, causing a tidal wave of sand and dust to fly into the air. The ground trembled around me, shaking violently, and started to give way; before I could do anything, I was sliding down the other side of the mound, headed right toward the swirling dust and the three fighters. I had nowhere to run or hide, so I stood up and stayed where I was, only a few feet from the three figures that were still in the middle of the dust storm. The dust finally cleared, and there they were. Two of them on one side faced the other, which was bigger than them both.

I knelt down to the ground, wanting to bury myself in the sand. The one closest to me was the bigger one. I now knew who he was: the shadow I had seen before. I knew because I saw the white scars covering his entire body, each of them glowing. He seemed to be moving, even when standing still; he wasn't transparent, but it was like looking at static. A black aura surrounded his body, rotating around him like a protective shield. His back was towards me, so I couldn't see his face. He had on black armor with golden edges, which shined in the sun. I didn't understand what the six slits on the back of his armor were for, since they exposed his flesh. They were too neat-looking to have been caused by a fight. He was holding a gigantic, black sword with a gold-tipped blade that matched his armor.

The two creatures that he was fighting each had white eyes and tangled dark hair. Steam rose from their bodies, and they breathed liked they were being forced to. They had no armor, but their skin looked like crusted dirt and was probably tough. The flying one had leathery wings with spikes along their edges.

"Is he really worth all of this trouble?" The spiked one took a confident step toward the taller being in front of me. "All we want to do is speak with him, after all. He *is* here." Both of their white eyes shifted to me, resembling how a fly moves on the ground.

"*Stay where you are.*" The strong voice I heard before spoke in my mind. The being with its back toward me turned his head to the side, looking at me out of the corner of his eye. I knew that it was his voice I had just heard.

"What is only a word? That is all we want with him: a single word." The spiked one's partner stepped closer as well.

The black aura surrounding the taller figure became thick, almost concealing him entirely. "He is with me."

The spiked creature's white eyes turned black, and as if he had been launched from a catapult, he shot up in the air. His partner sprinted toward the tall figure, screaming and grunting. The aura surrounding the tall figure seemed to get sucked inside of him. There was a crack, a blast, and a spark of light, and like the aftershock from a bomb, a sheet of blackness flew out of the taller being's body, knocking over the charging assailant pinning him to the ground, holding him there as he struggled to get back up. The spiked one attacked from above and latched himself on the back of the tall being, stabbing, punching, and biting. The tall being tried to grab him and throw him off, but he couldn't get a grip. Then the spiked creature was thrown off the tall being and sent to the ground. Two massive gold and black wings, which looked like pointed daggers, appeared on the taller-being. That's when I realized what the slits in his armor were for. But why six?

The spiked creature jumped up to his feet and charged again. The tall being then leaped into the sky with ease and dodged the attack. The spiked creature followed him into the sky and grabbed the tall being's wings but he managed to break away from the hold and turn around to face the spiked creature. They spiraled back to the ground like two fighting birds. Another explosion of dirt and sand sprayed into the sky. When the air cleared, I saw the tall being holding the other one by its throat.

"Show us mercy." It gurgled, flailing its spiked wings. Its black eyes had turned white again. "You're supposed to show mercy."

The tall being raised his sword with his other hand and thrust it into the side of the screeching creature; the one still being held on the ground screamed out, too. He removed his sword from the creature's side and sheathed it, still holding him by the neck.

"What would," the stabbed creature struggled for a breath, "your king do?"

The tall being stood motionless for a moment and shut his eyes like he was listening for something. "You tempters need to understand that my king is also yours."

The spiked creature groaned in pain and went limp in the tall figure's grasp. He dropped his bloody body into the sand and turned to the one who was squirming on the ground. The black aura lifted and returned to circling around the tall being. The other white-eyed creature stood up cautiously.

"Forgive me, forgive me. Show mercy." He had his hand raised, surrendering.

The tall being walked toward him and lifted its chin with his hand. "Mercy is not something you can request." In one quick motion he drew his sword and sliced off the head of the other creature, sending a spurt of black sludge in the air and onto the tall being's armor.

He turned to face me for the first time. The black aura surrounding him vanished inside his chest, revealing his face, which looked human with high, pointed cheekbones and a long chin. The dark sludge from the creatures he had just killed was stained under his glowing bright green eyes, the same eyes as those of the child who had been haunting me.

Then I remembered the day my mom died. I remembered she was describing a massive angel with burning green eyes. Was this him? Was my mom not crazy? Did he kill her? Was he going to kill me now, too? I started to back away as I thought of all these questions. He looked at me with a somber expression on his face, like he was seeing an old friend for the last time.

I blinked, and suddenly I was staring at Ashlin asleep next to me on the bus. I ripped out the earphone in my ear and hurried to the bathroom, holding in the vomit that was pushing its way out of my mouth. I threw up into the sink. I cupped the running water with my hands and washed my face. I knew I should believe that what had just happened was only a dream, but I couldn't. I needed to know who that tall, winged killing machine was. All I could think about was whether my mom was right all along.

18

I was surprised by just how many people came out to the capital in Des Moines to see Marcus speak. I was also surprised how the capital building looked. Ashlin had been saying how Iowa was nothing but, "flatland boringness" so I was expecting it to be a simple looking shack of a building. Instead, it looked like a massive cathedral with three domes. The biggest dome in the middle was gold, reflecting the sun to the spot where Marcus would be speaking at the top of the staircase before the main entrance.

The dome reminded me of the armor of the tall figure I had seen. I was trying to get the image of him out of my mind, but the dome only reinforced it. Why couldn't I get away from these images, these constant reminders?

Ashlin and I stood at the bottom right of the staircase with members of Marcus' team and some suits. The crowd was murmuring anxiously behind us.

"There's Gabe and Kale," Ashlin nudged me and pointed across the way to two men walking down the far side of the stairs.

"Which one is which?" I wanted to have a decent of idea of who I'd be working with.

"Gabe has the buzzed head and Kale doesn't. You'll see when you meet them." Ashlin waved at them. Only Gabe noticed and nodded back in our direction while smiling. Before I could ask any more questions, a cheer erupted from the crowd as Marcus came walking toward the microphone with a skinny looking guy by his side, who I assumed to be the governor. Erika and a few other important looking people dispersed down the stairs and stood by us or on the other side where Gabe was. Two suits moved into position at the bottom of the stairs blocking any path to Marcus.

The skinny man walked up to the microphone first, waving halfheartedly to the crowd.

"Good afternoon," his voice was as unemotional as his wave to the crowd. "It is my pleasure to introduce to you the only man who seems to really understand our country's needs." He turned his body to face Marcus while still leaning toward the microphone, "Senator of Arizona and my vote for president, Marcus Ammon." Before he finished talking, cheers overtook his voice.

"Thank you, Governor, and thank you, Iowa, for welcoming me to your home." Marcus flashed his smile while shaking the governor's hand. The ankh pin was shining on his jacket. I looked down to my own pin shining just like his and noticed the entire team wearing their pins as well. I felt connected. I was part of something big. I turned to Ashlin and saw that she wasn't wearing hers.

She probably just forgot.

Marcus turned fully to face the crowd and lifted his hand in the air to try and calm the cheers that were still being screamed out. "Today," his voice echoed louder than the cheers, "let it be known that today is... ." His index finger pointed to the sky on his raised hand, "Day one in our war with Washington, friends." The crowd's cheers grew louder, but Marcus continued to speak over them.

"I am asking you, Iowa," With the same hand that was raised he now pointed to the crowd, "Join me in this war and help me take back what is yours. For too long..." he lowered his hand to his side. The cheers started to quiet. "Washington has sat by and done nothing to rebuild our nation. They have let us rot with no protection, no fuel, and no hope."

I think for anyone else it would've seemed awkward standing up there with no podium or anything, but this felt like Marcus was actually preparing us for a battle.

"My plan for this nation begins with the people. How the founding fathers of this great nation would've wanted it. They freed themselves from what our nation has become. It is time for us to free ourselves." His voice rose with passion and the crowds cheers answered the same way. They began to chant: "Ammon, Ammon, Ammon." Marcus continued to try and speak over them but it was no use. I started to clap with the crowd.

I looked over to the other side and saw that Gabe was no longer there. I felt the need to search for him and, as I was still looking in that direction, I saw people fall violently to the ground. No one else seemed to notice what was happening. I was about to tell Ashlin to look when a man came sprinting out of the commotion with a knife raised in the air. He was immediately tackled by the closest suit and held to the ground by a few cops.

"What's happening?" Ashlin along with everyone else now saw the crazed man managing to fight off the massive suits and cops.

"Time to go," I heard a deep voice from a suit behind me push me along with Ashlin toward the direction of the bus. I managed to look back and see Marcus being led in the same direction.

"Dad?" Ashlin tried to shove her way through the suits that were pushing us forward. "Sam, is he OK? Did you see?"

"He's OK." I grabbed her hand and kept walking away from the mayhem behind us. I honestly didn't know, but I didn't want her going back in that direction.

We were forced into the bus as if we had no choice to get in or not.

"I knew this was going to happen. I knew it." Ashlin looked out the first window. More team members came running on the bus like a tornado was right on their heels. "Where is he? Where is he?"

"He'll be here, Ash." I looked with her out the window. "Here he comes." I tapped the glass and saw Marcus, Erika, and Dante surrounded by a blob of suits escorting them to the bus.

"Thank you, thank you," Ashlin held onto my arm wiping away tears with her free hand.

I brought her in close to me. "He's OK." I was still watching them approach when I could've sworn I saw the bum with the aviator sunglasses walk right in front of them. I forced myself to blink and looked to where he would've been but he wasn't there. No way he'd be here in Iowa.

"Dad." Ashlin cried. As soon as Marcus was on the bus Ashlin latched onto him. He didn't seem fazed by what just happened; instead he almost seemed excited.

"Everyone here? Everyone OK?" He looked at me for the answer. I nodded, not knowing what to say. I never thought this would happen. I only knew of Marcus being loved; I never thought there were people who wanted him dead. As I watched Marcus try to console Ashlin who was still hugging him, I felt the scar begin to burn on my wrist. I wondered if it was trying to tell me something.

Once we were on the road, things began to calm down. Ashlin and I finally learned that we were headed to the town next to Des Moines, where Dante would connect with his half of the team while Gabe, along with a few others, would be joining our bus until the next destination.

My scar had stopped the weird burning sensation as we got further from the capital. Erica, Kelly and a few others were all talking intensely on their phones. Marcus was in the back office with Dante going over their next moves. I couldn't believe how calm Marcus had remained during all of this.

"I can't get over the fact that he has no issue with what just happened back there," I said. Ashlin couldn't believe it either. She held her knees up to her chest with her back against the window as she sat facing me.

I know she was upset and she had every reason to be, but Marcus showed just how fearless he was. For the first time since meeting him, I was starting to understand why he was loved so much.

"Well," I offered, "at least he, along with everybody else, is OK. Ya know?"

"Yeah, of course, but... . " she dropped her head down onto her knees while letting out a deep sigh.

"What is it, Ash?" I wanted her to feel better about this but I had learned that the worst thing to do to someone who is hurting is simply tell them "feel better," as if those two words were the most powerful two words in the world. I got that a lot after my dad's funeral from family friends who I never saw again. They'd walk up to me with their sympathy faces and pat me on the back or give me a hug. I know they didn't mean to but that just made me feel worse after a while. So I knew Ashlin wouldn't want to hear those two words now.

"It's only the beginning, and this already happens." Her voice was muffled since her head was still on her knees. "I hate it." She slowly looked up at me while using her kneecap as a chin rest. "I'm glad you're here with me, though." She reached for my arm and pulled me into her.

"Me, too," I wrapped my arm around her and leaned my head on top of hers. I felt exhausted and I'm sure Ashlin was, too. We remained quiet and watched as people flowed in the middle aisle like tiny fish in a thin creek. I didn't think anyone was really doing anything important, but they all made sure they looked like they were. I think that's how life is most of the time; everyone has a dream of being important some way or another, but only a few select people actually understand what importance is. I don't think I do. I wondered if I'd ever done anything important and not realized it.

Without thinking, my eyes drifted to my scarred wrist. As I stared at it I felt the need to control it. I wanted to feel the burn again just to prove to myself that I can. This mark was on my body, so I declared to myself it will do what I want.

Burn, burn, burn. I refused to blink. I leaned with the bus, as it turned. I didn't look up though. The feeling was faint but I felt it. The burn began to return, so I tried to keep it going as if I was actually creating a fire.

The bus had stopped moving, but I was too entranced to even care.

My vision went black for a second. When my vision returned, I didn't move my eyes off the scar. Another blackout occurred, this time longer. I waited to see, but now I was standing underneath the massive tree from the painting, instead. The green-eyed tall being was in front of me just as he was in the desert. Before I could even react, I was back in the bus.

"Let's go, Sammy," Ashlin said.

My eyes ached as I regained my focus and stood up with Ashlin to get off the bus. I looked out the window and saw a mix of police cars and black SUV's in a parking lot of a roadside diner.

I had no answers yet, but I knew this scar was something much more than just a marking.

19

Stepping off the bus, I felt like I had been transported to an alien planet. All I thought about was that tree and my scar. Trying to think of anything else almost felt wrong. I put on a smile and forced myself to pay attention.

"This is my boyfriend and your new co-worker, Sam."

"Addison, right?" Gabe stood with one hand raised shading his eyes from the sun and one extended to me. He looked to be in his late 30's and was about the same height as Marcus, but with a stronger build. He wore a blue button down shirt with the sleeves rolled up to his elbows and black slacks. I noticed a dark purple and red rash splotched down his arm and hand that was waiting for mine.

"Yes," I shook his hand, "and you are obviously Gabe." I was waiting for him to tell me his last name.

"That's me." He nodded once. He looked at me as if remembering something important. "I had a whole detailed introduction planned, but honestly, after today, you've experienced enough." His voice sounded like he'd just got over a cold. "I'm happy that everyone was OK."

"Me, too," I agreed. We all had to move out of the way as people were transferring carts of supplies and other campaign related items onto the bus from a few SUV's.

"I'm sure you were told that you'd be working with Kale, too." Gabe put his hand that he was using as a shade down into his pocket. "Well, that's changed."

"How so?" Ashlin asked with a bit of concern in her voice.

"He resigned on the way over here," he chuckled and shrugged at the same time.

"Does my dad know?"

"Yeah, he's not worried." He glanced back to the diner where Marcus was standing by the entrance talking with police. "He told me Addison here, will be more than enough help."

I hoped to live up to Marcus' expectations of me. "I'll do the best I can." I wasn't sure why he was calling me by my last name, but it seemed natural for him.

"Good." He turned to me fully and, as he did, I noticed his eyes for the first time. With a closer look I noticed one eye was dark and the other was light colored. I couldn't tell the exact color of either because of the way the sun was hitting him.

"I'm sorry about Kale, though. I know he was your mentor." Ashlin put her hand on my back, getting my attention. "Kale had been designing for my dad since I can remember." She ran her other hand through her hair to keep it from blowing in her face. "I'm a little shocked."

"I'll live. I trust your dad," Gabe nodded once more. He was probably trying to convince himself that I was going to do my job. I knew I'd have to prove that I would to him.

"Do you mind if I talk to Sam for a bit?" he asked.

"Oh, sure, sure. I'm sorry," Ashlin started to walk toward the diner while looking at me. "I'll get something to eat. You want anything, Sam? Gabe?"

I shook my head no. I was more concerned with what Gabe wanted to tell me.

Ashlin gave us a thumbs up and walked away toward the diner.

"I know today was crazy, but in a way it was a good thing," Gabe said as he walked closer to the side of the bus right next to some luggage waiting to be loaded.

"How so?"

"This was a good day for Marcus in terms of marketing." He just looked at me like I was supposed to know why.

"I don't understand," I said, puzzled.

Gabe put the sole of his shoe on the bus tire behind him and leaned back. "The press will be covering this story for the next week or two. Marcus' face will be all people see." He opened the palm of his hand and moved it in one wiping motion across his body. "He's already the more popular candidate, so to start the campaign this way was brilliant."

"What're you saying?" It sounded like he was saying that Marcus may have known this was going to happen.

"I feel like I'm obligated to inform you, since I'm Mr. Teacher now." He paused and grimaced. "Listen, Kale was the best. He just quit." He pushed himself off the tire with his foot and chuckled. "All I'm trying to say is, our job is to help Marcus win anyway we can."

"I understand... . "

"No, Addison. You don't understand." With his hands in his pockets, he put his foot on a bag of luggage and rocked it back and forth. He wasn't looking at me. "When I first started, I thought I understood, too."

A shock of pain from my scar stormed through my entire body. With my other hand I squeezed my wrist until the pain subsided.

"I still don't, though." He turned his head to the side and looked at me as the bag of luggage toppled over. He faced me and took a step closer. "All I need to know is that you will be committed to this process. If today freaked you out, then you may not want to do this."

He made it sound like I was joining a group of assassins. "I'm committed, even though this seems to be some sort of warning you're giving me."

"If it sounded that way, then you were actually listening to what I was saying."

So I was right when I thought Marcus knew what was going happen at the capital. I wondered if Kale was the plan designer. "You'll find that I'm a pretty good listener."

"I hope so, Addison." He glanced toward the diner where Marcus was making his way inside still surrounded. "Let's end this crazy day with some diner food. We have all the time we need to talk about work." He motioned his head for me to follow him.

Before we went to the diner, I needed to ask him a question. "It was confirmed that no one was hurt today, right?"

He nodded.

20

A month passed, and Gabe was right; the attack in Iowa was a great way to start the campaign. Since then the country was falling in love with Marcus more each day. I thought of all that had happened during the first month as I waited for Marcus in his office. We would try and meet every morning if possible.

In New Hampshire, the crowd chanted his name, "Ammon, Ammon, Ammon!" for ten minutes before he said a single word. Florida was our biggest crowd. Marcus was just going to speak in a local park in Miami, but the governor insisted that Marcus speak in the abandoned football stadium. Within an hour, it was filled. Marcus' message to unite and begin fresh without Washington's politics was hitting home with a lot of people. Marcus was the symbol of a new United States. His competitors were labeling him a "rebel," but that only seemed to feed his popularity growth even more.

As for my job, I was enjoying my time with Gabe. We worked well together. He didn't talk much, but he didn't need to. Our first deadline was coming up for the nation-

al sign campaign that Gabe had started before Kale quit.
I helped him with the slogan.

"Ammon, the answer to our prayers."

My job was to also help him spice up the visual
elements of the sign, not hard at all. The background was
a dark red with a white font. Both Marcus' and Dante's
names were underneath the brief statement. This would
be the first big exposure of the ankh cross symbol as well.
We decided to place it at the very top of the sign, also in
white. Marcus stood by his belief that the symbol would
be accepted.

Dante was off campaigning throughout different cities
of the country. Both he and Gabe would be rejoining
when we arrived in Montgomery, Alabama.

During the entire month, I hadn't had any weird
dreams or whatever they were, like the last time I saw that
winged being. The scar on my wrist had grown faint, but
I wasn't satisfied. I just knew that there *had* to be more.
When those answers still hadn't come, I started to
blame it all on stress from the drastic changes in my life.
Not a day went by without me thinking about that
winged creature's bloody face as he looked at me.

Ashlin was my biggest concern, though. She had kept
her distance from Marcus after Iowa. That seemed odd to
me. She did a lot of writing and helped out Erica as much
as she could. But, I felt something was off with her.
She was there, but her mind was running in a different
direction.

"So Sam, my boy, how're you doing today?" Marcus
came shuffling in and sat at his desk. He leaned his
elbows forward and hunched over. His usually perfect
hair was disheveled, and his eyes had sleep written all
over them.

I stretched my arms out above my head, cracking my knuckles. It was early in the morning and waking up on a bus still took some getting used to. "I'm doing fine. Did you get the latest polls yet?"

Marcus got up and went to the coffee machine, which was bolted to the wall by the window, and pushed a button. "Coffee?" I should've been the one getting the coffee for both of us, but that's just how Marcus was.

I nodded, still waiting for his answer about the polls. I did find myself getting more involved with the details of the election and liked feeling like I was part of a team.

"Not yet. Erica will have them by the time we get to the hotel, I'm sure." He handed me a Styrofoam cup steaming with coffee. "We're out of cream and sugar. We're out of everything." He shook his head, frustrated. "Alabama couldn't have come soon enough." He took a sip and grimaced from the bitterness of the coffee.

He was right, though: we all needed a break from the road. After New Hampshire, we had stopped in four different states, but only long enough to clean up, since we had to be in Florida at a certain time. Marcus left and flew to a few more cities before meeting the bus in Florida. I couldn't imagine how he had any energy left.

Alabama was next on the hit list, with about a month left to do some serious campaigning. He only wanted to stop in a few more cities before the major debate in St. Louis.

"How's Ashlin holding up? I haven't had a lot of time to talk to her," Marcus asked as he sat back down in his chair and wiped his hand across the table as if he was cleaning it.

"She's good, she's proud of you." I wasn't even sure if that's how she felt. We never talked about campaign stuff.

"I'm proud of *her*. She's one girl I can trust." He took a careful sip of coffee, trying not to burn his lips. "I remember the day I brought her home. I had no clue what I was doing." I could tell it had been a while since he had thought about this.

"If you don't mind me asking, what made you adopt?"

He wasn't smiling, but his face was pleasant. "Bree, my wife, wanted to. Actually, we both wanted to." He stared at the steam rising from the coffee.

"What happened?" The question slipped out. I didn't want to overstep anything. This was the first time he had mentioned his wife.

His intense, fixed gaze felt like he had just grabbed me by the shirt collar. "I haven't talked about Bree in a long time." His stare softened and he moved his eyes away from me.

I remembered almost every magazine printed the story about Marcus' relationship with his "deceased love." That was about the time Marcus was becoming popular nationally. I never read it. I was tired of death and love.

"I understand. Don't feel like you have to tell me anything."

"No, no. I know some of your story; it's only fair you know some of mine." He relaxed in his chair, and so did I. "We had been married for a little less than a year, and Sam, I was the happiest man in the world."

The biggest smile I had ever seen stretched across Marcus' face. This, I believe, was the first real smile I had seen him give.

"She was beautiful, like she didn't belong on this planet. Her blonde hair was like butter. Her eyes were soft and warm, always welcoming. She always did this thing with her nose when she laughed." He scrunched his nose slightly. "I loved her laugh. She had the kind of laugh that made other people laugh, not because it was weird or anything, but it was contagious, you know?"

I couldn't help but think of Ashlin and me.

"We were young and dumb. We both thought that as long as we were together, we could handle anything. I was struggling in law school, and even though she had no idea how to help, she still sat with me every night and tried to. Every night." He was fiddling with his hand, looking at it like he was remembering when she used to hold it. He chuckled to himself. "I would've made a horrendous lawyer, by the way. But that's another story."

He took another sip of coffee. "Anyway, we were young, poor, hungry, and married, making the ultimate recipe for disaster, right? Anyone would think that, but not us. Bree was just different. The harder life got, the stronger she became." His eyes widened. "She *really* believed in God. She said that was why she was the way she was. I'd just go along with it. She would pray and pray. I didn't mind it at all, though. It was soothing to see someone believe in something so much. Sure enough, the answer to her prayers came. I graduated, somehow, thanks to Dante." He motioned towards the door, like Dante was standing there. "I was hired by his uncle's firm. We were no longer hungry or poor. It was time to start a family, something Bree wanted most."

He brought his hand to his forehead and massaged it as if he had a headache. "She became pregnant." He stopped massaging his forehead but kept his head down and his hand where it was. "When something seems perfect, run. Perfection is only a mirage for suffering. Nothing is perfect, not even Bree's God." His hand dropped to the desk. "We lost our first child three months into the pregnancy." He pushed his chair back and started to walk around the office. He squinted his eyes, as if he were looking into the sun.

"Marcus, we don't... ." I began.

He shook his head, raising his hand stopping me midsentence. "Bree started to fade. That year, Dante convinced me to go into politics. I needed to clear my mind from everything, and that was my answer. Bree wouldn't eat. She wouldn't talk. She just prayed to her God, always telling me to have faith. I did have faith, but in *her*, not a ghost." He threw his hands in the air, feeling for something, proving nothing was there. "Later on that year, I was elected to my first political position, to sit on some dull committee, but my main concern was Bree. Then," he snapped his fingers, "she just came out of it, like I had awakened her from a nap. All she wanted then was to adopt a child."

He stood silent with his head lowered. "I didn't want to. I should've just said yes. That's all she wanted, and I was too selfish, even after all she had been through, to even consider it." His voice was an intense whisper. "I wanted us to have our own, together. I promised her it would work this time, that everything would be OK. So we tried, and just like before, she became pregnant. When we found out that we were going to be having a girl, Bree knew instantly what she wanted to name her." He looked up at me and smiled. "Ashlin, that was going to be the name, no matter if I liked it or not."

He held his smile, and I smiled with him. "I loved it," he said. "The time finally came for baby Ashlin, 3:22 a.m. to be exact. I held Bree's hand the entire time." He made a coughing noise, then cleared his throat. "I can still see her looking at me. She was pale, with her hair sticking to her forehead, damp with sweat. She kept her eyes on me. I didn't understand why or how she could." He slowly sat back down in his chair. "Something happened. I'm still not even sure what. Her grip became flimsy in my hand. Her eyes shut. She didn't even scream. It just happened in silence." He took a trembling deep breath. "Doctors shoved me out of the way and took her hand from me. I didn't know whether I should yell or cry or what. I watched them pull out my daughter and try to resuscitate them both. Nothing happened."

He sniffed, nodding his head, forcing himself to continue. "The most haunting sound is silence. Because with silence, there are no answers, only your own questions hanging in your mind like an overgrown vine. Even I," he slammed his finger into his chest, "prayed to Bree's God, only to be given more silence." He looked up to the ceiling. "I adopted Ashlin, at first to keep Bree alive in my heart, but people are right when they say, 'with time, everything fades.'" He changed his voice to a mocking tone and forced out what sounded to be a laugh. "You simply begin to forget. No one will tell you that, though. Well, I guess I just did."

My hand started to cramp from squeezing the armrest so tightly.

"I sometimes look at Ashlin and forget that Bree isn't her mom."

That's when it hit me. That's why Ashlin and her dad have such an odd relationship. Ashlin reminds Marcus of Bree, and he doesn't want her to.

"I haven't thought about this in a long time, Sam. Forgive me." He had a concerned look on his face. "Why haven't I thought about this?"

"I know why."

His eyes met mine, looking for an answer.

"You said that you begin to forget. I think that's impossible." For me it was.

He nodded. We both held on as the bus slowed down to exit the freeway.

"Nothing is impossible." He smirked and let out another short laugh.

I didn't know how to respond to that.

The office door opened and Erica stuck her head in. "We're a few minutes from the hotel in Montgomery."

"Any crowd?" Marcus seemed to gather himself together and bring the business side back quickly. Erica opened the door all the way and stepped in. I don't know how she did it, but she always looked clean and proper, no matter what.

"I spoke to the hotel manager. No crowd yet. The area where you'll be speaking later on I expect to be filled." She folded her hands in front of her. She always did that. I didn't mind her though. All I knew was that she was a working machine for Marcus.

"Polls?" Marcus stood up and stretched.

"I'm waiting for the text." She pulled out her Smartphone, and pushed a few buttons.

"Looks like you have it under control, as usual. Thanks." Marcus smiled as he put his hands in his pants pockets.

"We'll have a few hours once we get to the hotel... ."

Erica kept on talking, I did a quick wave to Marcus, and he nodded back as I slipped past Erica in the doorway to go back to my seat to see if Ashlin was awake. I wanted to tell her what Marcus and I had talked about, but I knew I couldn't. I wondered if Ashlin knew that story of Bree. I was glad Marcus had told me though.

All this time that I had known him, I still felt like I really didn't. As I walked down the aisle toward my seat, I felt something I hadn't felt in an entire month. I held onto my wrist like it was falling off of my body and almost collapsed onto the ground when a searing pain ripped across my arm.

"No, no, no." I spun around in the aisle, almost hitting Erica.

She slid into a seat to get out of my way. She looked to my death grip on my wrist and then to my eyes. "Are you hurt?"

I froze in the middle of the aisle, looking at her like I had never seen her before. "I'm fine." Another sharp pain stretched along my arm. I hurried into the bathroom and locked the door. I let go of my now-shaking arm and saw the scar that I hoped was leaving, glowing brighter than it ever had.

"Don't fight it, Sam." I heard my dad's voice in my ear like he was in the bathroom with me. I looked at my arm again and saw every vein begin to glow beneath my skin like the scar. I went to grab my wrist to try to squeeze it out or something, and a bright shock like I had just blown a fuse sparked off of the scar, but it didn't burn me.

"Don't fight it." My dad's voice said calmly again. Even though I couldn't see him and the voice I was hearing was probably just my own internal one, I listened. I sat down on the floor with my arm out and took relaxed breaths.

"What's happening to me?" I gritted my teeth as I watched the veins on my arm glow like burning tree branches. I was hoping for an answer from my dad.

"Shut your eyes." There it was. I listened again. The pain vanished, and I could smell salt in the air. I opened my eyes and saw my dad standing in front of me, smiling. Behind him was the massive tree from the painting.

My dad pulled me close to him and hugged me. I was *hugging* my dad. I sort of laughed and sobbed at the same time.

Was he really there in front of me? I grabbed a handful of his shirt to make sure. He wasn't transparent like the last time I saw him.

He leaned his head back and looked me in the eye. His hair wasn't graying; it was still dark and wavy as ever. As I looked at him, it was like he had never died. He let go and stood beside me in the lively, bright side of the tree. I remained where I was the last time I was here, directly in the middle of both sides.

My dad reached across my body and grabbed my wrist, examining the scar, which was no longer glowing. After taking a quick look, he smiled and started to walk toward the tree.

"Come on." He looked back and waved for me to follow. I caught up to him and tried to cross over all the way into the lighted side, but couldn't. It was like I was on a railroad track and had no choice but to go wherever it led me. For the first few steps, all I did was look at him. He acted like he had never died, like I had never *seen* him die. I had so much to ask him, but all I could think about was how everyone always told us that we looked like we were twins. For the first time, I actually agreed. The only difference was our eyes. He was glad I had my mom's eyes though. He scratched the stubble on his cheek, like he always did when he was thinking.

"Dad, what's happening?" I blurted out the obvious question on my mind. Then more came spilling out, hoping he could answer any of them. "What is this tree?"

I opened my arms toward it. "What is *this*? I showed him the scar, again. "Am I going crazy?"

He stopped mid-step. "I can't answer any of those questions. I wish I could, but I simply can't."

"Why? Why are you in front of me, right now, all of a sudden? Not once did any of *this* kind of stuff happen after… ."

He started to walk again, quicker. "Come."

I was tired of not getting any answers. For all I knew, I was just dreaming all of this.

"You need to meet him now." My dad had stopped and turned around to say that before starting to walk toward one shadow figure standing underneath the tree. I already knew that it was the winged being I had seen a month ago. I stood there watching my dad until he was right next to the giant shadow. I saw two huge silhouettes in the shape of wings sprout up behind the tall being.

"Don't be afraid," a voice whispered in my head; it was his.

"I'm not."

As I got closer to the winged being and my dad, I started to feel like I was getting pulled in, as if the tree was a planet pulling me into its orbit. I felt the half of my body that was on the darker, burnt-looking side become hotter as I approached the tree. My other half, on the lighter side, cooled. I had no choice but to stay in the middle. I noticed my dad looked worried as he watched me, and then he would look up to the winged being with concern, as if he would know what to do. The winged being had on his black and gold armor, with his sword sheathed by his side. The black aura surrounding him flowed around him calmly before sucking inside of him when I reached the pair. His eyes burned green, and he still had a somber expression on his face as he observed me.

"It is an honor to meet you, Addison." The being dropped his head slightly, but his mouth did not move when he spoke. I heard his voice in my head. Why would he be honored to meet me?

"Who are you?" I looked to my dad for reassurance that this thing, whatever it might be, was safe.

"My name is Michael. I will not harm you."

"*What* are you?" I watched his two massive wings shrink into his back armor and disappear. I heard faint voices to my right on the darker side of the tree. I noticed Michael turn to look. He must've heard them to.

"I am the sword for the King of Kings," he said still looking for whatever made those sounds. He then turned to look at me again. I wanted to look away, but couldn't. "I bring a message for you." His eyes continued to smolder like magma from a volcano. "Trust and prepare."

"For what?"

The black aura spewed out of him, surrounding him, and started to billow in every direction, until it cloaked him entirely, turning him into a shadow again.

"For what?" I asked again, taking a step closer to reach for him. I needed something more than that. "What is happening to me?" I looked to my dad, who was getting overtaken by the black aura now.

"Trust and forgive Him." My dad seemed to dissolve in midair.

"Who?" I felt something tugging at me from behind, pulling me away. "Who?" I needed to know who I needed to trust and forgive.

"GOD." Michael's voice thundered from within the black cloud, and I was yanked away from the tree and lifted off the ground. I slammed my eyes shut to find myself back on the bus, sitting in the bathroom.

I was staring right at my scar, which was no longer glowing. I leaned my head back against the bathroom door. "God?" That word came screaming back and punched me square in the face. "Do you exist?"

21

When we arrived at the hotel in downtown Montgomery, I was still shaken by what I had just been through. I felt like a fisherman casting out into the middle of an entire ocean that contained only a single fish, but that one fish would give me an answer to what was happening to me.

The hotel where we were staying was in the middle of the city, so as the bus drove down the much smaller side roads of Alabama, people knew that Marcus Ammon had arrived. We parked in the back and tried to remain as hidden as possible. It was still morning, so we had until that night to rest and clean up for Marcus' speech at the Alabama River. Signs and banners welcomed Marcus and advertised his speech. I needed to take a long walk and forget about the campaign for a while. I knew Ashlin would have no complaints about that either. I could tell she was ready to sprint off the bus as soon as the doors opened, like a caged animal being freed into the wild for the first time.

I washed up as quickly as possible and was waiting down in the main lobby, which smelled like every other hotel. The place was fancy, though, for sure. I could see my own reflection in the patterned floors as I sat and watched the few people who came in. I felt the urge to ask anyone who passed me if they believed in God. I felt like I needed to take a poll for evidence. I couldn't wrap my head around what I had just seen-not only my dead dad, but some winged creature who calls himself the sword of the King of Kings. I recognized the term "King of Kings" from my dad when he was actually alive. Was God the one causing all of this to happen? I dropped my head into my hands and just looked at myself in the shiny floor. I unbuttoned the first few buttons on the gray shirt Marcus had given me for tonight's speech and saw Ashlin and two suits headed toward me. She was wearing a dark green sundress that hugged her body perfectly. She waved to me like she hadn't seen me in a year. I just couldn't help but laugh. She was all I needed to get through whatever the hell was happening to me.

"What do you wanna do?" Ashlin was stroking her hair, which hung over her left shoulder. She balanced on her tiptoes, ready to move. I kissed her lips and took her hand.

"Let's just walk." We stepped out onto the main street and started to walk. The city had an old-town feel to it, with older-looking brick buildings with columns. There weren't a lot of people walking around yet, so it was nice to have the quiet city hum, and the sound of our feet against the pavement the only sounds beside some birds and a few cars driving by. Ashlin was holding my scarred hand and was brushing the marking with her thumb. I was paranoid that it was going to start glowing like it had on the bus. I wouldn't be able to explain that to her without telling her everything. I *wanted* to tell her everything so badly, but I couldn't do that to her. I knew I'd sound absolutely crazy to anyone else, like my mom had to me.

"What're you thinking about?" Ashlin leaned into me with her shoulder.

"Everything, really." I watched my feet as I walked.

"So, you're thinking about the theory of relativity?" She gasped. "Me, too." She smirked.

"Smart-ass," I joked, stopped walking, and pulled her to a bench outside of a small shop. "I guess I'm just thinking about why bad things happen." We both sat down on the bench. I sat on the top, with my feet on the flat part where you're supposed to sit, and Ashlin sat next to my feet. "Why do we lose what we love? That just doesn't make sense to me. I don't know." I watched a guy ride by on his bike wearing a "Vote for Ammon" shirt.

Ashlin untied one of my shoes and was twirling one of the laces around her finger. "We lose what we love so we can love even more when we are given the chance." She started to tie my shoe. "At least, I like to think that's why."

"I guess that makes sense, but when that chance *does* come, aren't you afraid you'll just lose it again?"

She tightened the last knot on my shoe and turned to me on the bench. "That's when I just trust in God and his plan for me." She kissed my knee.

"I can't understand that." I thought of Marcus' wife, Bree, when I looked at Ashlin. I wondered if Marcus knew Ashlin felt the same way as she did.

"What?"

There was that word again. Trust. "Putting your trust in something you don't even know exists for sure." I sat down all the way on the bench.

"Didn't you ask your dad about this?"

"He told me, whether I listened or not. I never really listened though." An image of my dad tied to the pole came screaming into my mind.

"Why not?"

I thought about why, and I didn't have an answer. I just didn't want to. Even with my parents always talking about God, I had learned to tune it out. "I don't know." I shook my head and shrugged.

"It's just not for you, right?" She moved a few strands of her hair aside from her face.

"Right." But was it for me? Marcus was right. You can't trust a ghost.

We sat silent watching the city come to life minute by minute.

"Ash, can I ask you something?" After my talk with Marcus earlier I just wanted to see if she was doing OK.

"Of course." She tugged at my shirt-sleeve and smoothed her finger over it.

"Your dad was asking about you this morning."

"So he sent you to spy on me?" She arched her eyebrows and pushed her finger in my shoulder.

"No, no. You've been quiet lately and he's probably noticed, too. Are you doing OK?" I asked.

"I guess I've just been in writer mode. That's all." She moved her hand away from my shoulder and looked out toward the street.

I didn't want to be nosey but I could tell something was on her mind. I wasn't that good at this. "Well, what're you writing? I'd love to read your stories."

"It's not a story." She hesitated but brushed her hair back with her hand. "It's a letter."

"To who?"

She quickly looked at me with a pained look on her face. "You know how you just said God isn't for you?"

"Yeah, you don't need to tell.... "

"No, I do need to tell you because you are a part of this." She twisted on the bench to face me and sat cross-legged. "This campaign isn't for me. This kind of life is not for me."

My heart sunk as I watched her struggle.

"My dad didn't notice me being quiet. You did." She tilted her head to the side as if waiting to hear a specific sound. "He has his own agenda. I want mine."

"Is this what the letter is about?" I reached for her hand.

"Yes." She held my hand between both of hers. "No matter what the outcome of this election is, I'm leaving." She lightly pulled me closer. "I want you to come with me."

Her words just hung there in front of me. I wanted to be with her but I didn't want her to leave her dad at the same time.

"Your dad needs you, Ash. I know you may not think he does, but he does."

"He doesn't." Her eyes watched our hands in her lap.

"You're all he has left, and both of you are all I have left."

She brought my hand up to her lips and kissed it. "I have to do this. I will do my part for the rest of the election. I will be the proud daughter for him, but I can't continue my life not knowing what I could've become besides the adopted daughter of Marcus Ammon."

She faced the street again and stretched her legs out. "I know this is where I am needed, now. But I just feel that *we* are needed elsewhere once this is all over."

"Maybe you're right, but maybe you're not." I didn't know what else to say.

"A decision that you feel in your gut is never wrong." Ashlin hopped up and grabbed my hand to pull me up. "Come on, speaking of my gut, I'm hungry. Let's eat." We spent the rest of the time we had exploring the down-town area, eating at a sandwich shop. The entire time, though, my thoughts didn't drift too far from both what Ashlin had said and hearing Michael's voice saying "God" with a sound of finality in it.

With only an hour or so until Marcus was scheduled to make his speech, Ashlin and I walked back to the hotel to meet up with the group. I noticed the two suits following us were drenched with sweat. Ashlin got a kick out of that but still offered them water every chance she got. She even got them both a sandwich from the place we had lunch. They didn't eat *with* us, of course.

"They return," Marcus noted while he fixed his shirt collar in a mirror when we walked into the main suite of the hotel that was now headquarters. "You both look lovely." He hugged Ashlin, "You missed the good news." He smiled at Erica, who was reading over something as she sat on one of the couches. "As of right now," he pointed to the ground, "we are ahead in all of the polls, comfortably."

"More than comfortably." Erica stood up from the couch, putting on lip balm. "Fredricks might as well drop out. Henderson is our only worry now, and trust me, he isn't that big a threat."

"Let's not get ahead of ourselves," Marcus said.

"Either way, congratulations, Marcus." I said.

"Yeah, Dad," Ashlin smiled with me at Marcus who was looking at us from the mirror. He gave us both a professional nod.

"Dante is here, preparing a speech of his own." Erica smiled like she had been thinking about this moment for a long time: both Marcus and Dante on stage together. Ashlin moved away, probably to explore the suite, when Dante walked in, looking how a politician should look. That meant Gabe was around too. Marcus walked over to me.

"You have your pin?" That's when I realized everyone in the room, including the suits, had the ankh-cross pin somewhere on their clothes. Ashlin was putting one on the top of her hair, as was Erica. I pulled mine out of my pocket, glad I hadn't forgotten it, and pinned it to my shirt pocket.

"We're ready to move now," Erica patted Dante's shoulder.

"Let's go make a speech," Marcus said as he shook Dante's hand, and looked to me and then to Ashlin, who came up next to me. "Stay close." Erica and the entourage of suits escorted Marcus and Dante out. We followed behind. They would be speaking by a bridge just outside of the hotel. It looked like a pier overlooking the steady stream of the Alabama River. A decent-sized crowd waited for Marcus, but the greater part of the crowd was the media presence with their cameras set up where Marcus was going to speak.

"Stay right here," a suit guided Ashlin and me toward the back by some stairs leading up to the main street. We stood on the top tier, looking over everyone, while

Marcus, Dante, and Erica made their way to the front. I hadn't seen Gabe yet.

"Good job, Sammy." Ashlin pointed at the backdrop. The sign that Gabe and I created was behind the microphone. I saw people passing out smaller versions to hold as well. I imagined all of the people watching and seeing the signs too. I had actually accomplished something, thanks to Marcus for inviting me along. I tried not to think of what Ashlin and I discussed earlier.

The crowd started to cheer like they always did during Marcus' appearances. Cameras sparkled like the sun on the river's surface as it set behind the bridge. I saw the red lights flicker on all of the TV cameras when Marcus reached the stage, waiving to the people. Dante stood like an army general next to him, along with a few suits and another lady, who was a city official, welcoming Marcus. The short-haired lady started to speak first, but I couldn't listen. Some people are too dull, and this lady was one of them, so I couldn't listen. I expected Dante to sound the same way.

"Count how many bald people are in the crowd," Ashlin squeezed my hand, fighting back a laugh climbing up her throat. I looked out into the crowd and started to count all of the bald heads I saw. Ashlin did too. I knew I was supposed to be taking this moment for the campaign seriously, but it felt good to let my mind go free, even if it was to just count bald heads.

"A lot of baldies out there," Ashlin said, under the cover of a loud cheer when Marcus was introduced. I was counting in the middle area of the crowd when I saw what looked like a man engulfed in bright-blue flames standing in the midst of everyone. No one else was reacting to this sight. Was he really there?

I could see his outline inside the blue light, but I could tell he wasn't facing Marcus and the stage; he was facing me. I looked to see if Ashlin noticed this, but she had her finger pointed out, still counting. She couldn't see it. I lowered my eyes to my wrist, checking if it was glowing or anything. It wasn't. When I looked back to the blue light, he was moving throughout the crowd, walking right through people like he was made of vapor. I noticed his body flicker brighter, then dimmer as he moved. A dark-colored mist appeared out in the middle of the river behind Marcus. It traveled quickly and overtook the stage and everyone on it, except for Marcus. The mist slithered into the crowd, cloaking every last person, forming a black dome. A thin trail of the mist stopped right before Ashlin and me. Along with Marcus and this blue light, we were the only people not inside of whatever this was.

"I'm at seventeen, so far." Ashlin giggled next to me. The mist pushed the blue-light figure up into the air, which formed what looked like a throne for the figure to sit. He had arms and legs just like a man's, but every part of his body was a beautiful blue that moved just like a burning candle flame.

"My promises will not be broken." Marcus' voice sent a streak of white light writhing throughout the black mist, feeding into the blue figure's throne.

"I'm crazy," I mouthed silently to myself as I gawked at whatever this blue being was.

"You're not crazy, Sam Addison." A smooth voice came from the blue light that I couldn't forget. It was musical, like the perfect song. He was the other shadow by the tree that stood on the charred-looking half. A trail of light came from his throne to my feet within the black mist when he spoke. "You're important." His entire body went from being blue to a dark ruby. "I've been waiting to finally meet you. Face-to-face, that is."

"I hear you, and I will answer." Marcus' voice broke through again.

"Who are you?" I asked.

"What?" I felt Ashlin looking at me. "Sammy?"

"I am your way out of all this." The now ruby-colored being opened his arms wide and closed his hands together, as if he was crushing something between them. The dark mist sucked into the ground wherever it lay and was gone. He was floating in midair, his blue color returning.

"Sammy?"

I turned to Ashlin, probably looking as confused as I felt. "Yeah," I looked out of the corner of my eye and saw that the blue being had gone.

She put her hand on my cheek. "You're on fire." She pulled her hand away.

"I'm fine." I wasn't fine. I was tired of all these weird episodes happening to me. What did he mean that he was my way out? I yearned to hear that being's voice again. It was addicting.

"It is an honor for me to introduce to you now the man who helped bring peace to so many nations when he represented our great country and served as the Secretary General of The United Nations, my running mate, Dante Wess." The crowd cheered and cameras flashed.

22

his is what God wants." My dad's voice startled me awake, but my eyes opened to see Gabe standing over me.

"Time to do some work," Gabe said.

I covered my eyes as he turned on all the lights. "How did you even get in here?" He looked exhausted. He had dark circles under his eyes, which made them look even more unique. He was wearing a black dress shirt that he was trying to tuck in to his pants.

"I just landed. I guess we're roommates. That's a good thing, because I was going to wake you up no matter where you were."

As my eyes adjusted I remembered we were in St. Louis for the final debate. The election was only a two weeks away, and I saw no way that Marcus was going to lose the way things were going.

"Let's go. Get up." Gabe pulled the covers off of me, sending a cold shock through my body. It had been a while since I had even seen Gabe, since he couldn't get to Alabama when we were there. I sat up and caught the clothes he threw at me with my face.

"What time is.... "

"Late, and it doesn't matter. Remember day one in Iowa? When we talked by the bus?"

I nodded before putting on a shirt. I felt disturbed as I remembered the attempted attack on Marcus and how Gabe implied it was all set up. What really disturbed me was that was the big reason why Ashlin started to shut down and want to leave once the election was over. I thought of her and felt the urge to go to her room and wake her up and tell her let's just leave together.

"We're needed again. And I need your help." He disappeared in the bathroom and I heard the faucet turn on. I used this opportunity to check the clock next to the bed. It was 4:03 in the morning. Part of me didn't want to know what we were needed to do, but another part of me couldn't wait.

I finished getting dressed and checked the scar on my wrist, which was the last thing I did every morning when I woke up. So far, it was faint. I started to understand that when my scar acted up I was about to be thrown in another episode. I began using it like a warning to myself.

The water shut off but Gabe didn't walk out. I got up and saw him just staring at himself in the mirror as if his reflection had just mocked him. I found myself doing that a lot lately too.

"Your reflection can tell you all you need to know, because when you look into your own eyes, you can never hide," I thought of my mom's words.

"Gabe?" I tapped on the bathroom door.

His eyes shifted toward me in the mirror. "Ready?"

"Yeah. Lead the way."

We hurried out of the hotel into a waiting SUV out front with a suit in the driver seat. Once we were both in the car, we were off.

"Where are we going?"

"The University." Gabe strapped on his seatbelt in the front seat.

"Where the debate will be tomorr... I mean, today?"

"Yep." He didn't turn back to face me just looked ahead. The drive wasn't long at all. We were already on campus and I was soon following Gabe toward the back entrance of the auditorium. The buildings were nothing but shadows with lights illuminating the pathway toward each structure. I didn't know how Gabe knew exactly where to go. We turned down a wider path and faced an illuminated building with banners hanging across the front, advertising the debate. We walked around the brick building to the back.

"Stay close and smile." He looked back just before opening the doors.

"Good morning." Gabe opened his arms out toward two security guards wearing red vests. We were in what looked like a loading dock area where boxes were stacked and pallets left abandoned throughout the place.

"Morning. What can we do for you both?" One of the guards who had a gap between his two front teeth straightened his posture as if he was trying to intimidate us.

"Yes. I believe the Ammon campaign notified you that we would be stopping by to check our equipment that was delivered earlier today. At least I hope you were." He forced out a cheesy sounding laugh.

The other guard who was a tall, freckly red head took out a walkie-talkie and walked a few feet away.

"He's checking for you."

"Thank you, thank you...what's your name?" Gabe reached out his hand to the gap toothed guard.

"Will." He didn't shake Gabe's hand.

The other guard whistled over to us. "They're OK." He motioned for us to follow him.

"Thanks, Will." Gabe said as we walked by. The other guard led us down winding white hallways with pictures of smart looking men with mustaches on the walls. I had no idea who they were but I didn't understand the point. These men had been dead for decades now and I'm sure they didn't want a painting of themselves hanging in the back hallways of some building. I'm sure they wanted to be hanging in the front rooms for all who entered to see.

We stopped at a door that looked like a storage closet. The guard inserted a key and opened it for us. Inside were a few opened crates and miscellaneous items that were supposedly needed for Marcus tomorrow.

"Thank you, we can handle it from here." Gabe placed his hand on the guards shoulder next to him.

"I'm afraid I've been asked to stay with both of you until you... . "Before he could finish, Gabe had swiped his leg out from under him and slammed him to the ground.

"What are you... ." I took a panicked step toward them both. Gabe raised a fist and slammed it into the guards face, knocking him out.

"Look in the corner for two small black rectangular boxes."

"Why did you do that?" I asked.

"It was needed. Don't worry and just do what I say. Please." He took the walkie-talkie out of the guards vest and held it to his mouth.

I went to the corner and searched through the only crate there and found the two boxes he asked for.

"Will, are you there?" Gabe spoke into the walkie-talkie. Static answered only for a second.

"Yes, who is this? Where's Brent?"

"This is Gabe. Brent slipped on a water spill left by the janitor. We need some help back here."

"On my way."

"Give me those, and you take this," Gabe ordered. I handed him the small boxes and he gave me the radio.

"Once he gets here, either keep him here, or move him back to where we came in. Tell him I went to look for help." Gabe went running out of my sight, leaving me with the unconscious guard. I still didn't even know what exactly was happening. I wondered what was in the two small boxes.

"What the hell?" I heard the other guard's voice down the hall. He probably saw his partner sprawled out on the ground. I stepped out and hoped I would be able to do my part of the job.

"Hey, let's get him to the back. My friend went looking for some help."

"Wh.... "

I didn't give him a chance to ask for an explanation.

"We can call an ambulance if we need to once we get him to the back." Will seemed a little spacey before, so I needed to take advantage of that. He just nodded quickly and we both put one of his arms around the back of our necks and shuffled him to the back door where we came in. Thankfully, it wasn't too far because big red was heavy. I felt bad, though. I didn't understand why Gabe had to hurt him. I replayed the image of Gabe taking the guard down with ease in my mind. He had definitely done that before.

We made our way to the warehouse area. Will shoved open a door with two desks and the smell of stale coffee waiting inside. There was an unmade bed in the corner and we put him down there. This was obviously the two guards' office area.

Big Red began to groan on the bed as he came to. Will rushed over to his side.

"Brent, you hear me?"

"I've got ice, gauze, some pain meds and water." Gabe walked in the office with total confidence. Whatever he did he did incredibly fast.

"Is everything OK?" A short-haired motherly looking lady followed Gabe into the office.

"I found the campus nurse as well." Gabe laid out the supplies onto one of the guard's desk.

"Thank you. All I know is that he fell," Will got up and faced the nurse. "He's waking up though." He pointed toward the bed behind him.

"Paramedics are on their way. But I'll still take a look" the nurse said, and as she moved toward the bed, I made my way next to Gabe in the doorway of the office. He closed his eyes, which I thought was odd. His lips were moving slightly as if he was talking to himself. My wrist began to burn at my side.

"Someone has to fire that janitor." I turned back to the bed to see Brent holding his head sitting up in the bed. "Hallway was slippery as freaking ice."

When I went to look back to Gabe, he was already walking toward the exit.

"We're going to take off." I said loudly enough for them all to hear. Will looked at me and nodded once.

"Feel better." I looked to Brent but didn't get a reaction from any of them. Brent kept saying how slippery the floor was. He was convinced that he had slipped.

I followed Gabe outside the same way we came in. The black SUV was outside waiting to take us back to the hotel, but I wasn't sure if I even wanted to go back there.

23

pretended to sleep for an hour or so back at the hotel. During that time I listened to Gabe snore in the bed next to me as a car alarm sang out in the parking lot outside the window. I didn't mind it though. The rising and falling of the shrieking alarm and Gabe breathing distracted my thoughts.

Before Gabe fell asleep, he told me the black boxes were a kind of electronic device that could distort the TV audio for the other two candidates as they talked in their microphones, meaning an Ammon team member could control the volume and the clarity from miles away. I wasn't sure why Marcus even felt the need to do this. He was leading in most polls. But one good thing was that learning this made my decision much easier.

I got up and left the room and headed toward Ashlin's room. I wasn't sure if she'd be awake yet, but I wanted to tell her that I was going to leave with her as soon as the campaign was over. After last night, I knew this was what I wanted most.

I only knocked twice before she answered the door, her hair in a messy ponytail that shifted to the left side of her head as she slept. She hugged me before I could even walk in the room, and I walked us both inside as she held on to me.

"I'm glad you're awake. The suits were staring at me out in the hall."

"They're just jealous that you get to see this in the morning." Ashlin chuckled, backed up away from me and did a lame dance move as she let her hair down. For a second she was back to the old Ashlin before the campaign, but her smirk vanished as she sat down in a lounge chair by the window. She held onto a pillow and threw a blanket off the chair and onto the bed.

"Not a fan of beds anymore?" I opened the blinds a little bit as I hoped to see her smile again.

"Not a fan of sleep, actually." She brought the pillow closer to her.

"Ash, I would've hung out with you if you couldn't sleep."

"It's not that I can't sleep; it's just that I don't want to." She rested her head sideways on the pillow while looking at me. "A lot of weird dreams lately."

"About what?"

"I don't really know."

"Well, if you want to talk about them, you know I'm here," I assured her, walked over to her and kissed her forehead. I understood not wanting to talk about dreams more than anyone else.

"I know, Sammy."

I dropped down to my knees in front of her, forcing her to adjust her position on the pillow to see me. Her eyes were half closed. "This is almost over and once it is,"

I held onto one of her hands, "I want to just live some-where else with you. I want a life with you; like you said in Alabama, I'm learning that this life isn't for me, either."

Her eyes shut and a small smile formed on her lips before she puckered them, waiting for a kiss. I moved closer and pressed my lips into hers tenderly. When I pulled away, she was asleep, her face calm and worry free. I realized that she must not have slept at all. I picked her up from the chair and laid her onto the bed. As I did, she mumbled, "Let's leave now."

"Soon," I breathed and rested next to her, listening to all the sounds on this side of the hotel. I wasn't completely against leaving now but I felt like I owed it to Marcus, despite my distaste for some of his methods, to at least stay until this was over. He was the one who gave me this chance in the first place. I stared at the ceiling and remembered a conversation I had with Marcus in his office on the bus one night after the first debate. He had asked me to take notes on his opponent's answers.

"Wow. I ask for notes and I get a novel," Marcus laughed as I handed him the notes. He shut the office door when I walked in.

"I just figured you'd want detail."

"I'm kidding, my boy. The more detail, the better." He threw the notes on his desk and sat in the chair. "I had a few others take notes as well, so when I combine all of them with my own, there should be no big details missing." He winked before kicking off his shoes and tossing them in the corner.

"OK, good. I'm glad I could help."

"You've done well here. I hope you are at least enjoying this process." He sounded like he was asking me a question.

"I am enjoying this. I hope Gabe thinks so, too."

"I know he thinks so. Once the sign was declared a success, I know he relaxed a bit more." He motioned his hand to one of the signs that Gabe and I created hanging on the sidewall.

"You were right about the ankh being accepted." We both stared at the sign.

"We create what a symbol means in our minds. I knew it would be accepted because to me, this symbol is the sign of a fresh start. A new nation."

I nodded and before I could say anything, Marcus continued.

"I remember you asked what I wanted to be besides being President of this country. I have thought about that a lot. I would want to be a twenty-year-old, like you, all over again." A small smile formed on his lips. "I'd take Bree and marry her even sooner, and then we'd just travel far away from here." He motioned his hand like he was telling me to back up. "I'm not saying I regret my life choices that lead me here, but to just travel with Bree would be my dream."

Ashlin scooted close and rested her head on my chest, nudging the memory of Marcus away. I wasn't convinced that leaving was the best thing to do. Was it even the right thing to do?

What was the difference between the right and best thing to do anyway? Making the "right" decision was constantly preached to me in school when I was a kid. After living in the world for a few years, though, the right decision never seemed to be the best.

Was it the right decision for my dad and me to go to Honduras? In my mind that was a definite no, but others would try to explain to me why it wasn't so bad.

They'd say, "He's in paradise with God," or something along those lines. That may have made those people feel better, but for me, my dad was still gone. The only thing that his death brought me was practice for how to deal with my mom's death.

I held Ashlin tighter and closer to me, trying to stop the thoughts that were multiplying in my head. I stared at the ceiling, begging it to open up and explode with answers to my questions. If God was really there, he or that winged being should burst into the room.

My eyes drifted to my scar that was propped on top of Ashlin's shoulder and hoped to see it start to glow. I realized that the mark was mine for a reason.

"What is that reason?" I knew I wouldn't get an answer from God, but I wondered if he was at least listening.

The whole rest of the day Ashlin was quiet and distant, tangled in her own thoughts.

I was the first to board the bus when it was time to head over to the university. I sat and watched the droplets of rain race each other down the window. I pictured the droplets to be boxcars winding down a hill. I never built a boxcar when I was a kid. I was never a Boy Scout either. I guessed that was when you did those kinds of things.

My eyes wandered to the entrance of the hotel, where there was a campaign sign for Marcus with the ankh symbol right below it. That symbol was becoming just as popular as he was. I looked down at the tiny pin on my chest and straightened it out.

Erica and Ashlin came walking outside, talking about something. Ashlin was facing the window where I was sitting. She wore a long black jacket that stopped before her knees, revealing a little part of the black dress she was wearing underneath, and a gray scarf wrapped around her neck, which dangled down the front of her jacket. She looked down to her boots before she saw me through the bus window. We both smiled the way we smiled when we first met each other. She continued to listen to Erica, but would glance back to me as she did. A few trails of rain slid down the window, causing Ashlin to look like a blur. Their conversation ended when the light drizzle turned into a downpour. Erica went running into the hotel, and Ashlin came onto the bus.

I got up from my seat and met her in the middle of the aisle, put my arms out and placed my hands on top of a seat on both sides, blocking her from passing. "You'll need a password if you want to get through."

"Let's see." She tapped her chin mockingly and then came closer to me. Our lips hovered inches away from touching. I could feel her breath against my bottom lip the way a breeze gently pushes a fallen leaf across the ground. We both gave in and kissed; the cold from the outside lingered on her lips.

"How'd you know that was the password?" I raised my arm as if it were a bridge opening for a boat to pass underneath.

She smiled and made an engine noise with her lips, ducking beneath my arm. She seemed to be feeling a little better. "Have you seen my dad yet?"

"Nope, I haven't. He's been in prep mode."

"Sounds about right." She sat down and turned her legs out into the aisle, facing me.

"What were you and Erica talking about?"

She thought for a second. "Nothing special. You know Erica - always business, like my dad. I could care less." She leaned forward, resting her head against my stomach.

I smoothed a strand of her hair behind her ear and said, "I know."

"I wish I knew what to expect after all of this." She leaned back and looked up at me with her big blue eyes. "I don't feel right, Sam." Something had changed in her; the girl who stole the SUVs and drove them wildly to "get where we needed to be" wouldn't have wanted to know what was next.

The driver came running onto the bus along with Erica and her blonde assistant, who was on the phone.

"Finally!" Ashlin scooted over to the window seat, and I sat down next to her. Marcus was next to board the bus followed by Gabe and the rest of the team. Dante was supposedly meeting us at the university. Marcus went straight back to the office without looking up from a notepad.

The bus headed for the university and the debate, rain curtaining the windows.

"Sam, can I see you for a second?" I turned and saw Marcus standing by the office door. I got up and followed him inside. Marcus slid one of his arms through his suit jacket. "Shut the door for me."

I shut the door and leaned against the wall.

"I need you to hang on to this until I ask for it once we're inside." He held out a notebook. I lurched forward and took it nervously. All of his notes were probably inside.

"I also wanted to thank you." He patted the top of his chair as he stood behind it.

"For what?" I asked.

"For keeping what we've talked about between us." He tugged forward on the suit and flattened the sleeves out. "And for listening to me. You may think people listen

to me all the time. They don't; they just *hear* me."
He walked around his desk and put his hand on my
shoulder. "You've earned my trust, and I hope I've earned
yours. We're in this together." Marcus squeezed my
shoulder and held open the office door.

"I wouldn't want it any other way."

The bus came to a stop outside of the university.

"Time to put this election to bed." Erica waived us all
off the bus, where security was waiting to escort us inside.
I was the last in line to get off, with Ashlin in front of me.
I shut my eyes to see if I could hear my dad's or mom's
voice again. Instead, I felt Ashlin's hand move into mine.

"Don't let go."

I squeezed her hand a little tighter as we both stepped
off of the bus.

24

he sounds of our shoes and the girls' heels hitting the tiled floor filled the otherwise silent theater lobby. The constant *click-clack* reminded me of a ticking clock. Each step moved forward with time. Thankfully, we arrived when we did, since we managed to beat Marcus' fans and the news reporters from swarming us like bees around their hive.

"Good afternoon. Mr. Senator, Mr. Wess, and the lovely Ms. Andrews." A slim, neatly dressed, middle-aged man with a crooked nose opened the two theater doors separating the lobby from the stage area. He held one door open with his back and arched his eyebrows, creating deep worry lines in his forehead. "Please follow me. How's everyone doing?" He bowed his head as we passed him. "Ah, Ashlin, you look stunning as always." It was weird to know that people I'd never met before knew who we were, or at least knew of us. Maybe not me, but Ashlin was now in the spotlight without even trying to be. Marcus couldn't stop that now. Not with the entire country wanting to know everything about his life. Ashlin gripped my hand tighter as we followed our new guide through the auditorium. As we walked past the three podiums on the stage I noticed that this place wasn't too big, and not a lot of people were going to be here because of that.

"Be careful," the man shouted at three scrawny workers struggling to position some cameras. I almost tripped Ashlin because I stopped so abruptly. Sitting on the stage with his legs dangling over the edge was the old bum with the aviator sunglasses from Phoenix.

"What's going on? You almost dislocated my shoulder," Ashlin gathered herself while I wondered how he even got here and with a job with the university. He was wearing the same work shirt as the guys setting up the cameras.

"Sorry. I just thought I saw someone I knew." We caught up with the group, but I glanced back to the workers to try to get another look at the old man. I couldn't see him though. I thought back to the first day of the campaign and the set-up attack; I thought I saw him there as well. Was he working for Marcus, too? I wondered where the audio devices were that Gabe had installed last night. Was the old man going to be the guy controlling them?

We followed our guide through a side door that lead into a narrow hallway, similar to where Gabe and I were the night before. We were forced to form a single file line, making our way to Marcus' "dressing room."

"Here we are, Senator Ammon. I hope all is to your liking. We will keep you updated with the time. Good luck." The guide bowed his head again and opened the door for us. The room was nice and comfortable, with two long leather couches and a table filled with food and drinks for us. There was a TV up in the corner, with the local news showing the outside of the university. Erica turned off the volume but kept the TV on.

"Sam, do you have that notebook?" Marcus took off his suit jacket and placed it over one of the couches.

"Yeah, here you go." I handed the thick notebook over to him. He buried his face into it, studying. I relaxed on one of the couches and watched the TV flash images of Marcus with the headline: "Final Debate Tonight."

Ashlin placed a cookie on my lap as she sat next to me, eating one herself. She was in mid-chew, trying to not drop any crumbs onto her dress.

"Thanks," I laughed as I watched her almost drop her entire cookie. Sometimes it feels like the harder you try to *not* do something, the easier it is to do it. Whatever that something is doesn't matter.

I started to unwrap the plastic around the cookie until I felt my wrist go numb and shoot with pain, causing me to flinch and shake it out of reaction.

"What happened?" Ashlin set her cookie down beside her while still looking at me, confused. "You OK? I didn't realize they were electrically charged."

I managed to smile at her, trying to fight back the pain that was steadily increasing. "It's nothing. My wrist is a little sore." I clenched my fist as I held it with my other hand. I had to get out of that room. I didn't want my entire arm to start glowing like it had before on the bus, not now. Before I could move, Ashlin had her hand on top of my own hand, which was covering my scar. I felt the marking throbbing slowly, pounding against my flesh. Ashlin started to unfold my fingers.

"It's nothing. I'm all right." I closed my fingers around my wrist tighter.

"You're in pain. I can tell. Erica can get a doctor, "
She looked back at Erica, who was talking with Marcus
and now Dante who walked in.

"No, no. I'm fine. I promise." I got up and headed for
the door, knowing she would follow me out. I didn't want
anyone else to think something was wrong. Out in the
hallway, a suit was standing guard by the door. He was
the only one in the hallway.

"Can you give us a second, please?"

He looked around, unsure of himself.

"No one is going to be coming, all right?" Ashlin
snapped. I had never seen her do that before, especially at
one of the suits. The suit turned on his heels and went
into the room to join the others. Ashlin looked to me and
softened her stare. "I'm not stupid, Sammy. Something is
going on. Just tell me."

Whether she was talking about what was causing my
pain, or whether she had a hunch that something else was
going on with me, I wasn't sure. I really wanted to tell her
everything about what I'd seen, the painting, and this
damned scar that was still shooting stabbing pains
down my entire arm. She'd think I was crazy, though.
She didn't need to get thrown into my spider web of
confusion with me. We'd be like two trapped flies waiting
to be eaten. She didn't need my trouble.

She lifted the hand covering my scar. I watched her
eyes narrow, then grow huge when my scar was out in the
open. The flesh was raised, puffed out, and bright white.
I pulled my hand away and shoved it in my pocket, still
wincing in pain. My body became weak and very warm.
I felt beads of sweat drip down my neck and back.

"Don't tell me you're OK when you're not. What is
happening with... that?" Her eyes darted to my pocket

like she just saw a mouse scoot across the hall. "Is it infected, because that isn't normal." She shook her head slightly, still looking at my pocket. "Let me see it again." Her eyes were now filled with curiosity.

"I'm fine. Please, trust me." I pulled my hand out of my pocket, and she grabbed it as soon as it was free.

The door opened and a nervous-looking lady rushed in. I could hear the crowd in the auditorium before the door shut again. I forced my hand from Ashlin, who was enthralled with my scar now, and put it by my side. The lady knocked on Marcus' door opened it and called softly, "Just a few minutes, Senator Ammon." She went all the way inside and shut the door behind her.

"Can we talk about this later? It's a big night for your dad. He needs our attention and support."

She reluctantly nodded her head. "Later."

"I promise." I kissed her lips and felt a drop of sweat trickle down my forehead.

Ashlin watched the bead of sweat fall to the floor. "You're burning up, and it's chilly in here." She ran her hand through her hair, not looking at me. She was frustrated, and I was the cause. I should've just blurted everything out right then and there, but I didn't.

"I'll be all right."

I heard a muffled voice coming from the auditorium, followed by a cheer. Something was definitely wrong with me, though. Just standing made me feel like I was trying to balance on a wooden beam five stories high. I thought my heart was going to break through my chest at any moment. I shoved my hand into my pocket and followed Ashlin back into the room, just as everyone else was coming out.

"You're already in the lead. Just relax." Erica was in Marcus' ear. Dante shook Marcus' hand firmly. The last two people he had to pass were Ashlin and myself.

"Love you, Dad." Ashlin hugged Marcus and kissed his cheek. "I'm proud of you."

I just nodded at Marcus, hoping I was hiding my pain successfully.

"See you guys out there," was all he said before he, Gabe and Dante followed the nervous looking lady in the opposite direction we came from.

"Ready?" Erica looked to Ashlin and me with wide eyes and her lips tightened. "Let's go to our seats." Once we stepped out into the auditorium, the crowd and flashes from cameras littered the entire place. People held signs for Marcus, wore campaign shirts, anything to support him.

"Ashlin!" Some fans shouted toward us. More flashes from cameras sent purple dots into my eyes, just as another wrecking ball of pain hammered my arm. A roaring cheer bounced around my head, making me feel like I was slipping down a spiral slide. I felt Ashlin's hand grab mine, keeping me steady.

We took our seats in the front row, directly in the middle, right where Marcus was going to be. I sat down in my chair, as if that would be the cure for whatever was happening to me, but no relief came. My vision went black; I heard nothing but droning voices circling around me like vultures over road kill.

My vision returned in time to see Ashlin's eyes filled with worry.

I tried my hardest to focus and not cause a scene, keeping my scarred wrist inside my pocket.

A burly man wearing a suit walked onto the stage. He began to speak, but his words sounded like mumbling to me. My scar throbbed to the beat of my heart.

"Ladies and gentlemen, your candidates for the presidency of the United States." I heard that clearly. From the left came Dean Henderson, a silver-haired, smooth-faced man, and from the right, John Fredricks, a tall, lean, military-looking man. Both were waving to the crowd. Then from the middle came Marcus. The crowd erupted into an orchestrated frenzy. Somehow I found myself standing with everyone else, but I hunched over as a tearing pain ripped into my gut.

"Do you need help?" Ashlin said in my ear, trying to talk over the cheers. I could no longer see where she was; I was looking through a distorted lens. Her voice was only an echo. I collapsed into my seat, my limbs stiffening. I needed to leave.

"I'll be in the back room," I stuttered, "I... I need to lie down," I leaned over to where Ashlin was. My voice was a hum inside of my head.

"I'll come with you," she insisted. My vision returned. She was scared.

"No, stay for your dad." Without looking back, I made my way to the side door. As I walked, I slipped in and out of blackness. My entire body shook like I was freezing, but I wasn't. I felt like I was standing on a glacier. I reached the door, flung myself into the empty hallway, limped down to the dressing room, and dropped onto one of the couches. I had no more energy. I was a car with no more gas. I sat up, and my head fell backwards. The crowd erupted into another cheer.

The room was quiet. The TV was still on mute, but I could hear buzzing when another image would flash onto the screen. I could hear the ticking of the clock on the wall, reminding me of when we walked into this place.

"We are in need of a new beginning." Marcus' muffled voice broke into the room. Then, faintly, I heard footsteps walking down the hallway.

"Ashlin," I didn't even hear myself say it; I must've just mouthed it. The steps grew louder. They were too heavy to be Ashlin's. Every step pounded into my head and caused my scar to throb at the same time. The ticking of the clock stopped. I didn't hear any more cheers or muffled voices. The handle on the door jiggled.

"Who's ... ." I couldn't continue; I had no breath to speak.

The door swung open with a gust of wind, and a bright light flooded the entire room. I managed to look toward the door and saw Michael standing there. The black aura surrounding him dispersed throughout the room, cloaking everything in sight. He walked calmly over to me, glowing as if he was on fire, and held out his hand toward me. I noticed the white scars pulsating on his arm. His green eyes blazed like comets darting across the night sky.

"It is time." His voice echoed in my head.

I couldn't even respond. He placed his massive hands on my shoulders. His eyes spit out a ray of green light, blinding me. I felt pressure build deep inside of me, then drop quickly, like I was on a rollercoaster. I couldn't see anything at all. The pressure inside of me came screaming back as Michael's grip on my shoulders tightened. I felt him lift me upward as easily as if I only weighed five pounds. A cold wind brushed against me for a few seconds when I felt him release me, but I was drifting, twirling, like a log flowing down a river.

A white light seeped into my eyes as my vision started to clear. Something was guiding me, rocking my body back and forth, until I landed on a soft, cushioned surface. Warmth rushed through my veins. I felt loved. I felt as if my family had never died, that they were right next to me in this moment. I felt every worry that I'd ever had melted away like ice on a road. Still blurry-eyed, I felt a burst of energy shoot through me, as if I had been injected with it.

"Welcome," I heard Michael's voice next to me, not inside of my head. "Stand up."

I didn't struggle to my feet. It almost felt too easy.

"Look," I felt Michael's hand on my shoulder, and my vision was instantly cleared.

"I… where… ." I dropped to my knees, astonished at what I was seeing.

25

"What is this place?" We were standing on a small hill with a white stone path that led to a breathtaking city made out of what looked like to be glass; each tall structure sparkled like a diamond would in sunlight. Some were pointed at the top, shaped like a pyramid, while others were vast domes. It was then that I noticed the sky, golden red like a permanent sunset, just like the sky by the tree. Dark green hills filled the backdrop behind the shining city, and beyond them two snow-covered mountains that seemed to stretch into the sky forever. Their height dwarfed the mountains my eyes were used to seeing in Phoenix. Two waterfalls streamed down the faces of the enormous mountains, the water dark blue as if it had been dyed. Everywhere I looked, radiant colors painted the entire place. I peeled my eyes away from the city and looked to Michael standing beside me, waiting for him to tell me where I was. Even *he* looked different.

He now had six wings that were bright white and speckled with gold. The black aura surrounding him was now purple. He wore his black and gold armor with his sword by his side, and was taking deep breaths through his nose with his eyes shut and his head slightly raised.

I knew where we were just by watching him: his home. We were in Heaven. I rose to my feet. "What have I done to deserve this?" I asked, waiting for his answer, listening to what sounded like music coming from the city. It sounded like the clatter of glasses, a tinkling sound, but with a melody and a gentle beat. I thought the buildings were making these sounds.

I then saw two figures walking hand in hand out of the city, headed towards us. I looked to Michael, who was still just standing there, silently, with his eyes closed. As the figures got closer, I saw who they were. Tears filled my eyes, but I felt no sadness.

"We've missed you." I heard my mom's soft voice. For the first time since the agonizing days I had lost her and Dad, I wrapped my arms around both of my parents.

"It's really you." I squeezed tighter.

My mom kissed my cheek. I felt warmth coming from their bodies.

"Of course it's us." I had my family back.

"If I'm here, am I dead?" I tried to remember just how I got here, and I couldn't. Both of my parents' eyes moved away from me and to Michael, who glided past us.

"Follow me, Sam." Michael's voice was back in my mind.

"I want them to stay with me," I said, looking at my parents, expecting them to agree, but they were now behind me. I was moving away from them. Something was pulling me forward.

My parents remained smiling, standing hand in hand by the hill. "We'll be right here." I continued to be pulled toward Michael.

We were at the entrance of the city, where there was a gate in the shape of an arch with engraved names covering the entire thing. On each side of us were two streams that flowed smoothly, ending by the arch. I leaned down and dipped my hand into the enticing water, now walking on my own and not being pulled. When I saw the shimmering structures up close, I felt like I had been there before. That was impossible though. How could I have ever forgotten all of this?

"Come," Michael interrupted my thought.

As we walked forward, going further into the city, the stone pathway was now shimmering glass, just like the buildings. I noticed that I hadn't seen another person, or whatever else lived here, the entire time, but I was hearing faint voices chanting something the more we walked. I heard one single, powerful voice, like the rumble of thunder, say Michael's name. The voice traveled through the entire city. Whoever he was only said one word, but when he spoke, I watched everything around me react to it. The structures glistened a little brighter, the music became quiet, and Michael stopped walking like he had just hit an invisible barrier.

Michael faced me, looking serious, like he was late, and for the first time, the fire in his eyes was extinguished, the irises now a simple dark green. He wrapped his two upper white wings around my entire body, and I felt like I was in a cocoon. I could no longer move on my own because of this, but Michael kept gliding forward with me in a bundle on his back. I heard the harmonized chanting grow louder and listened for what they were saying, but I still couldn't tell. Even submerged in Michael's wings, I felt a surge of warmth pour into every part of me, like the sun warming my bones after a cold, rainy day.

"Who was, who is, and who is to come. Who was, who is, and is to come." I could now hear what the voices were chanting. Above me, I could hear the whirring of multiple wings like a flock of giant birds coming in for a landing. More voices chimed in with the chanting.

A deep blast from a horn sounded into the air and shook where we were standing. I could tell Michael was kneeling now. I wondered what he didn't want me to see or what he was protecting me from. Then dead silence interrupted my thought. The chanting stopped, as if the voices had been practicing to cut off at that precise moment. The music went silent. I pictured a small room with just Michael and myself inside.

"HOLY, HOLY, HOLY. WHO WAS, WHO IS, AND WHO IS TO COME," a roar that sounded like a million voices all crying out at once, causing my heart to shudder. We were definitely not in a small room.

I could feel a presence walk over to wherever Michael was kneeling. I was hunched over, still covered by Michael's wings.

"Michael," the strong voice said lovingly like he was speaking to a child.

"My Lord," Michael's voice quivered. That's when I knew I was in the presence of God. I wanted to see Him. I wanted to confront him, if this was God I was actually feeling. What did he want with me? I tried to stand up and push my way through Michael's wings. But, just as I was about to try, Michael squeezed me tighter so I couldn't move at all.

"The scroll is now yours to give."

I tried to fight my way free, but it was like I was trying to kick through metal.

"Love as I love, and save as I have saved."

"AMEN." The crowd of voices echoed above me.

Michael then rose to his feet, and I had no choice but to stand as well. Another blast from the mighty horn sounded. As we walked further away from the presence, I grew weaker. Michael pulled back his wings from around me when we were back at the arch. He was holding a scroll in his hands.

"Why did you shield me like that? Why couldn't I see him?" I stopped myself from saying God. It was then that I realized how hard it was for me still to even say His name, and here I was standing in heaven, His kingdom.

"His will was not for you to see Him. It is not your time yet."

"Then why am I here? Answer me that. Why am I in Heaven?" I held my arms out like I was going to try to hold on to the entire city.

"You have not seen Heaven as it is meant to be seen. That is why I shielded you." He started to walk to the same hill we'd stood on earlier. "And you are here for this." He raised the scroll in his hand but kept walking with his massive back toward me.

A hand rested on my shoulder. I turned, and there were my smiling parents once more. I hugged them again. I didn't ever want to forget this feeling of having them.

"Don't worry about us anymore. We are here for you." My dad kissed the top of my head.

"We love you. Now please, follow him." My mom brought her hand to my cheek and watched Michael waiting for me.

"We need to leave," Michael sounded urgent.

"I love you," I called to my parents, wanting to say more to them, but I couldn't. This time I wasn't sad leaving them. I knew they were OK. I finally had peace.

When I approached Michael, he put his hand on my shoulder. When his eyes looked into mine, the green glow returned.

"When will I be ready?"

"You will know." He handed me the scroll he was holding. "This is for you."

The scroll had a red seal with a cross engraved into it. I was about to peel it open when Michael's grip on my shoulder tightened. Pain burst through my arm as everything went black. I watched the colors that surrounded us vanish and blur into nothing. It felt like I was free-falling downward, but I didn't look. I kept my eyes on Michael's. His grip tightened on my shoulder. I collapsed onto the ground wherever we were, in agony.

"Remember," Michael's voice roared, as the place we were in started to break apart and shake violently. He let go of my arm, and then I really did start to fall. When I did, the last thing I saw were three other beings that looked like shadows converge on Michael, thrashing him. I couldn't do anything but continue to fall further away from him. I could see one of the shadow figures break away from the fight and explode with blue. I knew it was the same thing I had seen during Marcus' speech in Alabama. He started to gain on me. A trail of vapor spit off of him as he reached out toward me.

"REMEMBER." I could no longer see Michael, but he screamed out in a pained voice just as the blue light was on top of me. He seemed to pass right through me, but when he did, he took the scroll out of my hand. I had no time to react.

"No." I twisted around so I was falling face first to catch up with that blue light, but I only saw blackness. He was gone, with the scroll.

Sam! Sammy!" I heard Ashlin's voice in my ear.

"Hang on." That was Marcus.

My heart felt like it was a punching bag getting slammed by fists.

"Ashlin?" I waited for an answer.

"Call an ambulance." Another voice screamed out.

"Remember, remember, remember." I repeated to myself as I continued to fall in this nothingness, waiting to see anything at all.

26

y eyes opened, and I thought I was waking up in my old bedroom at my parent's house. I looked around the pale white room and wondered where the window was that was right in front of my bed; it was now to the left of me. And why were the walls barren and chipped? I felt something tug at my arm and saw that I was hooked up to an IV. I then heard the monotonous beeping of the heart monitor behind my head. Once I realized I wasn't in my room, I thought maybe I had always been in this bed and was just waking up *now*.

I massaged my temples, which were throbbing in pain, and continued to observe the room. There was a whiteboard directly across from me with my name written in red marker along the top. At least I still knew who I was. I saw next to me a paper coffee cup with some lipstick on the edges, along with a few candy wrappers.

"Ashlin," My throat burned with dryness. "What happened to me?" I tried to remember something, but couldn't.

Ashlin walked into the room, carrying a water bottle. She went to the fold-out chair with the coffee cup sitting on top, moved it to the floor, and sat down as if she had been doing this same routine for a while.

I just watched her, not saying a word. It felt like I hadn't seen her in years. She put on a black beanie and yawned as she did. That's when she saw that my eyes were open.

"Sammy." She pushed herself up and was kissing all over my face, as if this is what she needed to do to keep her lips from falling off. She pulled back, with her hair hanging down in my face until she moved it out of the way. "You're awake."

I reached my hand out to touch her and saw my scar on my wrist, reminding me of the confusion that had consumed me. She held my hand in both of hers.

"How're you feeling?" Her big blue eyes searched every inch of me.

"I'm good. Just tired. What happened? I can't remember anything." I rubbed my forehead with my free hand, as if that would help me remember.

She held my other hand up to her lips, not saying anything, just looking at me like she had forgotten who I was for a second. "We found you passed out, shaking and screaming, in the dressing room at the university after the debate."

I tried to sit up in the bed, but I dropped back down and winced in pain. My shoulder was killing me. "I… I don't remember a thing." I pulled back the hospital gown's sleeve. "Is there a bruise or something? It's really hurting here."

She moved her head so she could see my shoulder. "Whoa."

"What? What's there?"

"There is a bruise covering your entire shoulder blade. You didn't fall or anything. You were on the couch when we found you." She grimaced as she examined my apparent bruise.

I reached over and touched my sore shoulder like I was touching an activated bomb. I couldn't remember if I had dreamed the entire incident or if it had been real. "Where are we?"

"We're back in Phoenix. I bet you're ready to head home," Ashlin slid my gown sleeve back over my shoulder.

Home? What was home anymore? My face must've shown what I was thinking.

"*My* home is your home, Sam." Ashlin moved her hand in mine once again. "Time for you to get healthy." She fidgeted with my fingers and brushed my scar with her thumb.

"How long have I been in here anyway?" The campaign. Was it over? Was the election over?

"About a week. They still don't even know the cause of your seizure."

"I had a seizure?" I slipped my hand out of hers and wiped my forehead even though I wasn't sweating.

"That's what they're saying, and it sure looked like you were when we found you." Ashlin looked around the room as if someone could explain better. "Let's see what the doctor says today. That's all we can do." She kissed my hand. "We'll get you out of here soon."

"Where is your dad? "

"Finishing the last stretch of the campaign. The final pull." She did the political thumb with her other hand, causing me to laugh which I regretted since my entire body hurt.

She looked at me like I was dying. I hated that; I was fine. I wasn't going to let what happened to my mom happen to me, whether that was what was happening to me or not. I just wanted to remember something that may have set off the seizure. I couldn't believe I even *had* a seizure.

The last thing I did remember was sitting on the bus, watching the rain slide down the window. Erica and Ashlin were talking. And the last image in my mind was Ashlin looking back at me, exactly how she had when we first met. I guess that's not a bad last image to remember before a seizure.

"How'd the debate end up going?" I wanted to keep talking. I didn't want to have Ashlin keep looking at me like she was never going to see me again.

"Do you really want to know?"

"Yeah. Are we packing our bags to take off yet?" My decision to leave with Ashlin was still made. But, she didn't react the way I thought she would've. She looked unsure about how to answer.

"Well, it seemed to go really well, but I guess something went wrong with my dad's microphone. Whenever he spoke, it sounded fine at the university, but the TV audience never heard anything he said. They heard both Henderson and Fredricks just fine, though." She popped her lips together while continuing to fidget with my fingers. "We're still leading, but barely."

An image of Gabe running down a white hallway came into my mind. It looked familiar and felt like a memory, but I just couldn't confirm with my brain that what I was seeing actually happened. Another image pushed its way through. I was holding two small black boxes with multicolored wires sticking out of them. Finally, the full memory of the night before the debate came at me all at once in a stampede.

"I know. It's crazy." Ashlin must've noticed my face as I remembered what Gabe and I did. "So it's kind of a mess right now." She took a deep breath and blew it out through closed lips causing them to vibrate. "That reminds me." She squeezed my hand tighter for a moment. "Gabe was released from the campaign yesterday."

"For what?" Marcus must've been livid from Gabe's mistake.

She shrugged. "Not sure. Erica called to check up on you and told me. It doesn't make sense to me either."

Even though I knew why, it still felt wrong.

"Enough about the campaign. You should get some sleep, Sammy."

I didn't answer her. I was done sleeping. "Have *you* been sleeping?"

"Yeah, don't worry about me." She fought off a yawn the best she could as she spoke.

I laughed, causing myself to cough and get lightheaded. Ashlin quickly gave me her water bottle like it was the last vial of medicine on the planet.

I took a swig of the water, which instantly cooled my throat. "I'm fine, Ash."

"I just hate seeing you like this. I should've done something." She let go of my hand and took off her beanie with one smooth swipe from her hand.

"What do you mean? You couldn't have done anything. Plus, I'm still here. I'm alive." I held her hand that was holding her beanie.

"I could've. You don't remember, but you were acting really strangely before the debate started, and your scar... . " She flipped my hand over and looked at it like she was trying to pick out a suspect from a lineup. "It looked awful."

Another memory came rushing back to me of Ashlin and me talking in the narrow hallway outside of the dressing room. She wanted to talk about the scar. I was not going to lay that concern on her head too.

"So yes, I could've stopped all of this." She was looking down at her beanie in her lap as she scrunched it in a ball.

"This was going to happen, no matter what."

"How do you know that?" She didn't look up at me.

"You're the one who told me that we're always in the place we need to be at the time we needed to be there. I remember *that*." I pushed myself up in the bed fighting through the soreness. "It was going to happen."

She looked at me like she was going to say something, but before she could the doctor walked in.

"Good to see you're awake." He walked to the other side of the bed as if he had been given a time limit to get there. "My name is Aaron Reed." His stethoscope was swinging around his neck. He brought his too-tan face right into mine and shined a light into my eyes. Every doctor I'd ever been to was the same. They all walked too fast and stood too close to me. He clicked the light off and stood with his hands on his hips. "Now that you're awake, we're going to be running some tests on that head of yours." He pointed to his own head and nodded while he spoke. "How're you feeling now?"

"Just tired."

"Good. Sit tight." he said and was out the door before I could've said anything.

The day seemed to crawl by, filled with test after test that brought back negative results. Their final diagnosis was a panic attack. I had a feeling it was something much stronger than that, though. I was going to be released the next day. Marcus and the bus were already headed to Arizona from Texas. They were going to be my ride home.

"Rest up, Sammy," Ashlin said as she helped me get comfortable in the bed. A nurse entered holding a syringe and fed medication to help me sleep into the drip line in my arm. I already felt the warmth coating my insides.

Ashlin sat down next to the bed, not moving her eyes away from mine.

"Thanks for everything," I mumbled, not certain she even heard me. My eyes were already shut.

The last thing I heard Ashlin say before I fell asleep was, "I love you." I couldn't wait to wake up and tell her the same thing.

27

No dream was waiting for me this time as I slept. My mind was quiet when I woke to see the sun breaking through the hospital blinds. Ashlin had somehow squeezed next to me on the bed and had fallen asleep with her head on my chest, with one of her arms up by my shoulder and her other arm curled up by her face. I looked toward the window again, imagining in the distance a line of mountains. I knew we were in Arizona, but I still hadn't seen it so I felt like I wasn't.

Ashlin's hand was twitching by my shoulder as she snored lightly. I moved a few strands of her hair behind her ear. The scar on my wrist caught my eye.

I tried to remember anything else from the debate night. Whenever I tried, it was like trying to spot a fish from above the water. I would get short glimpses of a memory, but then it would bolt away before I could do anything to grab it. That was the way my entire life had been since losing my parents. If my life had a road, it was pitch black, and I was driving down it without any lights.

The door to my room swung open and in came the noises of the hospital. An older woman nurse walked in, rolling a machine toward me, to take my vitals. Ashlin took a long, deep breath, stretched out the arm she had rested on and sat up on her side facing me.

"I love you too," I brushed more strands of her hair off her face. This time my IV line hit her forehead. She smiled and looked at me, either surprised from what I just said or surprised that she managed to sleep all night in the narrow bed.

"I'm glad you heard me last night. You make a pretty comfortable pillow, too." She slid out of the bed and made room for the nurse. "You want anything? I'm going to get some juice."

"I'll get it for you. What would you like, honey?" the nurse asked as she put on a pair of latex gloves.

"No, it's OK. I know where everything is. I'll get it. I need to walk around for a bit anyway," Ashlin said.

"Alrighty." The nurse cleaned the middle of my arm with an alcohol swab.

Ashlin peeked around the nurse as she drew some of my blood. "Anything?" She grimaced when she saw the nurse preparing the needle.

"Water, please." I turned my head away. I hated getting my blood drawn, and it seemed like that's all they did at hospitals. I heard Ashlin walk out of the room and waited for the pinch.

"Hate needles, huh?" The nurse wrapped a rubber band around the top half of my arm. I imagined my blood coming to a complete stop in my veins. "Ironic, since you have tattoos."

"Yeah. I guess." It felt like this was taking years. I didn't feel like small talk. I never understood why people even attempt small talk. It is obvious and sometimes worse than just saying nothing at all.

"I hate needles, too," she laughed to herself. "OK, honey. Think of the most beautiful place you have ever seen."

As soon as she said that, an image of a massive glistening city with a white mountain in the backdrop came into my mind.

I remembered. I had been to Heaven and I had seen my parents. A warm, comforting feeling consumed me.

"The scroll," Michael's voice swooped into my mind out of nowhere like a diving hawk, snatching the comfortable feeling away as if it were a field mouse. I remembered seeing the red seal that was stamped on the scroll floating further away with the blue being until it vanished completely in some other realm I had no idea how to reach again.

"All done." When I looked over, the nurse was taping a cotton ball where she had stuck the needle in my arm. "Not so bad, right?"

"Not at all." I said.

"Let me know if you need anything else. I'll be your nurse all day today." She winked at me and left me alone with my memory of why I was in here.

I remembered when I had tried controlling my scar one day on the bus. Maybe it was the key into that realm. I put the pieces together in my mind. Whenever my scar would burn or glow, I'd be thrown into a vision or dream. I needed to control it. I was done just sitting around waiting for the next thing to happen to me. I knew I couldn't be crazy. The doctors had performed every mental test on me imaginable since I'd arrived and found nothing, just like they did with my mom. I was tired of nothing; no answers come from nothing.

I held my other hand over my scar and shut my eyes, imagining it glowing. I began to think of the tree. I felt my hand covering the scar get warm like I had a flame hidden in my palm. I pictured the massive tree towering above me, with its colorful leaves and vines on one side and the charred branches on the other. I could smell both the smoke and the salty breeze again. I could feel the tree pulling me, could hear the chattering of the colorful leaves in the breeze as if they were welcoming me back. My scar was no longer just a flame, but a wild-fire under my palm. A loud crack of thunder caused me to open my eyes. The tree stood directly in front of me and a streak of lighting darted across behind it in the darkened half of the sky.

I'd done it - engaged the experience, but I wasn't sat-isfied. I began to run toward the tree. I still couldn't move into one side or the other, but I continued to run directly toward the thick base tangled in vines. I was surprised that nothing was stopping me. I began to see tiny flowers growing off the vines right in the path and ran even harder, because I was going to bring one of those flowers back with me.

One half of my body began to ache with fatigue while the other seemed to grow stronger. I was almost there when I started to feel something pulling me away from the tree.

"Sammy?" Ashlin's voice was in my head.

"Not yet," I put my head down and kept running. My leg on the charred side of the field began to sink into the surface only feet away from the flower. I heaved my body forward, falling onto the ground and started to crawl. My right arm was now stuck in the charred ground. I felt another pull from behind me. I was in reaching distance. I threw my left arm as far as I could and grabbed for anything now.

"Did it hurt?" Ashlin was leaned over, holding a cup of water for me to take.

"Did what hurt?" My entire left side of my body was completely numb, so I reached for the water with my right and chugged until I finished the entire cup.

"Geez, you were thirsty. You want more?"

"Please. Thanks." I tried to feel anything in my hand. I couldn't tell yet.

Ashlin set her juice and muffin down. "Of course. I'll be right back. I'll get a pitcher or something."

As soon as she left the room I pushed the bed covers aside and saw the flower sticking out from my clenched fist between my fingers. I still couldn't use that entire arm so I grabbed the flower with my other hand and held it in my palm, just staring at its white petals with bright blue specks.

"Here I got an entire pitcher for... where'd you get that?"

I looked to Ashlin and then back to the flower. She was seeing it, too.

"Not yet," Michael's calm voice sounded in my mind, and for the first time, I knew he was real.

"Was it in the bed?" Ashlin was reaching to touch the flower lying in my palm.

"Yeah, pretty weird, huh?" I blew the flower toward her and watched it ride my breath down to her feet. There was a part of me that wanted to take this chance and tell her where it was really from. But, I agreed with Michael, not yet. The weird part was that I wasn't even sure why I agreed with him. I just had this feeling that I had to trust. What frightened me, though, was that Michael obviously knew of Ashlin, too.

Ashlin had her eyes focused on the flower that was now in her hand, her eyebrows arched upward.

I watched her study the flower just as she studied my scar.

She laid the flower pedal down and poured me a glass of water. "Are you feeling any better? Do you remember anything else?"

"I feel a lot better." I took the glass of water she had poured me from her and watched her walk around the bed to the other side next to me while drinking. She looked bothered.

"I had the weirdest dream." Ashlin's eyes formed little slits.

"What was it about?" I asked.

"Weirdness." She squeezed next to me in the bed and pinched her bottom lip with her thumb and index finger.

I ran my finger across her jaw line. "Sometimes dreams are weird and unexplainable. I think that's why they freak us out so much. We want to understand everything we see, and sometimes that may not happen. I consider myself a pro dream-have-er."

"Dream-have-er? Geez, you are feeling better." She managed to smirk while still holding her bottom lip. She turned over on her side, making sure to not get tangled in the IV cord.

"You can tell me about it, if you want." I said.

"Thanks, Sammy. It's all right." She stared at nothing as if she were hypnotized before snapping herself out of it. "Let's get you out of here first."

28

"Whatever you do in life, make sure to listen to what your heart tells you. It beats not only to keep us alive, but to remind us that we are not in control." My dad pressed his hand against his chest. "I don't physically make my heart beat, you know? Yet, I and most other people like to live as though we control it all. Just listen and let go. God will reveal the rest." He poked the campfire in front of us with a stick, as if he was trying to quiet the popping wood. He tilted his head toward me, lost in another thought. A smile formed on his face that was illuminated from the orange glow of the flames. "Consider this the first of many Honduran jungle life talks."

The memory of my dad slipped away as I stared at the blinking road sign advertising the return of Marcus, **"Welcome Home, Marcus Ammon."** I was still getting used to being outside surrounded by life after my extended stay in the hospital. Everything seemed too bright or too loud. Of course, the doctors never found anything wrong with me. I knew they wouldn't, so I was released.

Two days remained until Election Day. A black SUV was dispatched to bring Ashlin and me to the abandoned stadium where Marcus was going to speak. Since the country had fallen into its current state, *all* pro sports had been suspended, leaving vacant stadiums throughout the country. The closer we got to downtown Phoenix, the weirder I started to feel. We were back where this all began.

The bus stopped outside of the stadium where a line of people had already formed to get inside. I could hear their cheers and see them all waving flags or posters. Thankfully, security had them barricaded off.

Marcus was in the middle of it all, his hand raised and smile still on his face just as the last time I saw him. I could see Dante and Erica and, of course, an army of suits close behind. I turned to Ashlin, who wasn't even looking out the window, but to her legs. I reached for her hand.

"Are you feeling strong enough to be walking around?" she asked and squeezed my hand.

"I am. Are you?"

"If it ends this quicker, then yes. I am." The SUV swung in front of the bus and stopped. As quickly as we stopped, a suit was already opening the doors, allowing the screams of Marcus' fans to hit me in the face like an ice cold wave of water.

I kept Ashlin's hand close to my side as we walked together silently, because being together was all we knew anymore. Like she said, it was another step closer to the end. I was starting to feel that the scar on my wrist, the tree, and everything else I had seen were connected with this campaign, so I had hope that, when it ended, I would understand. I could finally tell Ashlin and know what the purpose was.

I pictured the speckled flower in my mind to numb
my mind from the crowd and the cameras and everything
that came with the campaign. I understood now why
Ashlin didn't like all of this. I also understood why
Marcus tried to keep her out of the process as long as
possible. But as we came behind Marcus, I watched him.
He enjoyed this. He fed off of it all.

"Ammon! Ammon! Ammon!" the hometown crowd
chanted as they filled the arena. Marcus, Dante, and Erica
had been escorted to the staging area; Ashlin and I were
guided to our spots with a perfect view, with the stage
directly in front of us. We stood in the tunnels, where the
players used to run out to the court. Ashlin's hand had
never left mine since we had stepped out of the SUV,
though she hadn't looked at me once. I had to keep
fighting off the urge to ask if she was okay. I knew she'd
talk to me when she wanted to.

The crowd was still in a frenzy when a short, stubby
man with a microphone came waddling up onto the
stage. I thought he looked like a ringleader for a circus.
He was only missing the top hat. This sure felt like
a circus, though.

"Ladies and gentleman, it is my absolute honor to
introduce a man that needs no introduction. Our very
own Marcuuuuus Ammmmmon." He held one of his fists
into the air, and the crowd erupted when Marcus walked
out into view.

Both Ashlin and I remained still, holding hands, silent
in the tunnel. I looked at Ashlin and realized that both of
us had not been wearing the ankh pins. She just stared
straight ahead, lost in her thoughts. I looked down at
where my pin would usually be and swiped the empty
space with my hand. Signs of the ankh symbol were

scattered like weeds on an overgrown lawn. Signs that Gabe and I created were spread throughout the stadium as well. I wondered where Gabe was now.

The stubby man handed Marcus the microphone, patting him on the back like a proud brother. Marcus paced around the edge of the stage, still waving to his obsessed admirers. He tried to hush the crowd so he could begin.

"I'm glad I saved the best state for last." Naturally, this caused another round of cheering. Marcus spoke over the cheers, which only grew louder. "Together, we – will – overcome."

I noticed something forming above Marcus: multiple figures that looked like warriors carrying axes and swords. At first there were only a few, but after every word Marcus said, more appeared behind him. Their faces were concealed behind headpieces and masks that resembled those a pharaoh would wear when buried. I remembered from my art class that they were called death masks. The warrior closest to Marcus was directly above him, his golden mask shaped like a scorpion, its stinger curling out from the back, arching over his head. Each warrior wore black armor that entirely covered him. All of these beings had weapons drawn, and all of them in the same moment unleashed a pair of bright white wings from their backs stretching above their heads, making them look even taller.

I knew Ashlin wasn't seeing this, but I checked just to make sure. She was still staring straight ahead, oblivious to the show in front of us. Walking on the stage next to Marcus was the blue light. He mimicked every motion Marcus made. I tried to blink away what I was seeing, but nothing changed. What I was seeing was actually there.

Then I felt someone's hand on my arm and my entire body went ice cold, as if I'd been thrown into a freezer and locked inside for hours. I tried to look behind me, but I was locked in place, frozen. Out of the corner of my eye, I could see the hand on my arm was black, with long, slim fingers and no knuckles. I could feel my scar throbbing, as if it were trying to jump off of my skin.

"Hello," an unnatural but delicate-sounding voice spoke into my ear. I could hear whatever it was behind me taking relaxed breaths through its nose.

An explosion erupted in the air, and, with a flash of light, I saw Michael and hundreds of other beings like him come out of nowhere.

The hand on my arm tightened. Another surge of cold seeped inside of me.

I couldn't remember the last time I had seen Michael. His face was stern and covered in soot, with bleeding cuts like he had been fighting. The others with him looked the same. They each wore the black and gold armor, like Michael, but each of their eyes were glowing a different color: bright purples, blues, reds, and silvers. Each had long, dark hair, except Michael, and each had a pair of golden wings pointed like daggers as they hovered in the middle of the arena, not far from the other group of masked beings near Marcus.

Michael was the only one looking right at me. "Calm yourself," his voice spoke in my mind.

"My son told you that he could provide the way out of all this, did he not?" A finger on the hand on my shoulder moved, tapping on my collarbone. I looked and saw that it was pointing to the blue light and Marcus. I wanted Michael's help, but if this being could end all of this right now, then that's what I wanted most.

"Say the word and you will be freed from this life that *he* has put you in." The finger was now pointing in the air where Michael was. "He could have saved your father, but did not. He even could have saved your mother, but did not."

I looked to Michael, who had his eyes closed.

"I'll even return your scroll to you and heal that scar of yours, Addison."

Whatever was in that scroll was important, and could I now see what it said and be freed from all of this?

Michael immediately stood directly in front of me with his eyes and scars glowing fiercely. He looked to me, then to whoever was behind me. Blood dripped down his face from a wound on his head. His wings stretched out by his sides. His sword was drawn. Even through his intensity, I felt like I could trust Michael. I saw him attacked for that scroll. He would want it in my possession, wouldn't he?

Michael pointed his sword behind him without taking his stare off me. I saw the group that came with Michael fly toward the blue light and the masked warriors. Michael took a step closer to me, and I felt the hand on my arm leave. Michael pushed himself up into the air with his wings.

"Believe." His voice echoed in my mind. Behind him, I saw the two groups of beings about to collide. The crowd erupted into a cheer, and everything I was seeing vanished. I saw only Marcus walking off the stage, and I still felt Ashlin's hand in my own.

"Miss Ammon." A suit motioned toward the both of us. We followed like we always did. I shot a glance behind me and saw nothing.

29

shlin and I had to wait with the suit for Marcus and the group by the door. I could see Marcus signing autographs and shaking every hand that reached out to him like he was made out of gold. The suits surrounding him were having a rough time holding back the throngs of people.

"Welcome back, my boy." Marcus finally reached us, and while still smiling, he looked overwhelmed. One of the suits pushed open the emergency exit door, and we were greeted by another group of screaming people. At first I thought they were more supporters, but as we walked, I noticed a sign saying, "You are the REAL liar." Another one saying, "NO HOPE, Ammon!" I looked at Marcus, who was still waving and smiling. Now I felt like I was in the middle of an escort of a guilty murderer being released from prison. Police stood on all sides of us, acting as barriers, along with the suits that enclosed us into a small circle as we walked. Ashlin was squeezing the blood out of my hand. This reminded me of how the campaign started.

Out of all the protestors, one caught my eye. He was standing in the front of them all. It was the bum with the aviator sunglasses from my bus stop. I was certain this time. His sunglasses were on the top of his scraggly head and he was pointing at our group and not saying anything, just pointing. As we passed him, he spat at us. I wondered if he remembered me.

"This way, Mr. Wess." One of the suits pulled Dante away from the group, and he was escorted away along with most of the team that had been on the bus.

"Where's he going?" I leaned over to Ashlin, who just shrugged.

"Who knows?"

I could see the bus up ahead. The suits continued to push back the mixed crowd. We hurried inside the bus. As soon as the doors closed, people closed in on it, still screaming.

"What a madhouse out there." Ashlin was the first to sit, looking exhausted. Marcus was the last to get on the bus, having been pushed in by the suits.

"Take us home." He glanced at Erica, and then to Ashlin and me. "You two made it just in time for the final ride." He squeezed my shoulder and leaned over me to hug an unmoving Ashlin, then collapsed in the chair across the aisle and, with a groan, shut his eyes. If he had a battery, it had to have been almost empty.

The bus started to roll forward. This was the final time we would be on this bus together.

Ashlin took her hand out of mine for the first time since we had arrived at the arena. I realized my hand was numb from her squeezing it. I stretched my fingers out, cracking each one.

"Sorry about my death grip," Ashlin slouched into the chair.

"It's understandable. We were both just released from the hospital." She just nodded. "That was crazy." We sat silent for a few minutes listening to the bus's noises. Marcus had his head in his hands asleep.

Ashlin's head hit my shoulder as she let out a deep breath. "I feel weird, Sammy."

I wanted to say I did too. "What's wrong?" I pretended I hadn't noticed her acting weirdly.

"You know that dream I told you I had? It hasn't left my mind. I keep thinking about it as if it really happened." She moved her head off my shoulder and looked up at the ceiling of the bus. "I know it's a weird time to bring it up, but... . " I knew that look all too well: confusion, my archenemy.

"Maybe I can help."

She hesitated, struggling to think of the words to say next. "Have you ever had a dream that you took as a sign or a warning or something?" She shook her head slightly like she was disagreeing with herself.

Only for the past few months. Again I wanted to say that. "I don't know," I answered, though I hated lying to her face, but I remembered Michael's voice in my head. I was starting to believe my dreams and everything I saw.

"Well," she brushed away her hair from her eyes, "I think I'm doing that now." She tapped the middle of her forehead with her finger. "I've never had this happen before."

Now, I wanted to know what she had dreamed. This all sounded too familiar for my liking. "You can tell me."

She grabbed a handful of her hair, smoothed it back, and breathed a shaky breath. "It starts off where I'm in a dark, cold room." Her voice was hushed. "I can see my breath puff out in front of me. I take a step and the entire floor creeks and moans underneath my foot. There is a red door on the other side of the room, and I feel the need to go to it and see where it leads." Ashlin shut her eyes. I don't know if she was trying to remember or if she just didn't want to see me as she talked.

"There is a knock at the door, so I hurry over and open it. It's you, but your eyes are closed. I kiss you and guide you into the room, like I knew you'd have your eyes shut or something." With *her* eyes shut tight, worry lines formed on her forehead as she concentrated.

"I can still see it so clearly. You close the door behind you, and then you open your eyes, and they are glowing, an intense green-like flame, sparkling wildly. Yet I don't react differently when I see this. I act like it's a normal thing. I notice your scar on your wrist is flashing light."

I didn't like where this was heading.

"You're holding a rolled up piece of paper that looks torn and weather beaten."

Was she seeing the scroll?

"You tell me that it was given to you, that it's very important, and that I need to trust you."

I started to grip the seat harder.

"I start to feel scared for some reason, and you look back at the red door right before it opens. You stuff the paper in your back pocket and get in front of me, like you're protecting me. I move my head to see around you at the man standing by the door."

I noticed Ashlin's hands shaking in her lap.

"It's my dad, and sliced in his throat is the ankh cross symbol with blood dripping down his neck, staining his shirt red. He has this look on his face like he was trying to find us for a long time, and not to just find us, but," she smoothed back her hair again and looked over me to see if her dad was still asleep, "to hurt us. You run toward him, and right when you are about to hit him, I wake up." She opened her eyes but looked down, like she was ashamed. "I've had this dream multiple times."

"Just remember.... "

"I *know* it's a dream, but... ." she lowered her head into her hands, which were resting on her knees. Both she and her dad were now in the same pose. "You don't understand the look on my dad's face in the dream."

She was right. Who was I to keep saying it was only a dream? I should be the first person to know how that feels after everything I've seen. I knew there had to be more to these dreams. If that's how I felt, then I knew that's how Ashlin felt. I just hoped that it was not the case, though, with her. Let me be the crazy one. Either way, she had become a little more involved in things that I didn't want her to be involved in.

We both sat silently again. I couldn't stop thinking about the scroll. Should I ask her about that? I looked over and decided to not to. We were both tired. I shut my eyes and leaned my head into the chair in front of me. I listened to Erika ending a conversation on the phone with Dante, who I learned was going to be making a speech the next day. I could see Erica's feet pacing in the aisle. I didn't bother looking up, though, until I felt the bus slow down.

We were approaching a black steel gate with a pointed top that looked like a spear in the center where both sides met.

"Finally home," Ashlin said under her breath.

The bus driver stopped the bus, which screeched and exhaled. Even the bus was tired. The driver got out and opened the front gate to the Ammon compound. Erica stomped forward decisively to stand in the aisle by Marcus, almost in a panic.

"Can we talk?" She smoothed down the front of her shirt and stood straight.

Marcus stretched his arms over his head and stood up from his seat. "Not about the campaign."

"Some issues have *just* been brought to my attention," she pronounced, glancing over to her assistant, who was sitting at the desk. Marcus followed Erica's stare and laid his hand on the side of her arm.

"We *just* got home. I'm sure this can wait." He looked to the blonde assistant. I had forgotten her name. "Kelly, it can wait, right?"

Kelly squirmed in her seat. "I... I... . " She was shaking her head, wanting to tell Marcus no, it can't, without actually telling him that.

"What's going on?" Ashlin perked up in her seat.

"What's the issue, Erica?" Marcus massaged his neck while looking down.

I could tell Erica didn't want to say it here, but she couldn't hold it in now. "There have been multiple, serious threats made against your life."

30

The atmosphere in the bus was suffocated in silence until the door opened and the driver returned to drive toward the house ahead. Both Ashlin and I now stood in the front with everyone else.

"It was only a matter of time, right?" Marcus was still sitting but bobbing his knee up and down smiling.

"This isn't a joking matter." Erica blew out a breath like she had just taken a drag from a cigarette.

"Yeah, Dad," Ashlin pressed down on Marcus' leg to stop the bobbing.

"Listen, great popularity attracts psychos out there. This has happened to us before. This is a normal situation, nothing to worry about. We knew my push for unity would cause friction at some point." He was looking at Ashlin as he spoke. "It looks like that friction is starting to burn a bit." The bus had stopped in front of the house and I couldn't really see what it looked like yet.

Erica reached into her pocket and brought out her phone, almost dropping it. "Is this normal, Marcus?" She showed him the screen.

"What's it say?" Ashlin asked as she tried to read it too. Marcus' face change dramatically, but he shrugged off Erica's concern with a short, "It's fine." He stood up as if he was ordered to. "Why are we still on this thing?" he grabbed his suit jacket, which was around the back of the chair. "Let's talk inside." He got off the bus and stretched his arms out above his head.

We got off the bus and I could see the Ammon house, which I had heard little about from Ashlin. In the middle of a circular brick driveway where the bus had parked bloomed a patch of flowers around an ornamental white fountain spurting out water. I had never seen a house that looked like this one in Arizona. It had a high-peaked, dark-colored roof, and the house itself was made entirely from white stone, with spacious picture windows covering the front. A redbrick pathway lead up to the front-door steps and the porch, with six white pillars gracefully supporting the roof, a ceiling fan, and two padded rocking chairs. This manor belonged to nobility in the countryside of England, not out of place in the desert.

Ashlin grabbed my hand and pulled me along. I knew she wanted to keep listening to Marcus and Erica. As for me, after living in my small shelter of an apartment, a bus, and then a hospital, what I now saw seemed too good to be true. We walked inside as the suits rushed around like the knights of King Arthur, dropping off our bags and securing the house.

The flooring throughout was light-colored bamboo, and almost every wall I saw was covered in artwork. The kitchen was spacious and modern-looking. But my favorite part was the entire back part of the house, made completely out of glass.

"Where did they go?" Ashlin's forceful tone snapped me out of the trance the house had put me in. "Probably his office." She answered her own question.

"Why don't you show me around?" I asked. I wanted to keep her mind off the newest stress of knowing that Marcus had been threatened again. She smirked her usual way and agreed.

We started up a luxurious twisting staircase to the second floor and I stopped again to look out the giant glass wall that faced the desert and the pink sky.

"Gorgeous, huh?"

"I could get used to this," I nodded.

"It gets better."

I looked back and saw she was already on the move down the hall. I heard Marcus' and Erica's voices echoing from somewhere on the same floor.

"I knew they were in the office," Ashlin pointed at two closed double doors. I knew Ashlin wanted to talk about what had happened on the bus. I wondered what that message actually said, but I figured it was better not to dwell on it with Ashlin, unless she wanted me to talk about it.

I didn't realize we were standing in front of Ashlin's room until she opened a door that seemed to appear out of nowhere around the corner of the hallway.

"Home sweet home." She flung herself onto her bed, which looked like a cloud with purple blankets and clung to her pillow. "This feels... . " She didn't even finish. I walked to the back wall and knew what she meant when she said it got better. Her entire wall was glass, too. I pulled the string on the side and the linen blinds moved, revealing a view that *needed* to be painted. I realized I hadn't felt like an artist with the drive to create at any time in the entire campaign. The last time I wanted to paint something, it had painted itself and dragged me inside.

"Whadaya think?" I heard Ashlin roll off her bed behind me.

"This is amazing." I said.

I felt Ashlin lean her head against the middle of my back and wrap her arms around my waist. I moved her in front of me and held her close, my arms below her neck. We watched the sun meld with the shadowy mountains, burrowing under the purple blankets of the peaks, to rest for the night. For this one moment we were carefree as we watched the desert slowly swallowed up in darkness. I managed to forget about the election, the death threats, the dreams and nightmares, and my scar. For this one moment, it was just me holding the girl I loved.

"Everything will work out, right?" Ashlin somehow shifted closer to me.

"You know the last thing my mom ever said to me?" I asked her.

She turned her body so that she was facing me now, rested her chin on my chest, and looked up at me with a tiny smirk on her lips.

"She told me, 'You'll be all right.' I know that doesn't sound like much, but even in her last moment, she was thinking about me, and whatever she saw as she looked into my eyes for the last time made her think that I'd be OK." I brought my hands up to her face and pressed my palms against her cheeks, with her chin resting in the cup of my hand. "And I believe her. So when I'm looking at you now, I know that everything will be all right." I kissed her forehead. "We have to try to not think about it all too much, you know? We're in this together." I knew Ashlin was the only person I could put all of my trust in, and yet here I was telling her this, and I couldn't even reveal all that I've seen to her.

Ashlin pulled me gently down on the bed with her and cuddled up next to me with her head on my chest. I heard Marcus and Erica leave the office down the hall and continue their conversation downstairs. I pictured Erica right in Marcus' ear the entire time.

"Your room, for now, is right next to mine. I'll show … " Ashlin's voice trailed off as she yawned, ". . . you." She was soon asleep. Even with a bed, it seemed my chest was her favorite place to sleep. I heard the front door slam shut and the bus' engine start. Erica had left.

I carefully slipped out from underneath Ashlin without waking her and headed quietly out of the room. I wanted to talk with Marcus. Maybe he would share what was going on.

Once downstairs, I quickly found him sitting in one of the fancy chairs at the square, dark, wooden kitchen table, spinning a golden ankh cross pin and watching it wobble. I considered Marcus a friend, so it bothered me that he was like this, and it also bothered me that the blue light was so focused on him at the arena. That was a different worry for me, though.

As I sat down in the chair across from Marcus, he looked up to me and then waved off the two suits standing on the closest wall. They obeyed his hand motion like trained pets and walked away to patrol another area.

"I hope the house is to your liking?" Marcus ran both of his hands through his hair and sat back in the chair, almost slouching.

"Your house is beyond 'to my liking.'" It was hard for me to believe I was even here still. Marcus looked to his right out the massive window, which had no perceptible view now since darkness enfolded the house like a black hole.

"It's *your* house too, Sam. We'll figure something out. Oh." He straightened up in his seat with eyes wide as if he had just sat on a needle. "I almost forgot," He got up holding his index finger out toward me. "Wait here." He hurried out of the room, leaving me in the midst of this mansion. All I could do was tap my fingers against the surface of the table as I waited. After a few minutes he returned holding something large, covered with a sheet. He smiled like the day he told me about his wife.

"Ashlin told me that you weren't going to take your painting with, so, here it is," he raised the object in his hands, and it was just what I thought it was going to be: the painting of the tree of life and death.

"How were you supposed to bring a painting on a bus with you for three months? So, I called a few people who were able to recover it from your apartment before it was too late." He held the frame out for me to take it. "We decided to it here." He looked around the room with his eyes. "Where is Ashlin, anyway?"

I reached cautiously out for the painting like I was about to touch something that could've been hot. "She's already asleep," I had my hand on the edge of the painting. "You know what?" I took my hand off and nudged it back to Marcus. "I want you to have it."

"Are you sure?"

"I've seen enough proof that you love art just by looking around. It would be an honor if one of my paintings could hang on these walls," I tried my best to sound convincing.

"It is an honor for *me* to accept this. It's truly beautiful." He leaned it up against the bottom of the nearest wall. "I'll put it in my office." He sounded like a proud father.

"The Oval Office?" I smiled, folding my leg across my knee, tapping my foot on the bottom of the table's surface.

"Hey, not yet, not yet." He chuckled. "You want some coffee? I'm going to make some." He shuffled over to one of the kitchen counters while looking at me.

"Yeah, sure." I wanted to talk for a while anyway.

"I haven't even had a chance to ask you the obvious question. How are you feeling?" He opened a cupboard and reached for the coffee container.

"I'm feeling good. A little exhausted." I replied.

"That's understandable," he nodded. "I'm glad you're good, though. That was quite a scare you gave us." He scooped the coffee grounds into the paper filter.

"If I could've stopped that from happening, I would've."

"I don't doubt that one bit. Like I said, I'm glad you're OK." He gathered some spilled coffee grounds into his palm and threw them into the sink. "So, Ashlin is already asleep? I was actually surprised she was able to make it through the entire time on the road. I have you to thank for that. I know she'll be worrying about these threats though." He lifted the sink handle, turning on the water for a second washing away the grounds.

He just made my job a lot easier by bringing up what I didn't know how to begin. "She is. We *all* are, especially since the attempt when the campaign started." The bum with the scraggly beard came to my mind.

"Trust me, it's nothing to worry about." He shut the top of the coffeemaker and pressed a button. He walked back, looking a little delirious, and sat back down. "No one will go through life without crossing paths with evil."

"Yes, evil is everywhere, I guess," I stopped tapping the bottom of the table with my foot.

"We are all capable of being evil. What exactly is evil to you? I hope you don't mind me asking," Marcus continued. "I've missed our discussions." He folded his hands on the table and leaned forward.

"No, not at all. But I don't know." I wondered why he never talked like this with Ashlin. She was interested in this subject, too, probably because of her beliefs in God. I still wasn't too sure what I believed in. "Like I said, I think it's everywhere. I just don't know what exactly it is," I shrugged.

"You're right." He got up once the coffeemaker beeped three times. "I think evil is necessary somehow, but dangerous, of course." He opened up a cupboard and grabbed two blue mugs. "That's *why* it's everywhere. We decide what evil is and how evil we want to be." He poured the black coffee into the mugs. I watched the steam rise from both cups. "Any sugar or cream?"

"No, thanks."

He placed a mug in front of me and then took his seat again. "If evil didn't exist, there would be no battles in life. It does exist, though, and has all of us in its grasp, trying to break free." He motioned with his hands like he was tearing something apart.

"So, you think an opposite force also exists then, to battle against evil?" I blew off some of the heat of the coffee.

"That's where we come in. We have that choice. We *are* that opposite force," he emphasized with his hand on his chest.

My scar throbbed as I took a sip of coffee. When I looked back at Marcus, he was still in the same position, with his hand on his heart. His mouth was opened slightly, as though he was about to say something more, but he just kept completely still. The throbbing on my scar picked up speed.

I watched as the space underneath Marcus' eyes filled with a dark blue and purple color. The skin on his face began to thin, like something was sucking out all of his blood.

"Marcus?" I tried to get up but I felt that familiar frozen feeling I felt in the arena. My eyes searched the entire room. There was no strange mist or blue light or whoever it was that had been standing behind me in the arena. It was only Marcus and me.

My vision went black, but in an instant I saw a battalion of soldiers running through a burnt field with sulfur heavy in the air. I could taste it. The soldiers all wore the same tattered uniforms with a single stitched patch of a white cross on their arms. Then as if I looked through a macro lens, I saw every one of their faces in close detail: blue eyes, green eyes, gray eyes, brown eyes. They were men of every race and every age, and I felt like I knew each one. With a flash, they were attacked by something in the air. Their agonized screams filled my ears and an intense heat seared my face. A few men were able to fire shots in the air with their guns, but it did no good. Each soldier charred to ash by that unseen flamethrower. I was suddenly alone in the burnt, bloody field until I saw the blue-light figure appear in front of me, floating above the lifeless bodies. He reached down and touched each corpse as he passed, coming closer to me.

I blinked once and was staring at Marcus again. He was moving now and saying something. Did what I see happen to him actually occur, or was that, too, part of the vision?

"I know this is all confusing stuff. I wish she was still here for Ashlin." He took a sip from his mug and looked like he didn't notice anything that had just happened.

"I know." I stood up. Apparently we continued having a conversation. I tried to pass off my confusion as convincingly as I could. "I'm really tired," I stretched. "I think it's time for me to go to bed."

A look of disappointment flashed across his face from my response. "Oh, well, I am, too. You know where your bed is?" He reached across the table, took my mug, and carried mine and his to the sink.

"Yeah, Ashlin told me. Thanks again."

He nodded. "Get some rest."

I made my way upstairs with my mind in the midst of a whirlwind. Bizarre things were now occurring regularly when I was awake. I stopped into Ashlin's room where she was still sound asleep. I leaned over and pressed my lips into hers gently.

"I'll never let anything happen to you. I love you," I whispered. That was one thing I knew for sure: being in her room calmed my thoughts.

Before I left, something drew my eyes to the ceiling.

"What do you want with me?" I stood there listening, blinking in the darkness. I got the answer I expected.

Nothing.

31

It was the day before the election. I could hear many voices echoing off the spacious walls downstairs. Marcus' team was doing anything they could for the "Push to victory," which was the newest slogan for the last days of the campaign. I sat in my bed with my back against the headboard as the morning sun slanted through the blinds. My room was actually Marcus' library, one entire wall filled with books of all shapes and sizes. I wondered if any of them were Ashlin's. I thumbed through them before I went to bed and tried to find her favorite, *The Great Divorce*. I couldn't find it and guessed she kept that one close to her, maybe in her room.

I always loved the smell of books, even though I never really read them. I remember sitting on the floor underneath my mom's drawing desk, looking through a book about sculptures, which was filled with hand-written notes from my mom to herself. I must've been eight years old. I wasn't worried about the words in the book, but rather the pictures and the sweet calming smell of each page. I remember thinking that each page smelled differently, like the stickers I got in school that smelled only when scratched. Marcus' library smelled just like that book. I shut my eyes to stop the memory and think of more relevant things.

There were no more developments on the threats as far as I knew. I thought of everything I'd seen, and my scar, but that was like having the code to unlock a safe with no safe to open. I had all these images and memories in my mind, but for what?

"Maybe it *is* just my mind." I hated thinking about that, but I couldn't help it.

"You awake?" Ashlin poked her head into the room. Her hair looked like a wild mane. She had on a purple t-shirt, which was way too big for her, and sweatpants.

"Sweet socks," I admired. They were such a bright pink that her feet seemed to be glowing. I motioned for her to come into bed with me and she jumped in like she was diving in a pool. She looked up at me with her hair in her face. All I could see was her usual smirk. She burrowed next to me and flopped her arm across my stomach.

I dropped down flat next to her on the bed. She moved her lips to mine before pulling away slightly. "I love you."

If those were the only words she ever said to me that would be just fine. Those three words create the one sentence everyone wants to hear.

"I love you, too," my words brushed against hers as closely as we were lying in the bed.

Ashlin smothered her face into my chest and, without looking up at me, said, "One day left." She blew out a deep breath. "My Dad could be President."

He *was* going to be president. There was no way Marcus was going to lose. "He could."

"Should we join them down there?" I heard Marcus' voice over the rest giving out last minute orders about which states to push his focus into. We both got up and followed the voices in the kitchen. Before we even reached the bottom of the stairs the doorbell was ringing. Ashlin sauntered over to the door and opened it.

Erica walked in, barely acknowledging Ashlin and me. She was too busy chattering away on her phone. Behind her were three suits, who remained outside with their backs turned.

"Why'd she ring the doorbell?" Ashlin pushed the heavy front door closed. "I think she runs on batteries."

"Or solar power," I agreed. It was hard to believe that the house had been empty and quiet just last night, because it now resembled the trading floor on the stock exchange. People ran to others on phones to pass them notes. Multiple computers lined up on the kitchen table with workers on each one.

"When did my house turn into headquarters?" Ashlin led the way, closer into the cluster of people and ringing phones. Marcus stood in the middle of it all, holding a steaming cup of coffee with both hands up to his face, with his eyes closed. Erica paced through the jungle of people, talking with someone who obviously had a lot to say. When Marcus spotted us, he looked behind him and pointed his cup of coffee that way, too. I followed his stare and saw a nook away from this early morning madness. He started to walk that way.

"You guys want cereal?" Ashlin was already rummaging through the pantry.

"Sounds good to me," I said and looked to Marcus, who just nodded his head and sat at a small, wooden, circular table in the nook that overlooked the desert.

I followed and sat in the chair closest to Marcus. Erica pointed at me and waved her finger like it was a magic wand, directing me to move. I listened and scooted over to the next seat. Ashlin came and placed bowls of cereal in front of Marcus and me.

"I'll call you back shortly," Erica ended her conversation. She sat, catching her breath and adjusting her already perfect hair. Ashlin leaned on the entryway wall, eating her cereal. Marcus closed his eyes once more and resumed the same position as before, holding his coffee with both hands up by his face as if the cup kept him warm.

"Perfect morning today," Erica laid her phone on the table. "First, our flight to Miami leaves in three hours." She held up three of her slim fingers. "After hitting the major cities in Florida, we are eating dinner in North Carolina with the governor. Then we come back home." She cleared her throat nervously and glanced at a campaign worker who had just got up quickly from their seat causing it to squeak against the floor. "I have some more news that you need to hear."

"Mmm, okay," Marcus opened his eyes and took a sip of coffee, placed the mug down, scooped up some cereal, but didn't eat it.

"We received another message from the anonymous source," she placed the palms of her hands on the table and tapped each finger once, "regarding the... threats."

Marcus shoveled the bite of cereal into his mouth. "What's new?"

Erica fidgeted in her seat. "I've seen my share of death threats while working on campaigns." She looked to Ashlin as if she was hoping she didn't hear her. "These are different. It's almost like... . "

Marcus snapped his head up, frustrated. "Every presidential nominee has had threats, along with every president and leader of any nation. It makes no difference. I will not let this affect the campaign or me." He lazily pointed his spoon, dripping with milk, toward Erica. "It shouldn't affect you, either." He held his stare with Erica, then went back to eating.

"Do you mind if we talk in the office?" Erica started to scoot back her chair.

"We talk here. Everyone is part of this," Marcus said.

Erica nodded. "Please listen. These are different."

Marcus chuckled to himself with a mouthful of food. "You keep saying these are different. Enlighten me, please, about how they are. I'm interested."

"They," Erica's phone rang again. She ignored it. "They know information that only *we* should know."

Marcus just shook his head. "What do you mean 'they know'?"

Erica leaned in closer to Marcus. "Whoever it is," she twirled her hand above her head, "sent me another email - on my personal email that I don't give out, by the way – with the exact address of the Wiltmon Wells Resort, saying, " she sat up straight into her perfect posture once more, 'he will die.'"

I looked at Ashlin, who set her bowl down on the table, the spoon clinking around inside. She looked at me and dropped her stare to the ground.

"So, what do we do about this?" Marcus chewed his cereal the way a cow chews its cud.

Erica stood up and started to pace around the nook, thinking. "I propose that you watch the election unfold from here, in the safety of your own home, with security. It is the headquarters for now, anyway." Once again she looked at the workers just feet away from us. "Then we schedule an acceptance speech, assuming we win, somewhere else at the last second." She stopped mid-step. "Or we even do it here in your office."

"Absolutely not." Marcus pursed his lips together and dropped the spoon into the bowl.

"We need to be smart." Erica stopped him. "It's simple and easy. It's the only reasonable solution I can see at this time. And so you know, that wasn't the... . "

Marcus slammed his fist onto the table, throwing the bowl into the air and crashing into pieces on the floor. I was the only one who didn't flinch when this happened. A few of the workers in the kitchen stared at Marcus for a second as if they thought they were the cause.

"N-O. I will not be mocked by these, these ignorant fools, thinking they can control me." He got up from his seat, stepping over the broken bowl. "No. That's my answer." He inspected his hand. "I'm bleeding now, because of these pricks."

Marcus turned on the sink and started to wash off the blood. Ashlin moved to his side and helped him. He came walking back with his hand wrapped in paper towels.

"We stick to the original plan. After we vote, we go to the Wiltmon and check into our room. Then when I *win*, I will speak in the conference room." Ashlin handed him another paper towel, and wrapped his hand with it. "All you need to do, Erica - listen carefully - is release this plan to the public. In fact, send a Goddamned email response to those people saying, 'He will see you there.' Then you let the press know, let everyone know." He checked his hand for more wounds. "That – is – the – plan." With his good hand, he rapped his finger on the table after every word. "The citizens need to feel that I am just like them, not some corny, flashy politician who shows fear like the ones who destroyed this country in the first place. If I let fear in, it spreads like an oil spill, contaminating anything it touches." He threw away the bloody paper towels and shook his head. "It can't and won't happen." Ashlin was already handing him more.

Erica remained quiet, just nodding, agreeing with him.

"If you want to hire more security, go ahead and do that. But they will not mock me in front of the nation."

"I'll get right on it," the look on Erica's face told me she wanted to argue but knew he wouldn't hear another word she said, not yet, at least.

"Thanks." Marcus walked out of the kitchen, dodging his employees, not saying another word. Erica left the house entirely, dialing away on her phone.

Ashlin started to pick up the pieces of the broken bowl on the floor. I went over and helped her.

"It's almost over," I used my hand like a broom and gathered a group of pieces into a pile.

"No, it's not. I thought it was too. It's not." She aimed some shards into the pile with a frustrated throw.

I had no response. What could I say? We cleaned up the mess in silence, then went upstairs to Ashlin's room. She went into her bathroom to take a shower, and I lay down on her bed, just listening to the running water.

32

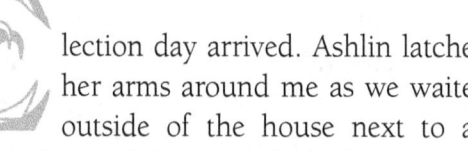lection day arrived. Ashlin latched her arms around me as we waited outside of the house next to an SUV for Marcus. The cool breeze lofted the scent of vanilla from Ashlin's hair up toward me, calming my nerves. Almost every second of the day, I was thinking about either that blue light or Michael. I hadn't had a chance to try to use my scar to find either of them. Part of me wondered if Michael still existed. I hated relying on myself for answers.

"What if we're cursed?" Ashlin looked up at me, squinting.

"Why do you say that?" I asked, startled by the matter-of-fact bluntness of her words.

She backed away from me in thought. "I don't know. I mean, you know the feeling when you think you've forgotten something, right?"

I nodded.

"I've been feeling like that ever since we left the campaign, and it got worse after that dream." She jammed her hands in her jacket pockets. "I thought it would go away once we got back home, but of course, it didn't."

"So, you're saying we're cursed?" I made a short but disconcerted laugh. Where did her thoughts come from?

"I don't know what I'm saying anymore."

"Well, if we are, then you're my beautiful curse," I shrugged, went over to her, and kissed the top of her head. "We're not cursed." My face was buried in her hair.

She leaned back and stuck her tongue out at me and smirked.

I didn't think we were cursed, but maybe we were. Maybe that was the purpose of my life: to be cursed. I just couldn't fully believe everything I had seen and heard.

Marcus walked out of the house, pulling on his wool jacket, with a few suits following close behind. He had returned from his flight with Erika for the important final push to finish the campaign.

"Let's go win an election." He climbed in the back of the SUV, and we followed. "You know where to go," Marcus touched the driver's shoulder.

This SUV wasn't like the others. The darkly tinted windows made it nearly impossible for anyone to see inside. I noticed how much heavier the door was when I closed it. I figured it was bulletproof. Erica was taking every precaution, I was sure of that and I could also tell that Marcus wasn't a fan of the heightened security.

Ashlin intertwined her arm with mine, holding on tightly as we drove to our voting station, a shutdown high school. No one spoke during the entire ride except the driver and the guard in the front seat, who was telling him directions. I looked out the window at the cloud filled sky the entire ride, picturing the city of Heaven in my mind and wondering just how close we were to it.

When we arrived at the school, a line already stretched out the front doors. Television cameras pointed in our direction, with reporters salivating like hungry wolves waiting for Marcus' arrival.

"Sir, stay seated until I open the door for you," the guard in the front seat turned around to speak with Marcus. Blood rushed into his face, turning it a dark red, since it was so hard for him to twist in his seat because of his hefty size. Before we even stopped, a crowd rushed toward the SUV like termites to a piece of wood.

"Back up, back up, back up!" the suit in the front ordered as he got out and extended his arms, creating a barrier and pushing away as many people as he could from the vehicle, allowing time for the local police to assist in clearing a path for Marcus. As soon as the door opened, screams and cheers assaulted my ears. Marcus gave us a confident look, then put on his smile and got out. Ashlin and I stayed in the SUV for the time being. The driver parked a little further away to escape the crowd. We had our loyal suit assigned to us, as always.

"What's your name?" I realized I never knew any of the suits' names during the entire campaign. I thought now was the last time to ask, before it was over.

We climbed out of the car and he looked at me as if I had just offended him. "It's Jack. Now let's go." He walked close behind us, almost pushing us forward into the mayhem.

"That was my dad's name. Nice to meet you finally, Jack," I said, but he didn't acknowledge hearing me. It was weird hearing my dad's name aloud, though. Even though it was a fairly common name, I wanted that name to *only* be my dad's.

As we neared the crowd, I saw more people looking over toward us, and then the looks on their faces brightened when they saw Ashlin. She squeezed my arm as some people pressed closer to us, wanting her autograph. The suit stepped in front of us, like a shield. Somehow we'd beaten Marcus to the entrance. He was inching his way through the mass of people, as if he were trying to swim through quicksand.

Erica greeted us as Ashlin and I opened the entrance doors, her arms folded in front of her. Behind her were two lines of security guards on each side, blocking off people and opening a pathway to the voting booths.

"Welcome to the madness. Looks like we have this election won already," Erica walked confidently over to us just as the doors swung open again and Marcus walked in surrounded by guards. The people inside erupted into a frenzy. I couldn't believe I was a part of all this.

"Let's vote," Erica moved Marcus forward with her hand on his shoulder. The noise in the hallway was deafening.

"Smile," Erica looked back at Ashlin and me with a big, cheesy smile stretched across her face. We reached the line of square, black voting booths lined up against the far wall like the guards of the electoral process, the hope for real change.

Marcus faced the crowd, waved, and beamed his bright smile before going in to vote first.

"So, who you voting for?" I leaned in close to Ashlin to try and fight over the cheers. She just smirked like she always did.

"Ashlin, Sam, over here," Erica pointed out the booths we were to use.

"Happy voting, Sammy," Ashlin let go of my arm and headed to her booth. I knew she was nervous. So was I.

Before I went inside my booth, I saw Marcus exit his and work his way through the crowd, signing autographs and posing for pictures, with security looking like they wanted to climb on his back, becoming his second shadow.

I stepped into the small cubicle and slid the drapes shut. Marcus didn't even need my vote. I was pretty sure this entire place would be voting for him.

I stared at a blank screen in front of me. "Let's see," I looked around, and it buzzed and flashed directions on the screen. "Touch here to begin." I tapped my finger directly in the middle of the glass. "Please look into scanner located above." I noticed three circular lights on a small box on top of the device. I moved in closer and stared into the lights for a few seconds. A laser of red swiped across my eyes. I remember Marcus mentioning that he was behind the installment of the optical retina scanners. This was the first time they were being used in an election. It was unnerving to think that somewhere the codes existed for every eye in the nation. A robotic woman's voice spoke from the screen: "Identity found. Welcome, Sam Addison." All of my personal information, along with a picture of me, appeared on the screen; then a page filled with names of candidates and proposed laws appeared on the screen with blinking dots. "Vote now," the voice ordered. I randomly touched the screen.

"Finally." The final screen appeared, and on this one, I knew what I was looking at. There were five names: the candidates running for the presidency. I recognized the three main candidates. Marcus' name was the third listed. My finger hovered over his name until I tapped the glass and highlighted it.

"Please wait." There was a ticking sound. "Congratulations, Sam Addison, for voting," the robotic voice said.

I slid the drapes open and returned to the Ammon frenzy and an anxious Erica, who was more than ready to get out of this place.

"You figure it out?" Erica asked as guided me to the group.

"Yeah, no problem."

We both walked over to Marcus and Ashlin, engaging the crowd. Erica forced herself next to Marcus and said something in his ear. Calm but laser-focused suits surrounded us and plowed our way to the doors, their eyes scanning the crowd and surroundings for any sign of something or anyone, even the tiniest sliver of a threat. The SUV was waiting for and we hurried over and crammed inside, including Erica this time, making it an even tighter fit.

"Hope you guys voted for me," Marcus laughed as he stretched his arms out along the top of the seat.

We headed to the Wiltmon Resort, the newest resort in Arizona, built strictly for special occasions to host the powerful people of the country. Here we'd find out if Marcus would be the next president. Our nation's next leader and hope for a new start could be sitting right in front of me, and I was completely in love with his daughter, yet all I could think about was why my scar had begun to sear and burn again.

"Now the real fun starts. We wait." Erica glanced at Marcus.

I turned around in my seat to view the caravan of police cars and SUVs behind us. What a journey this had become.

33

he final step in the campaign staircase was upon us. Actually, I thought, there never was a last step to anything; there would always be something else waiting once something ended. The threats against Marcus hung in front of our faces like a noose about to be tightened around our necks, yet Marcus still showed no sign of concern. I knew Ashlin was starting to dwell on them. We both wanted out of this lifestyle but I think we both didn't want to leave Marcus. I couldn't blame her. People had promised to kill her dad, the only family she had left.

I was excited to see the Wiltmon; it was known for its unique architecture and for being built within a mountain, like some secret shelter. As soon as we stepped out of the SUV, a storm front of reporters gathered around us.

"Can you handle the presidency? Do you think you have done enough to win this election? What will you do if you lose?" Questions rained down on us from the reporters, who hurled them our direction like a hailstorm over the suits.

"Dante is on his way." I overheard Erica.

"No press inside, not yet. Keep them out here." Erica ordered a few suits.

Once we were inside, a thin, tall, elegant-looking man with round glasses was waiting expectantly for us in the lobby. He adjusted his tie. "Senator Ammon, welcome to the Wiltmon. My name is Eli. I'm the manager here. It would be my absolute pleasure to show you to your room, sir." He almost seemed to bow, but instead folded his hands together and slightly moved them up and down twice.

"That'll be great, thank you." Marcus held out his hand to shake Eli's, and we all followed.

The entire building had marble flooring with glimmering chandeliers hanging from huge, spacious ceilings, as if we were walking through a cathedral. The lobby was built against one face of a mountain, and water trickled down the boulders into a large shallow pool, which had flowers anchored in the middle like lotus blooms floating with nothing underneath. We turned down the first hallway and walked out a pair of French doors into an open courtyard with benches and tables, then walked on to a deserted-looking trail with colorful, exotic flowers on each side. Eventually I saw a single story house completely separated from the actual resort.

"Perfect." Erica sounded happy with her work already. The house wasn't large, constructed in a dark adobe with a red tile roof and dark brown shutters covering large windows in the front. I could already tell it would be extravagant on the inside. Eli reached into his pocket and brought out a silver key card and fiddled with the door before it clicked and swung open. A suit held the door as we walked in.

"It's beautiful. Thank you, Eli," Erica was the first to state the obvious. Marcus remained silent.

"I hope all is to your liking. If you need anything else, I will be more than happy to provide it for you."

"Thanks again." Erica wasn't even looking at him anymore.

"Goodnight," Eli nodded and shut the door. The two suits remained outside as another pair went around the back entrance by the patio.

The entire house was filled with luxurious leather furniture and modern art, with glass tables and extravagant rugs sprawled across its wooden floor. Erica turned on the TV, which took up an entire wall. I didn't know if we were staying the night here after the election was over, but I wanted to.

"Sam, there should be a suit hanging in one of the bathrooms for you, and a dress for you too, Ashlin," Marcus grinned, "for tonight."

"Thanks, Dad. This is still hard to believe," Ashlin hugged Marcus.

"Believe it." He made his way into one of the bedrooms. "Call me when you need me." He closed the door, and just like that, was locked away. I think Erica was relieved to know where he would be at all times.

"Sweet patio," Ashlin was looking through the blinds of the back door. "Minus the two giants standing there, of course." She laughed to herself, and I think she was even talking to herself. I knew she was agitated. Calm lay over everyone and this place, but eerily it reminded me of a nature program about Yellowstone Park in the winter that I saw on TV: snow peacefully blanketed the park while processes deep underground pressure-cooked boiling hot, gas-infused water just waiting to erupt.

We were there now in this serene place, waiting along a railing of watchful security men while the geologic clock ticked. Everyone was agitated; Marcus was the only one who really didn't show it. Maybe that's why he locked himself in the room.

Erica, Ashlin, and I sat down to a grilled chicken dinner delivered from the resort's kitchen. No public appearances now. Marcus was still locked away in the room, and Dante was nowhere to be found. Our eyes were glued to the TV and waiting for the ring on Erica's phone.

"Polls on the east coast are closed. We should be getting results soon," Erica checked her phone as she chewed. Ashlin flinched when Erica's phone rang, sending her fork flying.

"Dante," she answered and walked away.

Ashlin got up to get her fork, now in the middle of the room, and instead of coming back to the couch, she just sat on the ground with a worried look on her face.

"What's wrong?" I asked; she was just sitting on the floor and seemed misplaced.

"I'm scared."

I wasn't expecting such a direct statement from her.

"This should be a happy time, a time to be celebrating. But for me," she pointed to her head with the fork in her hand, "that's impossible lately."

"I want all of this to go away." She swiped the fork through the air, as if that would erase everything. "I want a normal life for once, I want a normal life with *you*." Her eyes sparkled with tears. "Let's leave. Let's just go, right now."

I dropped to the floor alongside her and brushed aside a warm tear just below her eye with my thumb.

"We are needed here, Ash. *You* are needed here. Your dad... ."

"Besides you, he is all I have left. I know," she sniffed and wiped her eyes with the tip of her pinky finger.

"That's why you need to stay. Especially now."

"I know, I know."

"I didn't know what to expect with all of this. After I met you, every day was a surprise, and that felt good for a change, because I knew that every day I would get to see you. Every day I would have *you*, and that was enough for me. All I *do* know is that I love you."

"You're right. I love you too," she sniffed again and leaned into me with her head.

Erica came back into the room from the patio with her phone in her hand and her face flushed. "Dante..." she began, then looked at both of us like she was seeing the freak show in the circus, ". . . why are you on the floor?" Her eyes focused on Ashlin. "Are you crying? Is everything all right?"

"Just... ." The phone rang and cut off Ashlin again as Erica pointed her finger at us.

"What've you got for me, Meg?" Erica answered her phone and began to pace around in the same spot. I knew she was nervous not only because of the threats but she wanted to know she had done her job well enough, especially after Gabe's mistake with the debate. I wondered if he was going to be watching tonight.

Ashlin managed a tiny smirk as she watched Erica, then kissed me before she got up and went into the bathroom.

"Thank you, keep 'em coming." She hung up and stared at me, smiling. "First states' votes are in. New York and Jersey are both ours." Erica said.

"What's going on?" Ashlin walked out of the bathroom with a tissue with black smears over it.

"We officially won New York and New Jersey." Erica laughed I had a feeling that this was how the entire night was going to play out.

Ashlin sat on the arm of the couch, trying to seem excited by the news. She fidgeted and cleared her throat. "What's going on with the threats?" Her voice was stiff.

Erica's smile disappeared. "Your Dad is smart, Ashlin, and we have him protected very well."

"We have received word that Senator Ammon has officially won New York," the TV announced.

"Do you think these threats are real, though?" Ashlin was tearing the tissue down the middle.

"We have to take every threat seriously, and we have with these. I know you're scared, honey." Erica got up and rubbed Ashlin's back. "I assure you, we've got it under control. Like your dad said, these are just a bunch of harmless psychos." Erica's slight Southern twang coated her words like sugar over a bitter pill. Her phone rang again: probably more states voting for Marcus. She left the room and went outside once more.

I wrapped my arm around Ashlin and brought her close to me. She looked up at me with tears filling her eyes. My heart felt bruised to see her like this.

"I need to stop crying," she buried her face in my chest, letting out deep breaths.

"Senator Ammon now holds a commanding lead," I heard the TV in the background say before I tuned it out.

Ashlin breathed a shaky breath.

"It's OK. It's OK." I felt her relax a little. I wanted to see her smile again.

"Why do I believe what these crazy people are saying? He's my dad." She moved her head back and looked at me blankly.

"Don't let them get to you." That's all I could think of to say. I didn't have an answer for her. Every time I thought I knew something, a new puzzle piece would form in this elaborate picture.

As the night continued, the votes piled up for Marcus, taking state after state. Ashlin remained silent, both of us sitting with Erica, who got up every few minutes to take another call. More members of the campaign arrived, all of them dressed in fancy attire ready to celebrate.

I held Ashlin close to me, when Erica came bursting into the room from the patio. "It's over. We did it!" she beamed, shouting. "Marcus, we won!" she knocked on the door hopping up and down. "We already have enough votes." It wasn't official, but it looked like Marcus was the next president of the United States.

34

I looked into my eyes in the luxurious bathroom mirror. My thin, black tie, part of my new suit from Marcus, dangled in the sink as I leaned on the counter. "What happens next?" Of course, no answer came to mind. My hands clenched the bathroom counter as my scar started to sting underneath my shirt. I wanted something to happen, so I didn't mind the pain this time. I concentrated on the burn, bringing it closer until it was my only thought.

Shrieks rained down like meteorites from above me. Hot, dense air hit me like a wave of pressure. The image of the bathroom disintegrated behind me and Michael walked up with his eyes glowing brightly; he had transported me to wherever he was. His armor was in perfect condition, with all six of his wings outstretched behind him and two swords sheathed on his hip. The black aura that surrounded him flowed calmly around his entire body.

I turned to face him. Wherever we were, the sky was swirling red, and we were in the middle of a dry, barren field. I started to see a black haze form in the distance behind him, growing in size and moving closer to us. Another cluster of black formed in the sky, resembling a brewing thunderstorm.

"What is that?" I moved right beside Michael. He remained still, his face solemn, turned around in one quick motion and screamed something in a language I didn't understand. A roar of voices answered with such ferocity that it almost pushed me over. I slowly turned and saw a sea of massive beings in silver armor, all with glowing, colored eyes.

No words could describe what I was actually seeing. I looked back to the weird black haze, but now it was no longer a haze. I could see individual bodies walking closer. The sky tumbled with churning clouds like a tornado was directly above us, but that, too, was made of flying creatures. I realized I was in the middle of a battlefield.

"Michael," I began, but everything was gone, and I was back in the bathroom at the resort, staring into my own eyes. I let out a deep breath and rubbed my forehead. I wanted Ashlin to see all of this. I wanted someone else to *know* that what was happening to me was *real*. I slammed the sink handle to turn on the water and rinsed off my face to try to clear my thoughts. Every minute in life is a blank page, waiting to be filled with a story, but I never wanted to know something as badly as what the next pages said. I unhooked the suit jacket that was hanging on the door handle and slung it over my shoulder.

"Mr. Fancy," Ashlin admired, waiting for me, already wearing her new dark blue dress, making her eyes stand out even more. She looked stunning. "Not too bad." She fixed my tie and slid her hand down the bottom of it.

"How did I ever manage to get you?" I kissed her forehead. I was already trying to push back what I had just seen.

"Because you have amazing taste," she smirked the usual Ashlin smirk that I loved.

"We can now confirm that Senator Marcus Ammon from Arizona is our next president," the TV blared toward Ashlin and me. Erica was drinking a glass of freshly popped champagne with members of the victorious campaign. More people had arrived, crowding into and filling the entire place. The bedroom doors swung open, and there stood Marcus.

The people in the suite began to cheer and chant his name. Marcus smiled, waved and nodded in approval. Erica was the first to meet him. I watched her face filled with excitement deflate as Marcus spoke in her ear.

Erica tried to talk, but Marcus didn't let her. He shut the doors again. Erica stood there briefly, probably waiting for him to come back out as if he was playing a joke on her. She whipped around, started to run out, but I cut her off to see what was going on. Before I could say anything to her, she answered my question.

"He wants to speak outside."

I could feel Ashlin's stare behind me. Erica hurried out of the suite to do her job. I turned to face Ashlin and stopped her thought.

"It'll be fine. Let's just relax," I wrapped my arms around her petite shoulders. We walked over and sat at the kitchen table alone amid the crowd. I poured her a glass of water from the pitcher in the middle of the table. She couldn't sit for long, though.

Erica erupted through the door. She looked exhausted, as she was muttering words to herself. She went to the bedroom door, knocked on it, and entered without Marcus even answering. They both came out of the room with Erica pleading to Marcus.

Marcus looked at his watch on his wrist and walked over to sit with us at the kitchen table.

"You've already won. These threats are real and I'm afraid we won't have.... " Erica placed both of her hands firmly on the table, bracing herself like she was about to fall over.

"I *do* have something to prove. I have to prove that I'm not afraid. That I will stand up to any threat that comes against this country," Marcus insisted. "Even if it means that my life may be put in jeopardy."

Erica covered her face with both of her hands and exhaled slowly, calming herself. Ashlin stood up timidly and walked behind me.

"This is nothing, Erica. When I'm in office, I'm sure there will be even more threats."

"I know. We will have the resources to .... " Erica still had one hand on her forehead as she stared at the table as if it was the only thing listening.

"Maybe you're not ready," Marcus said.

She straightened her posture immediately. "What do you mean?"

"Are you?" Marcus didn't even look in her direction.

"After all this time, you ask this now?" Her face filled with red. "Fine. I tried to help you. You want to speak outside? Go speak outside. I told them already. They're setting up the stage in the middle of the damn courtyard with no protection, just for you." She was pointing out the window in the direction of the courtyard.

"Good." Marcus nodded once.

Erica stomped toward the front door.

"Where's Dante?" Marcus shut his eyes.

I didn't think she heard him at first, but she then took two strong steps back toward us. "On his way. I'll let you know when it's time." Erica opened the door as if she wanted to rip it off the hinges.

"Well, we did it," Marcus turned to face Ashlin and me, ignoring what just happened.

"I'm happy for you." Ashlin moved to the seat beside me, across from Marcus. She pressed her lips together. I'm sure she didn't know what to say after what just happened.

"Me too, Marcus," I didn't know what to say.

He moved his head slightly to look at me. "You've been a big help. You'll always be a part of this." The kitchen light shone behind Marcus and placed an odd shadow across his face. "You're lucky to have a great man like Sam, Ashlin. I hope you know that."

Ashlin fidgeted with a bracelet on her wrist. "I do know."

"*I'm* the lucky one," I tried to subdue the mood that was quickly thickening.

"Dad, are you feeling OK?" Ashlin laid her hand on top of Marcus'.

"I've never felt better. Why?" He held her hand in his.

With a flash, I saw a quick image of the battlefield I had seen earlier. I saw the two massive armies charging toward each other with weapons aimed, picking out their targets. My vision returned, and I saw Marcus and Ashlin talking, but I couldn't hear them. I heard nothing, until I heard my mom's voice in my mind.

"You'll be all right."

Another image of the battlefield exploded in my head, an image of Michael leading a group toward the tornado of creatures in the sky. Light engulfed his entire body and he drew both swords, his mouth open wide, screaming along with the other beings behind him.

"Marcus, we need to go. The courtyard is almost ready," Erica's voice snapped me out of wherever I was. I winced and took a quick breath, like I had been under water for too long. Ashlin glanced anxiously at me.

Marcus stood up and moved the curtains aside to peek at the courtyard. "Good job, like always," he nodded toward Erica.

Dante, accompanied by security, walked into the suite. Another cheer soon followed when people noticed that he had arrived. "We did it," he shook hands with Marcus. "I knew what I was doing when I met you. This was what you were meant to become."

"You showed me the way. I'll always be grateful," Marcus said.

"Shall we?" Erica motioned her hands like she ushering them to open seats in a theatre. Security encased both Dante and Marcus. Before they exited, Marcus went to the front of the room where everyone could see him.

"I just want to say something quickly to all of you," he waited for the talking and celebrating to die down. "I just told my new vice president the same thing." He raised his hand in the air with his palm facing them. "We did it." He rejoined Dante and the suits and walked out of the suite to cheers. Two more suits escorted Ashlin and me right behind Marcus.

I took Ashlin's hand and kissed her lips. "He'll be all right." I figured that if those words from my mom gave me hope, then they could give Ashlin hope as well. A chilly breeze whirled through the trees as we walked toward the courtyard. I heard the anxious crowd waiting for Dante and Marcus.

"Good, there you are," Erica walked rapidly back to us from where she and Marcus had been standing just out of my sight. "We're all going up there with him." Both of us nodded. "It'll be safe," Erica assured Ashlin one last time before hurrying back to Marcus. I could feel my scar pulsating underneath my jacket sleeve.

"Ash." She met my eyes with hers.

"Yeah?"

There was a screech from the microphone. "It is my honor to introduce to you the next president," A loud voice boomed through the speakers.

"What, Sammy?" Ashlin tugged at my arm getting my attention.

"I love you."

"I love you too." She was the same lovely vision as she was the day she stood outside of Hunt's, waiting for me with cookies. Her eyes narrowed with joy when she smiled, and she moved a few strands of her hair from her face when another cold gust of wind blew in between us.

"Marcus Ammon and Dante Wess!" the voice shouted over the cheering crowd.

"Let's go, let's go." Erica waived us forward. The roar from the crowd hit me like a shock wave in the face. Where did this vast crowd even come from? Flashes from cameras sparkled like lightning in the midst of a massive storm cloud.

Two men were setting up a Plexiglas screen around the microphone on a raised platform in the middle of the sea of people. Marcus was the first on the stage and told the workers something while waving to the crowd. The two men started to take down the glass pieces. I saw

Erica's smile vanish and felt Ashlin's grip tighten as each piece of glass was removed.

Only two suits could fit on the stage with us, a mere arm's reach away from the nearest fan. The rest of the suits were attempting to push back the crowd, but Marcus waved them off too. Erica had to be screaming inside as Marcus bent down to shake hands with his supporters. I looked to Ashlin and saw that her eyes were closed and her lips were moving. She was praying.

My eyes drifted upward as if I would see God listening to Ashlin. Instead, I saw the full white moon staring back.

"There is just something about a full moon." I watched as my dad set another log on the campfire, sparks fluttered upward before extinguishing in the darkness. "I think God created the moon to remind the darkness that it will never rule over the earth. He uses darkness to create the brightest shine."

The memory evaporated just as quickly as it came. I decided to do something I had never truly done. I said my first prayer. I looked at Ashlin for a second, her eyes open, still praying to herself as she watched her dad interact with the crowd. My eyes drew back up to the moon.

"I'm listening, God. I'm right here waiting to hear what you have to say to me. You have put her through enough and have left me clueless my entire life. For once, I need you to give me a clear answer. For once, give Ashlin what she wants. I'm listening."

A thick silence fell over the courtyard, pulling my eyes away from the sky. Trees that had been swaying from the wind froze in place, and the flashes from cameras were no longer flashes anymore, but steadily bright as if they were flashlights. Marcus was leaning over the crowd but completely still. Was this my answer?

I looked within the crowd: mouths were open, eyes were wide, hands were in the air, yet there was neither sound nor movement.

A furious burn wrapped my scar and hand that was holding Ashlin's. I tried to pull away but our hands seemed to be welded together. A white flame encased Ashlin's entire arm and shoulder.

"Ashlin?" I noticed her eyes filling with tears as she looked upward. I tried to pull my hand away from hers again. She was in pain. I began to panic.

"Stop this." I looked up to the sky and saw a cluster of clouds, solid and darker than the sky itself, begin to swirl. An opening appeared in the center of the churning clouds and a single beam of light drilled its way through and moved around like a spotlight searching for someone lost. The light shone over the entire crowd, moving over frozen bodies. Then it stopped in the back and shone on two men. I recognized both of them. One was the bum from the bus stop. He didn't have on the aviators and his once scraggly beard was now dark and thick. His pale blue eyes were now bright, almost glowing. Could he see me, see that I wasn't part of the crowd but thrown into this supernatural reality?

The man next to him was even more familiar to me. It was Gabe. Both Gabe and the bum seemed taller. I realized they were walking forward, somehow free from this lurching halt in time, pushing the frozen audience out of their way. At the same moment, both sprouted two towering black and gold wings from their backs like Michael's and both were clothed in shining silver armor.

With a quick movement Gabe launched into the air, holding a spiked sword. Bleeding and cut all over his arms, he floated onto the stage and landed directly behind Marcus, never even looking in my direction.

I heard the trees come to life again and the leaves rustle in the wind. A single flash from a camera clicked.

Ashlin started to twitch next to me. The white flame disappeared from around her arm, my scar was instantly cooled, and our hands unclamped from each other's.

"Ashlin?" I looked to her but made sure to see where both Gabe and the other being were as well. Ashlin was still frozen in place like everyone else, yet tears streamed from her eyes. The crowd slowly started to move, along with the noise of the cheers.

Ashlin, released from the hold, looked at me frantically just as a blast from a monstrous horn like the one I heard in heaven bellowed across the sky, shaking the ground like a magnitude five earthquake. The entire crowd leaped to life but was silenced by the horn.

"Oh my God, the sky!" a person yelled as screams split the crowd. Everyone's attention riveted on a light show in the heavens, oblivious to what was happening in front of them. Gabe swung his spiked weapon over his head just above Marcus.

"Gabriel." Like a crack of thunder, the horn blasted again and the blue light flashed behind Gabe, stabbing him, reaching through his armor to the other side of his torso. The being that used to be the bum flew into the air to come to his aid but a burst of energy from the blue light threw Gabe into his partner throwing both of them into the resort's walls.

"Are you seeing this?" Ashlin's voice shook. A roaring streak of light burst through the swirling clouds and crashed into the ground, blinding me. I saw nothing but milky whiteness. Another blast from the horn screamed out.

"Ashlin!" A gust of wind rolled me across the ground like tumbleweed. The happy cheers I had heard just moments ago were gone and replaced with terror-filled cries. I crawled on the ground, blind. I grabbed nothing but handfuls of dirt and rocks, searching for both Ashlin and Marcus.

The whiteness mutated into blackness, and Michael now stood in front of me, his face gashed and bleeding, his armor tattered and dented. The black aura flying around him looked broken and violent. His wings were fully extended and he held out his hand to me.

"Now you will know."

35

All I could hear were panting, quick breaths - my own breaths. I knew I wasn't in the courtyard anymore, but I couldn't see anything in front of me. I felt the wet, hard ground around me with my hands. I could smell sulfur and burnt wood, but I saw nothing. The darkness felt alive and moving, and I sensed a presence close to me. I heard something heavy drop to the ground a few yards away.

Light trickled in and I could see the sound was Marcus falling. He was bleeding from his head, the blood sliding down his face and dripping off his chin onto his white shirt, spreading into a deep red patch. I reached towards him to help.

"Watch." Michael's voice ordered in my head; I had no choice. Marcus began to move and sat up, looking around the room. He started to laugh as a thick cloud of smoke poured out above him, a dusty, miserable haze. Every breath I took pushed threads of smoke aside. The mist reminded me of the vision in Alabama.

"Where are you?" Marcus yelled to the sky, holding his palm against his head. I wondered who he was talking to but got my answer quickly, when the blue light appeared within the haze in front of Marcus. He was sitting in the smoke throne I had seen in Alabama. Walking underneath the throne and approaching Marcus was the pale white being who had placed his hand on my shoulder. He wrapped his long fingers around Marcus' arm and lifted him to his feet. In a way he was beautiful, pale but sparkling, even within the smoke. His face looked like a man's, but it was too perfect, and he was taller than any man I'd ever seen. His eyes glowed ruby as he looked upon Marcus like a small child.

"You told me I'd live," Marcus regained his balance, still holding his palm to his bleeding head.

"And you will," the ruby-eyed being placed his elongated hand on Marcus' hand holding his wound. The bleeding stopped, and the wound was gone when Marcus pulled his hand away.

"Welcome, my brother." The blue light's throne disintegrated as he floated down from it, landing next to the massive white being. He glided right up to Marcus. "The wait is finally over."

"What's next, and where is this place?" Marcus seemed completely comfortable around these beings. Had he been seeing visions similar to mine the entire time? I wanted to sprint over to them, not even caring what they would do.

The pale being didn't give the blue light a chance to respond to Marcus. "You do not need to worry, my love. I have been with you since your birth. I have watched you grow and have seen you fall. I have counted the seconds until this day. You have done what I have asked, and that's all I wanted." He brushed the edge of Marcus' hair with his skinny thumb.

"When can I see Bree?"

"Trust me. All you deserve will come to you." The pale being turned his back to Marcus as the blue light drifted into the air and floated above them both as if he was trying to entertain himself while they talked.

"I do trust you," Marcus watched the blue light while taking quick glances back to the pale being.

"And you should. I've given you things no one else has or ever could."

The blue light turned black and blended in with the smoke, making him almost impossible to see.

"I never wanted this life, though. You know why I agreed. Now please let me see her."

Without looking, the pale being raised a single finger and moved it slowly up and down. In the corner of the room a door made of light appeared, and there stood a woman: Bree. Marcus dropped to his knees, crying as she ran over to him. He held her to himself as close as he could. She *was* beautiful, as Marcus had described her. Her blonde hair hung over Marcus' entire face as they kissed.

"I'm here now," she breathed as Marcus held her face in both of his hands.

"Shh, shh," the pale being, his back facing them, motioned his finger side to side now. Bree crumbled into a pile of black rubble right in Marcus' arms. "How selfish of you to simply think that all of what we've done was to let you see a girl who could *never* be with you again," he sneered, turning around to face a stunned Marcus with his ruby eyes shimmering down at him. "That is why *your* time is over, too, my love."

Marcus buried his head in between his legs, still gripping the dust of Bree. He groaned and rocked back and forth.

"You must die in order to rise through me."

The blue light exploded in a fury above us, illuminating the entire place, flying down to Marcus and wrapping himself around his body like a boa constrictor.

"Now, take your last breath as who you are, and become who you were always meant to be." The pale being knelt down and looked into Marcus' eyes.

The blue light dissolved into Marcus, disappearing inside of him. The pale being smiled and hovered over Marcus' lifeless body until I saw Marcus sit up straight, looking around the room, blinking as though nothing happened.

"My son," the pale being kissed his own fingers and pressed them on Marcus' forehead. The Marcus I knew was gone and replaced with a being I knew nothing about, but its cruel, twisted origin.

"Shut your eyes, Sam," Michael's voice thundered in my mind, and I felt myself flying through the air. The smell of burning wood and sulfur was gone, and the smell of crisp salty ocean air replaced it. "You were chosen."

I opened my eyes to see Michael standing in front of me, with the tree of life and death stretching into the red and orange sky behind him. I stood directly in the middle like every other time I had been there. "Chosen for what?"

"To see," Michael stepped to the bright side of the tree and dropped to a knee to take a handful of grass.

I thought of the scroll that was supposed to be mine, but which was still in the possession of the pale being. I thought of Ashlin and wondered if she was safe.

I thought of Marcus and knew he had made the wrong choice. I wasn't going to let that blue light simply do whatever he was planning to do next. I knew he had to be stopped and that I was the only one who knew the real Marcus Ammon. But most of all, I thought of my parents.

I looked into Michael's eyes. "Were you there? Were you there in the jungle with my dad and me? Did you and God let them kill him as I watched? Was it *you* my mom was seeing?"

"You were never alone."

I was instantly transported back to that night in the jungle under the canopy of sticks, my dad in front of me with a blade pushed up into his neck. My eyes slammed shut, and my voice cracked as I screamed as loud as I could, a scream frozen in time, frozen in my brain, suspended since that horrifying moment, but I stopped when I heard nothing around me anymore, as if the sudden silence frightened me. I opened my eyes to see trees flowing beneath me like a green rushing river. I was somehow freed from that prison and was now flying through the air. A massive arm was draped across my chest, holding me. I looked up, and it was Michael. *He* was how I got out of there alive.

The vision vanished, and I was back in front of Michael and the tree. I dropped to one knee like him and placed my hands on both surfaces, grabbing a handful of darkened soil in one hand and lush green grass in the other. Why couldn't I ever remember that until now? "I just need to know, *why?* What was the reason for God to let those things happen to me? Just to get me to where I am right now?"

"So you could ask these questions. To understand would not be the answer." Michael looked behind me for a second and tilted his hand allowing bits of grass to fly away within the light breeze.

What was the answer, then? After everything that I'd seen, I knew there had to be some purpose for me. With this scar on my wrist, I knew I was marked for a reason. I looked up at the stunning tree in front of me. My eyes searched the colorful vines for answers.

A hand reached down from behind me on the same side as Michael and pulled me up to my feet. I turned and saw Ashlin next to me with the same glowing mark as mine etched on her shoulder.

"Ash?" I squeezed her hand making sure she was actually next to me in this place. "I... ."

"I think I always knew something was going on with you when we first met." She looked to Michael who stood up and nodded once in her direction. "And I understand why you didn't tell me what you were seeing, because I never told you all that I saw either." She took a deep breath and looked upon the tree. "I told you certain things I saw, like this tree I always dreamed of for example." Tears started to fill her eyes, but she was smiling. "And when you showed me your painting, it was too perfect."

"I didn't even paint it. The thing just appeared." I shot a glance at Michael who was looking at us with the slightest smirk on his face.

"Either way, it was *this* tree," she pointed with her other hand and tightened her grip with the hand in mine. "I knew that you had seen it like I did, but I never would've thought that it would be you holding my other hand and you my dad told me to ask why that side of the tree is dead?"

I remembered Ashlin asking me on top of the mountain, and I remembered her answer. "Your answer that day was right. That side of the tree is dead, because it was meant to be that way. Your dad once told me, that we decide what evil is. I don't think we decide, but we actually *know* what evil is. And that entire side, " I looked to the burning and smoldering part of the tree, "is our proof."

Marcus's face appeared in my mind. The handsome, perfectly structured face I thought I knew had been something different this entire time, until he finally gave in and revealed his hidden layer, the blue light.

I turned to Ashlin and wondered if she knew everything about her dad. Before I could even ask she kissed me.

She leaned back and said, "All I do know for sure, is that this is where we needed to be all along."

This is Matt's first novel, but be on the look out for the sequel to ADDISON'S MARK coming soon. To keep track of his other projects you can go to **www.mattkuvakos.com** or other social media outlets like:

https://twitter.com/mattkuvakos
https://www.facebook.com/addisonsmark
and https://mattkuvakos.tumblr.com

Matt is twenty-four years old and grew up in Chicago, Illinois. He now lives in a house with three friends and a massive German Shepherd in Tempe, Arizona. Besides going to school for writing, Matt loves to hike and cheer for the Chicago Bears, Blackhawks and Cubs.

Matt would love to hear from you.

If you would like to contact him via email please send your message to:

addisonsmark@gmail.com